BEASTS & BURDENS

Book 8 of
THE WARDEN

FELICIA JEDLICKA

Felicia Jedlicka (FelJed)
Find me on Facebook: www.facebook.com/feljedauthor
Visit my website feljedauthor.wordpress.com

For those who understand the importance of friends.

SISTER WITCHES
THE DEVIL'S SHADOW
THE DEVIL'S SOUL

DESTINY REJECTED
DESTINY RECLAIMED
DESTINY RAZED
DESTINY RESTORED

DÉJÀ VU

SAVE THE HUMANS

THE NECROMANCER'S CHILD

<u>**THE NEBRASKA APOCALYPSE NOVELS**</u>
CORN COWS AND THE APOCALYPSE
COW TIPPING AFTER THE APOCALYPSE
CORN HUSKING AFTER THE APOCALYPSE

<u>**THE WARDEN SERIES**</u>
SUCCESSORS
RIVALS
LOVERS AND LIARS
BAD BLOOD
TENANTS AND TYRANTS
THE RING BEARER
GODS AND MONSTERS
BEASTS AND BURDENS
MAGIC AND MAYHEM
FORK IN THE ROAD
DETAILS AND DEADLINES
*CURSES AND SACRIFICES**
*WITCHES AND WOLVES**
*SAINTS AND SERPENTS**
*ENEMIES AND ALLIES**

MARRIED TO DEATH*

Beasts & Burdens

Felicia Jedlicka

1

"REMIND ME WHY I have to do this," Cori said, nibbling on carrot sticks as she walked with Belus. It wasn't the Cheetos she really wanted, but she couldn't have predicted that Danato's disinterest in his own eating habits did not extend to her while she was pregnant. Six months of a nearly vegetarian diet was making her a little cranky. That and the fact that she was now toting around a bowling ball belly that had another month of expansion to go.

"I presume you're looking for a better answer than, 'because I said so,'" Belus offered dryly.

"Yes, I am. I don't see why you need my help with Efrat, especially if you aren't going to let me wear my rings."

"I'm not going to argue with you about that again. Both Danato and I feel the rings are dangerous while you're pregnant. As I recall, Ethan was also in agreement with that decision."

Cori stopped on the gravel path and stared down Belus. He stopped to offer his impassive attention. "Do you know how ridiculous that sounds to me? Three *men* condescending to me about my safety, but then turning around and taking away the one weapon I can actually use in this blimp condition."

"Excuse me, Princess, but it wasn't just *you* we were concerned about," Belus scolded. "And you are by no means incapable of using your gun." He looked her over acutely, searching for the weapon. "Where is it, by the way?"

Cori sulked, looking down for her weapon even though she knew it wasn't there. Tears sprang to her eyes without warning. "The belt is too small. I had to order a shoulder holster," she sniffled, trying not to cry in front of Belus, thereby proving the instability that was keeping her from her rings. To her relief and annoyance, Belus chuckled. "It's not funny."

"Sure it is," he said warmly. "Kid, you are not the only woman on Earth to have a baby under unusual circumstances. Despite what you might think right now, you will survive. Just one more month." He held up a finger to signify it. "We're all counting with you," he mumbled as he walked on.

She followed him the rest of the way around the prison to a clearing between Belus's house and the two large cement buildings that were used as quarters for the guards and the rotating medical personnel. Cori hadn't been inside any of them, including Belus's house.

His home was still fifty-some yards away, but she could see that it was a simple construction: an A-frame house with corrugated metal siding. It looked like a cross between a shed and a cabin.

Cori sat with Belus on a rock to wait for Efrat's escorted arrival. He had been working with him for some time on his powers, but hadn't made any real progress. Mostly, he was just ordering medical tests and treating him like a lab rat. For some reason, Belus had decided to include her in today's session, but she wasn't sure why. Without her rings, she had no protection from him—which scared her. And in terms of camaraderie, Efrat could jump off a cliff for all she cared. Consequently, she wouldn't be much help there either.

She glanced back at Belus's house, wondering why he had never invited her over, or anyone, for that matter. "Belus?" she asked carefully, and he looked up through hooded eyes. "Am I the reason you don't come over more often?"

His eyes widened before his brow furrowed. "What?"

"In the other version of things... with Gypsy, you apparently ate over at Danato's quite often, or at least often enough for no one to question your arrival. Do you think if I didn't look like... her, that you would be inclined to visit more?"

"Is this your roundabout way of asking me over for dinner?" Belus smirked, trying to lighten the subject.

"No, this is my roundabout way of asking if you can't stand being around me," she said, not willing to downplay her concerns.

He sighed and shook his head. "Damn it, Cori, does everything have to be dramatic with you?"

"Does getting an honest answer out of you always have to be like pulling teeth?"

"Of course not!" he growled, answering her prior question as he rose off the rock.

"Okay, I'm sorry. I just can't get the image of you pointing a gun at me out of my head."

"Cori," Belus said and sounded composed again, "I can count on one hand the number of times you've invited me to dinner." She opened her mouth to respond, but the answer she found wasn't the one she wanted. "I can't even walk through the damn door without an invitation."

Cori huffed and hugged her bulbous belly. Perhaps her emotions *were* getting a little out of hand. She was about to apologize when she saw Efrat sauntering over with two armed guards. Despite his captivity, he always strutted wherever he went. It ranked pretty high on her short list of reasons she hated him.

"Well, well, Corinthia, you look pleasantly plump. I'd heard you'd gotten knocked up."

"Don't call me that." She stood and squared her shoulders as he passed by Belus to greet her.

"Okay, Kitten." He grinned.

She didn't prefer that nickname either, but anything was better than staring into his baby blues and hearing her full name. Too much time and trust had been put into Efrat on account of those eyes. She didn't need to be reminded of why.

"May I?" he asked congenially and put his hand toward her belly, stopping just shy.

"No!" Cori withdrew, covering her stomach.

"She's not wearing the rings, Efrat," Belus offered further explanation after he dismissed the guards to return to their posts.

"She's…" Efrat withdrew his reach and looked over her hands thoroughly before his usual embittered facial expression returned. "Why not? Why did you bring her here then?"

Belus ignored his question and ushered her to move farther into the clearing. She obliged, hoping to gain some distance from Efrat. Unfortunately, he followed right along behind Belus.

"Belus, she could get hurt," Efrat grumbled just behind him like he expected she wouldn't hear him. She peered back, surprised that he would have any concern for her welfare. His responding scowl seemed to put the blame on her for the scheme.

"I don't want to be here any more than you do," she said.

"This is far enough." Belus stopped, giving Cori a stern look. He must not have approved of her bickering with his pet project, but Cori wasn't sure she could be near him without getting into an argument. "Efrat, I brought you out here to stretch your legs, so to speak. Are you uncomfortable using your power in front of Cori?"

Efrat's face twisted with amused disgust. "I'm not uncomfortable with... electricity isn't exact, you know! I'm trying to... damn you, Belus!"

Cori bit back her smile. It was a relief to her to see someone else getting just as frustrated with Belus's no-nonsense teaching method.

"Are you going to cooperate today, or shall I just mark this down as one of your moody days?"

"I'm not moody!" he defended *moodily* and Cori sputtered trying to contain a chuckle. Efrat glared at her as if she was the one who had suggested the word.

"Surly then, or perhaps morose," Belus continued. "I'm not sure if discontent is the right word, but I'm afraid I've used up my vocabulary for the day."

"How about asshole?" Cori mumbled. Belus gave her a drive-by glower. She mimed a dramatic mouth-zipping to appease him, but that only brought a longer, more severe glare. She lowered her eyes and crossed her arms, offering a surrender, albeit a pouty one.

"What do you want me to do?" Efrat asked.

"You see that little shack by the front gates?" Belus pointed.

From his angle, Efrat couldn't see it, so he moved closer to him. Cori took an unintentional step back, but pretended she was also trying to get a better view. She hated showing fear to Efrat, but the fact was, without her rings, he was dangerous to her, whether he wanted to be or not.

The small one-man guard shack by the gate was old and hadn't been used in years. The drawbridge's installation eliminated the need for a guard. It amused her that the only way to protect this prison properly was to use antiquated technology.

"I want you to put everything you've got at it," Belus offered him leave to proceed, but Efrat just chuckled. "Something amusing to you?"

"You want me to give it *everything?*" Efrat clarified with a smirk. Belus nodded. "You sure about that?" Belus took a step back and crossed his arms.

Efrat shrugged and swaggered into position. He took a deep breath and held his hands out, grasping at nothing but air. Rivulets of blue energy crawled up his arms and snapped in his face. He held his head back as far as he could without losing sight of his target. His fabric sleeves burned and fell away. A few static shocks snapped around his belt buckle, which made him tense his stomach.

Cori felt Belus nudge her. She looked over and saw he was covering his ears. She did the same. Almost as soon as she did, Efrat released the energy. A white-hot flash blinded her, and despite covering her ears, the boom was deafening.

Cori doubled over and cradled her stomach as she felt the baby kick harshly. Apparently, she/he didn't like the disruption any more than Cori did.

She blinked away the stars in her eyes while the ringing in her ears subsided. She heard Belus ask if she was okay, and she nodded. She looked up to see what damage Efrat had done to the guard shack that stood over 100 feet away.

It was no surprise that the guard shack had been destroyed, albeit in far smaller pieces than she might have predicted. What gave her pause was the upturned soil creating a thick ridge that ran from Efrat's feet to the shack. The gash he left in the soil was deep.

She didn't even know that was possible.

A fine layer of steam rose from the rut, hinting at how long it was going to take for the grass to grow back.

Cori turned away, unwilling to put her shock on display. Efrat had always hinted at the power he had. She had never given it much credence, since Efrat was usually more bluster than action. Apparently, it wasn't all lip service.

Belus touched her hand, and for a moment she thought it was to comfort her, but she was mistaken. He urged her to turn around and lifted his chin ever so slightly. She took the hint and crossed her arms over her chest. She put on her best stone-cold Belus impersonation and observed the scene with feigned interest rather than the awestruck horror that she was really feeling.

Despite her spike in hormones that was causing her to have rampant, abrupt emotional outbursts, Belus was trying to train her in the art of concealment. He valued his own restraint in difficult situations. Since Cori had the similar disadvantage of not being able to bully her way into getting respect, he was advising her to keep her reactions in check.

"Well, that's a little messy, isn't it?" Belus said sardonically. "This time, aim into the sky. The clouds won't mind as much."

Efrat was panting and sweating from the strain of using his power at full strength. Between that and his shredded shirt, he just needed to turn green and start roaring to complete the theme.

"Full strength?" Efrat sounded reluctant, but another smile crossed his face when Belus nodded. Cori imagined it had been a long while since Efrat had been allowed to turn up his amps this high, if ever.

Efrat went through the same routine, releasing the bolt into the sky where it splintered through the clouds, creating a tapestry of phosphorescence.

When it was safe, Cori unclenched her eyes and unplugged her ears. Belus did the same.

Efrat raised his hands in question. "Well, did you see what you wanted to see?" he said between gasps.

"No. Again, full power."

Efrat rolled his eyes and shook his head in disbelief, but didn't hesitate to do it again. When he was finished, Belus offered him the one-word command that once upon a time drove Cori insane: "Again."

After the first few times, Efrat gave up the buildup and went straight to the blow-up. Somewhere past a dozen strikes, he collapsed to the ground, dripping with post-marathon perspiration. Belus offered him the same one-word command, but Efrat could only flip him off in response.

"What did you just prove?" Cori whispered beside Belus. She could see his gears turning, but she couldn't quite see the rainbow in this storm.

"Nothing yet." Belus shrugged and led the way over to Efrat.

"No more." Efrat panted.

"Light this bulb." Belus pulled a small candle flame bulb from his pocket and handed it to Efrat.

The bulb lit easily. "Happy?" He let his hand drop as he coughed. The bulb still pinched between his fingers flickered and went out as he did.

Belus nodded slightly and summoned her with a wave of two fingers. "Efrat, take Cori's hand."

Cori stopped mid-step, gawking between the men with wide eyes, but she didn't object. She wouldn't jeopardize Belus's authority. She continued her approach a little less bravely.

"Are you shitting me?" Efrat yelled, and the bulb in his hands lit brightly before shattering. "I could kill her."

"Right now, I doubt that," Belus said indifferently. Cori couldn't help but feel insulted by his ambivalence to her potential demise, but she knew it was just an act. "But just in case, you'd better concentrate really hard," Belus added.

"I can't." Efrat flicked the stem of the bulb away like a cigarette butt.

"Yes, you can," Cori interjected, despite being less than enthused about being the rat in this lab experiment. "I don't have a lot of Dr. Frank's memories left, but I do recall she hoped you might eventually gain some control over your powers."

"Hope? Is that why she kamikaze-d the prison?"

"Efrat," Belus said. "This process could take years. You agreed to try things my way as an alternative to amputation. If you wish to change your mind, just say so."

Efrat's eyes narrowed. "I don't want to hurt her," he hissed and stood up.

"I'm aware of that. That's why she's here. I'm more than willing to be the guinea pig in this scenario, but I think you'll try harder for her."

Cori wasn't sure Danato or Ethan would like the risk that Belus was putting her at—especially in her current condition—but she understood Belus's reasoning. Efrat couldn't control his power because it was too significant. Since it was temporarily drained, he would have a margin of control, but only if he focused. Efrat wasn't a particularly optimistic person; if there was no motivation to try hard, he simply wouldn't try at all. She didn't entirely agree that *she* was that motivation, but there was only one way to be sure.

Cori extended her hand to Efrat. He stared through the proffered hand, stricken by whatever thought he was stuck in. When his eyes finally rose to meet hers, he looked forlorn. "You know I can't control it," he said hoarsely.

"Try," Cori said.

"You'd risk your life for me?" Efrat smiled humorlessly.

"I've done enough for you already. This is for Belus. He's trying to help you. I suggest you try to help yourself as well."

Efrat took a step forward and extended his hand next to Cori's. He closed his eyes and slowly pressed his fingertips to hers.

Cori could sense the tension rippling off him. She could feel the hum of potential energy behind his touch, but he didn't shock her. His fingers traced along the palm of her hand and up to her wrist. The delicate touch tickled, but she didn't pull away.

Efrat's breathing hastened, and he ripped his hand away, before a snap of static could hit her. He looked down at his trembling hands. "That was... pointless."

Belus groaned and rubbed his forehead. "Okay, let's start from the top. Efrat make it storm. Cori, earplugs," he said before clamping his own ears.

2

C ORI IMPATIENTLY JAMMED HER finger into the elevator button for the top floor, trying to induce some speed into the contraption. For the last few months, the elevator had been getting slower and slower, and considering it had never been prompt to begin with, it was beyond irritating. Unfortunately, climbing several flights of stairs was no longer appealing to her inflated belly.

Somehow she had gotten roped into taking Efrat back up to his cell instead of going home to put her feet up. She was certain that Belus intended it to be a declaration of trust—an attempt to get the same back from him—but it still felt like babysitting to her.

Luckily, Efrat was exhausted from his efforts to drain the bulk of his power, so he wasn't likely to be his usual snarky self. He leaned against the back wall of the elevator and pressed his forehead against the side.

She kept herself by the front panel, hoping to avoid all conversation, but his silence was short-lived.

"I've never used that much power in such a short span," he mumbled into the wall. "Short-Stack is very persistent, isn't he?"

"Don't call him that," Cori said gravely. The irony of her defending Belus from insult did not escape her. "He's the only one willing to help you right now. So don't screw it up."

"Sorry, habit." He sounded sincere, but it might have been his waning energy. "I'm not quite sure how to approach all of this. I don't know if I'm a prisoner, another science project, or... something else."

"We don't know either. Fortunately for you, Danato is too busy trying to prevent an audit to figure it out for us."

"How is that to my benefit?" He looked up from his wall.

"Because maybe, just maybe, you can find your humanity again, and convince Danato that you don't have to be a prisoner *or* a science experiment."

"You mean he might let me go?"

Cori felt a pang of guilt for getting his hopes up for that particular privilege. "I don't know about that, but you wouldn't be the first prisoner to be outsourced for non-optional employment. At the very least, you might be able to earn yourself a guard position."

"Why are you telling me this? I thought you hated me."

She scoffed in frustration. "Because my choices in life are based on *my* morality, not other people's. Just because you are a conniving bastard doesn't mean I need to lower myself to that standard."

"You really do hate me, don't you?" he murmured. "I just want you to know I'm going to try to change that. I haven't a clue how, since I'm very aware of how badly I pissed you off—"

"Pissed me off?" Cori whipped around. "You tried to cut my hands off! I was the only one on your side and you—" She stopped her castigation to hold a hand to the wrenching pain in her side. Yelling was apparently not good for the baby. Efrat took a step forward, but stopped, since he was clearly not going to be able to help her.

"Look, don't strain yourself to make your point. I know I fucked up on so many levels it's hard to keep track, but what I'm trying to say is that I'm sorry."

"And that makes it all better, does it?" she snarled in a less than mature tone.

"No, but I'll work to earn your forgiveness."

"Why?"

"Because I'm hoping I'll find that humanity I've been missing on the way."

Cori frowned at his seemingly honest statement. She didn't want to forgive him. She wanted to yell and scream and throw things at him until one of their heads exploded. Civility and a decent upbringing, however, left her with only one response. "Good luck."

She was more than happy to hear the sound of the elevator stop at its destination, but the loud clank preceding the abrupt rollercoaster descent was not quite as joyful to her.

C ORI GASPED AT THE feeling of her stomach going into her throat. The roar of metal grinding on metal screamed all around her. The flickering lights added to the horror movie feel. She wanted to scream, because she knew in mere seconds she was going to be dead, but nothing came out.

Efrat lassoed his arm around her back and pulled her impermissibly to him. "Grab onto me!" he yelled into her ear over the noise.

She hooked her arms around his neck while he extended his arms toward the adjacent walls. She felt the tingle of electric blue and she buried her face into his neck.

They both lifted from the floor, held up by Efrat's magnetism. His knees lifted beneath her, cradling her further. She could feel his heart racing and his ragged breathing from the effort.

The noise crested with the elevator landing in the sub-basement. Efrat's energy fluctuated, and they landed on the splintered floor of the elevator. He absorbed most of the impact, as she was essentially still in his lap.

She listened to him pant, but didn't bother to look up at him. She wanted to cry, and she was pretty sure that it wasn't just her hormones talking. She had not been this certain of her death since she fell off the roof.

Some part of her was shaking—it could have been all of her. Efrat wrapped his arms around her, pressing his hands flat against her back. Since she wasn't getting shocked, she made no attempt to stop him.

They stayed like that for several seconds, possibly even a minute. Cori was about to collect herself and pull away from him when the elevator door ripped off with a horrific squeal that made her jump. She looked up and saw Danato, along with several guards, peering into the half-lit elevator. His eyes widened at the scene he witnessed.

"What the hell did you do, Efrat?" he yelled, maneuvering into the trashed elevator sans cane.

"Nothing!" Efrat's brow knitted, and he pulled her tighter, as if Danato was another dog threatening to take his bone.

The big man did not miss the shift, and he narrowed his eyes. "Let her go, before you fry her." His voice was low with threat and promise, but Efrat didn't release her.

Cori pushed herself out of his grip to keep a fight from breaking out. The movement seemed to snap him out of his canine antics, and he released her. He assisted her to rise, and he finally noticed his hands freely touching her arms. They exchanged a look, silently acknowledging contact without consequence. He released his lingering touch, and she stepped away.

"This wasn't me," Efrat announced, masking his ire behind assertion.

Danato looked to Cori for verification.

"It wasn't him. The elevator just started dropping. He... saved my life." She waited for Danato to question her interpretation of the accident, but he didn't. She wasn't sure if it was his effort to trust her at face value, or if he just didn't want to argue with Efrat.

"Come here." He opened his arms, and she tucked herself against him. "Help him and get someone to look at the elevator," he barked at the guards. They gave him and Cori a wide berth to clear the elevator.

Danato kept Cori close to him as they weaved through the pipes and ductwork of the sub-basement. She wasn't particularly afraid of the sub-basement, but it definitely had the feel of a haunted submarine.

When they reached the open stairwell, Danato lifted her into his arms to carry her up the stairs. "Danato," she objected, "I can walk." She could see his face contort as he climbed the first step. "Where is your cane?" She looked over his shoulder.

"I'll be fine; you're light as a feather."

"Yeah, right," she mumbled. "Danato, please, I can see you are in pain."

"Nothing new." He grunted.

"I don't want to be the reason for your pain."

"You're not, sweetheart. Trust me." He gave her a squeeze and continued to carry her up the stairs.

4

"WHAT'S GOING ON?" ETHAN burst into Danato's office.

"Gun!" Belus and Danato yelled, and he leaped back out to stash his pistol in the bin before the repercussions took effect. Danato was on the phone griping at the maintenance staff for not having the answers he wanted. Belus was listening to Cori's stomach with a stethoscope that he no doubt stole from the infirmary. Cori looked none the worse for wear, and was, in fact, eating... again. "My men said the elevator crashed."

"It did," Cori said, crunching on Cheetos.

"Holy crap, are you okay?" Ethan tried to embrace her around Belus and her orange hands, but all he could do was pet her hair.

"I'm fine. Danato let me have Cheetos!" Cori grinned at him with cheesy teeth, and he couldn't help but chuckle at her. "So worth it," she whispered. Belus sighed and pulled away from her belly. "Are we good?"

"Yeah, your digestion is healthy, too."

"Don't tell me that there is no reason for it!" Danato yelled into the phone. "Elevators don't just fall!"

"How did you come out unscathed?" Ethan brushed Cori's hair behind her ear.

"Efrat," she admitted reluctantly. "He did some magnetic mojo to keep us from splatting."

"What the hell were you doing with Efrat?"

"Her job," Belus said, not leaving room for questions. Ethan had a good number of them lingering in the back of his throat, but unfortunately, the debate about Belus's authority over Cori was off limits to him.

Ethan kissed the top of Cori's head. She seemed fine, but he imagined she hadn't been as calm pre-Cheetos. Ethan wasn't sure how to feel about Efrat saving her. He still blamed him for his role in Cori's current situation, but he was thankful he had been there to save her.

"I don't care if it's working fine now! Just look at it again!" Danato hung up the phone and exchanged a troubled look with Belus.

"Maybe she should go with him," Belus murmured inexplicably.

Danato's eyes widened. He looked fearful. It was a strange emotion to see on him. He had only seen it a few times, and it usually involved Cori's safety. "No," Danato said with sudden composure. "That shouldn't be necessary. She shouldn't travel in her condition. I think we'll just make the elevators off limits for a while."

"Go where?" Cori asked with her mouth full.

"Ethan has been *invited* to join Annette in China," Danato explained, glancing between him and Cori. "She is very interested in your ability to hear the dragon's thoughts."

"What?" Cori looked back at him. Judging from the shock on her face, he must have neglected to mention that little discovery. Truth be told, he had forgotten about it himself. "You can hear Penelope's thoughts?"

"Yes, with the dragon's blood. She likes the name, by the way."

"Ha!" Cori pointed a finger at Belus. "Told you." He gave her a look like he might break her finger and she retracted it immediately. "Wait." Her face crumpled, and she looked between all of them before settling on Danato. "When is he leaving?"

"Yes," Ethan added with a good deal more earnestness. "When am I leaving?"

Danato lifted his chin high and clenched his jaw, not letting his firmness go unchecked. "Tomorrow."

"How long?" he asked, as Cori jumped up to offer her objection.

"I don't know, Ethan." Danato managed to offer some sympathy in the statement. "That will be entirely up to Annette and her compatriots."

"But..." Cori looked back at him, fearful of what was being said. "You'll be back for... the baby." She was doing her best to remain calm, but he could tell that no amount of snack food was going to fix this. "Danato?" she whimpered and looked back to him.

"I know, sweetheart, but you have to understand that being able to communicate with dragons is unprecedented. It is not something that we can simply reschedule."

"I can't reschedule this either!" Cori pointed at her rounded belly. "And it's pretty unprecedented for me," she muttered, starting to cry.

Ethan gritted his teeth and pulled her into his arms. She already knew how this conversation was going to go. He did too. Danato would offer a list of reasons to comply, including income for the prison, building allies, and overall sucking up. Unfortunately, especially right now, they needed to take any opportunity they could to suck up.

Danato mouthed, "I'm sorry," at him. He looked excessively disgusted with himself as well, but Ethan couldn't find it in his heart to forgive him just yet.

"Cori and I are taking the rest of the day off." Ethan gave both of them a look, daring them to challenge him, but they didn't. He took Cori by the hand and led her home for a good and proper sendoff.

5

DANATO SIGHED AND RUBBED his face after Ethan and Cori were gone. "That went about as well as I expected."

"It could have been worse," Belus said.

"Someday, Belus, I want to go back to being the hero instead of the bad guy."

Belus shook his head. "You can't blame yourself, blame the job."

"It's hard when your job is to break hearts."

"Men have missed childbirths before. It doesn't make them less of a father."

Danato nodded. For a change, he was appreciating Belus's diplomatic appraisal of his duties. However, judging by the way he was avoiding eye contact with him, that was about to change.

"Have you taken into consideration that the elevator wasn't an accident?" Belus asked.

"Why do you think I'm being so insistent that they check again?" Danato met Belus's gaze, and for a moment, they were at a standstill. "She wouldn't do that."

"I'm not saying *she* would, but *it* might. Cori is pregnant. You are a good deal happier. Jealousy is the universal motivator for murder."

Danato was up before he could stop himself. He wasn't angry, but he wanted to get away from the conversation. His leg erupted in teeth-clenching pain. "Damn it!" He leaned on the desk, shaking from the ache that he could never get away from.

"Danato," Belus said quietly. It wasn't a question, or a scold, simply a plea. There was little that he could do to help, but he still wanted to try.

"There's nothing more to do, Belus. I promise. I would try if there was."

"When do you want to schedule the surgery?" he asked, giving up the fight to keep him from amputating his leg.

"After Cori has the baby," Danato whispered. He felt his eyes watering, but he no longer cared what judgment was passed on him regarding his representation of manliness. "I'd like to hold my adoptive grandchild before I'm crippled. Ethan's ready to take over my duties. He has been for quite some time." Danato felt a tear dribble down his cheek. "I'm sorry, Belus."

"For what?" His face was somber, but he could sense the sorrow hiding behind his impassive eyes.

"For everything." Danato shook his head, unable to contain the emotion that had built up for seven years. "I never apologized for everything I put you through. It was all my fault, and I regret that I wasn't strong enough to finish it myself."

Belus looked away, his eyes no longer pokerfaced. There was anger there, but when he looked back, it was gone. "I would never have let you do that yourself. No man should have to do that."

Danato nodded. He wasn't about to argue with him, but deep down inside, he always wondered how much Belus resented him for imposing on him to kill his best friend.

6

E THAN LED CORI INTO the house and removed her coat to hang it up. She wasn't speaking to him, nor was she yelling. He didn't like that. He would have much preferred she be impassioned with anger, rather than crying quietly beside him. It told him she was truly pained by this decision and there was nothing he could do to make her feel better about it.

He had only just been told that he was leaving, so he didn't have time to make preparations for her beyond instilling his unconditional love for her.

He guided her by the hand upstairs to their apartment. The small studio-style apartment had a set of parlor doors separating the living space from the bedroom, and the bathroom had finally grown to accommodate two people getting ready in the morning instead of one.

The house had yet to offer them a nursery, which he thought was strange, but he imagined the house didn't readily understand pregnancy as compared to an actual baby.

Cori immediately went into the bedroom and sat on the edge of the bed to sulk. She wiped away a few tears while he unloaded his weapons belt and slipped off his black t-shirt, leaving his chest bare. He slipped off his boots and socks. Before he could get his pants off, Cori decided to speak.

"Making love to me isn't going to make me feel any better about this," she grumbled.

"Oh?" he queried seductively. She looked up at him through pained eyes. Her pout was enough to make him want to send a "bugger off" letter to Annette and her dragons. "Who says I'm going to make love to you?"

He was going for playful, but she just looked back down at her feet without a hint of amusement. He moved to the end of the bed and kneeled down before her. He helped her slip off her tennis shoes. Her boots had become too uncomfortable with the swelling in her limbs. She was plumper in more ways than one—none of which he objected to, since it was resulting in the creation of a child. His child.

He massaged her calves, and despite herself, she closed her eyes and moaned in enjoyment. He smiled when she peeked open to glare at him. "I know what you're doing, and I'm telling you I'm not going to crack."

"That's fine. I can wait until you do. I'm patient." His smile turned into a smirk, and he saw her gulp under his gaze.

"Do you think they'll really keep you there all month?"

"I don't know any more than you, Cori. I'm trying to think positive."

"I know, but... I just don't want to be alone for this."

"You won't be. Best medical staff in the hemisphere, an overbearing father figure, and a surprisingly clingy uncle."

"Clingy?" Cori's brow furrowed.

Ethan chuckled. "I just mean you will be taken care of."

"But I want you here." Her lips pursed in an adorable sour face that didn't draw his sympathy as much as something else.

"I know, sweetness, but whether or not I am, you are still going to be brave and strong." She shook her head, ready to say that she couldn't. He pressed his hand to her cheek to stop the movement and draw her attention. "Yes. You are," he stated in no uncertain terms.

"Please don't leave."

"Please don't make me feel guilty for following Danato's orders."

Her eyes lit with understanding, and fell again, meeting the defeat she wasn't quite ready to embrace. She nodded. "Okay."

"Now, Ms. Reiger—or was it Mrs. Pierce?—what are we going to name this baby?"

She smiled broadly, finally coming back to him. "Reiger-Pierce, I think. I thought we were going to make love," she complained.

"You said that, not me," he chided her, but held his lascivious smirk. "As I recall, you objected to the idea, anyway."

She stood and walked away. "Fine."

He grabbed her quickly and carefully. She squealed as he tripped her back into his arms. Her heart was beating fast from the scare, but her eyes weren't fearful of him. She wanted him. It made him grin all the more. He loved bringing her desires alive. It was one of his favorite pastimes.

Since she'd had her experience with the genie, she had been far more receptive to his playful side. He was curious about what had happened to her to make his aggressive play more palatable, but he wasn't about to ask. He just wanted to enjoy it.

He lay her down on their bed and slipped in beside her to admire and caress the bulging mass that appealed to his primal instincts. She, of course, considered the changes to her body to be hideous, but he found the entire process mesmerizing. He hated to miss any part of it, but if he had to, he was going to make sure she was taken care of.

7

CORI YOWLED IN FRUSTRATION at the truck distancing itself from the main dock. The cold air whipped through her hair violently as the outer door slipped shut. "Why am I always on this dock saying goodbye to him?"

Belus glanced up at her, but didn't offer an explanation. There either was none, or she should have known it already.

"Give me one good reason that I shouldn't hate all of you right now!" She stared him down point blank, but he didn't flounder under her gaze. In the end, it was she who winced and looked away. "Why can't you humor me, Belus?" she grumbled as she headed off the dock.

"I am amused by you, does that count?" Belus said, following her.

She sighed as she entered the hallway. "I guess it will do. Where is Danato? I'm surprised he didn't come see Ethan off."

"He is taking the morning off to rest his leg," Belus said casually, like it was an everyday occurrence.

"I don't think Danato has taken a minute off since the day I arrived. Is he really in that much pain?" Belus nodded. "Can't the doctors do something?"

He paused before answering. "They will. Come on, time to see Cleos again." Belus passed her up when they reached the main foyer.

"Great, the cherry on my week." Cori followed Belus to Danato's office, where Cleos was waiting in his hooded robe. He always looked worldly and benevolent in his robe. It made Cori smile, since she knew Cleos was anything but benevolent.

"What are you doing here?" Cleos eyed Belus with disdain.

"Monitoring your services. What do you think?" Belus said with a snarl, but Cori thought she detected a little amusement in his tone. "Cori, take a seat. Let's get this over with."

Cori sat down in the chair next to Cleos and reached her hand out to him. He looked over her proffered hand carefully. "And the other?" He nodded to her other hand. She rolled her eyes and held up her other hand for him to inspect. Even though she hadn't worn her rings since Belus took them away six months ago, he still insisted on checking her.

"Are you really that afraid of me reading you?" she asked.

"We've been over this. You have no understanding of the barriers that shouldn't be crossed in the mind.

Your amateur explorations are an invasion." Belus snorted, and Cleos offered him a fiery glower. "Something funny, Belus?"

"The pomposity of that statement; like rules for a cat burglar."

"Indeed," Cleos agreed, though Belus was making a joke. He turned his look to Cori. "Just remember, it's *my* services that are required here. If you take issue with my rules, then you can take your request to another psychic, though I doubt you will find any like me." His eyes sparkled with amusement.

Cori offered her hand again, but Cleos reached for her face instead. She tried to pull away, but his grip unleashed a flood of memories. He was searching for the erroneous ones—the memories of Dr. Frank that didn't belong in her head.

He had been removing them slowly, so he didn't harm her, though she suspected he was enjoying getting a break from his prison cell as well. So far, with each *treatment*, she was feeling more like herself again, but Cleos was also concerned about the vacancy in her brain scan. He hadn't provided an explanation for it, but again, he was taking his time.

His mind latched onto her with such force, she could only describe it as painful. Whatever he was doing, he wasn't being gentle about it. Then it all stopped. She opened her eyes to see what had changed, but she didn't see Cleos. She saw herself. The mirror image—that wasn't a mirror—opened her eyes, and the connection broke like the whiplash of a rubber band.

Cori flew back, grasping at her body and cradling her stomach. She was panting heavily, and ready to run, but she was okay otherwise. Cleos, on the other hand, looked livid. He was on his feet, towering over her with teeth bared.

"You!" he seethed. "You are an endless reign of bad luck!"

Cori wasn't particularly mad about him yelling at her, but what she was mad about was the last six months of passive-aggressive attacks on her, and his refusal to offer her any leniency for ignorance. She stood so suddenly that Cleos drew back.

"What the hell do you want from me?" she yelled.

Belus stood up to break them apart. It wasn't their first argument, but it was the first time they were head-to-head preparing for blows.

"I want you out of my mind!" Cleos yelled back.

"I'm not in your mind! I can't undo what I've done! Why can't you just let this go? I'm sorry! I'm sorry! I'm *so sorry*!" Cori panted and took a step back. She felt Belus pressing his hand against her back. Consoling her? Pushing her forward?

"Stupid, stupid girl!" Cleos groused.

"Go to hell!" she screamed so loud her throat hurt. "Get off me!" She shoved against Belus's hand, but he pressed back, keeping her trapped between him, the desk, the chair, and Cleos.

"Are you finished or not?" Belus asked him.

"I've gotten all of Dr. Frank's personal memories out, but I can't fix the vacancy," Cleos answered Belus with a good deal more respect than he had offered her.

"Why not?" Belus didn't hide his distrust in his conclusion.

"Because she did it to herself."

"What?" Cori balked. "I didn't—"

"What did she do herself?" Belus interrupted.

"She put her unconscious mind in mine."

"What does that mean for her?" Belus asked before Cori could formulate a question.

"It means her mind is vulnerable to being encroached upon."

"How vulnerable?" Belus asked, drawing her back behind him by the arm, since she would no longer be helpful to this conversation.

Cleos rubbed his chin thoughtfully. "The vacancy in her brain is like a flood plain. Any extraneous memories that aren't readily absorbed will pool there. That's why she was getting confused between herself and Dr. Frank. She couldn't distinguish." Cleos glared at her like that was somehow something she should have read in the handbook that came with her brain.

"So she should avoid absorbing any more memories?"

"To say the least; I would also advise that she doesn't use her rings on any more psychics." Cori felt uncomfortable under Cleos's scrutiny, but all she could do was cross her arms and pretend that it didn't hurt like hell.

"Can we undo this?" Belus glanced back at her, probably checking if she had run out of the room.

"No, the only one who can undo it is her, and she is far too underqualified to do such an extraction."

"You can't do it?" Cori asked.

"Since I would be the one that requires the extraction, no. And just so we are *all* perfectly clear, you will never be allowed back in my brain, certainly not to do anything as complex as removing your own subconscious."

Cori shook her head. She didn't really understand what he was saying, but she didn't dare fertilize his condescension.

"What about long-term effects?" Belus asked, indifferent to Cori's heart being ripped out right before his eyes.

"I don't know. I imagine, with Cori's luck, we'll be in for a few surprises." His lips curled in a smirk that faded as soon as he looked at her. She closed her eyes and tipped her head back so the tears that she couldn't hold back trailed down her temples instead of her cheeks.

"What about you?" Belus mumbled as if he didn't really care about the answer, but felt obligated to ask. "What effect will this have on you?"

Cori looked back to see his answer, and she found his eyes boring into her. "Let's just say it's a good thing I'm such a nice guy."

"Nice?" Cori scoffed.

"Yes." Cleos pulled back the chair to get around Belus. She backed herself into the wall. He put one hand up on the wall behind her. "I have part of you in my mind, Cori. Do you have any idea how easy it would be to puppeteer you with it? I could ruin you."

Cori shook her head. It was too much. She shrank down the wall to the floor in tears. "Please, stop. Please, just stop." She buried her face in her hands since she couldn't reach her knees anymore. "I hate you. I hate you so much."

"Enough, Cleos," Belus threatened, too little too late.

"Yes, it is," he said, his voice reeking with the pride at breaking her.

8

"Cori, you have to understand Cleos," Belus said, hanging up his coat before he joined her in the living room. She half expected Danato to be home in bed, but he wasn't. He must have been receiving some kind of treatment in the infirmary.

"I do understand him. At least, I thought I did." She sat down on the couch and put her feet up on the coffee table. The instant she did, she took them off again.

"You understand the Cleos that has spent the last few years beating himself up for his perceived sins." Belus helped himself to the liquor cabinet as usual. "You never knew the asshole he was before he walked through our doors."

Belus set out two glasses on the coffee table. Cori furrowed her brow. "Belus, I can't drink with you."

"Sure you can." He smirked playfully. "I'm having a gin and tonic. You're having a tonic."

She smiled and reached for the glass of tonic that he poured her. She couldn't quite reach. She tried again, but was still too far back on the couch to reach it over her belly.

"What's wrong there, Humpty Dumpty?" Belus grinned at her.

"You could just bring me the glass," she scolded.

"I don't know. This is pretty entertaining to me."

"Yeah, I know how you like big women." She smiled at her joke, but instantly blanched from panic. She wasn't sure if he would take offense to it. "Sorry."

He eyed her suspiciously, but didn't lose his amusement. "Don't be." He brought the glass of tonic to her. "It was funny."

"You were saying about Cleos," Cori said, desperately trying to change the subject so she didn't put her foot right back in her mouth.

Belus finished pouring gin into his tonic and sat back in Danato's chair. "Cleos isn't the type of man to keep friends. His vulturine business tactics tend to scare away associates. He may have been your fallback friend here, but out there..." Belus motioned his drink to the proverbial *out there*, "...he's not going to help anyone but himself."

"What does that matter while he's in here?"

"Because he isn't going to be in here much longer. He's going to get a parole review and, given your admission about the circumstances that put him in here, we may release him."

Cori frowned. She didn't know what to feel about that. Part of her relished the idea of having him out of her life, but the part of her that held onto hope far too long wanted to repair their friendship. "If he's going to be rid of me anyway, why is he running me into the ground first? Why can't he just cut his losses and forget about me?"

"I think he's about to leave behind the only friend he's ever had in his whole miserable life, and the only way his demented little brain can deal with it is by making you hate him."

"You mean that was all an act?"

"Cori," Belus's voice was soft, but he was scolding her with it. "There is a reason that Danato didn't want you socializing with him. There is a reason I didn't attempt to intervene today. He is not a good person. He may not be as evil as we all thought, but he is definitely not someone worth keeping as a friend. Please let this be the end of your relationship with him."

"Is that an order?" she said, swirling the liquid in her glass.

"No," Belus said. "Just friendly advice."

9

DANATO BREATHED IN THE smell of chicken and mashed potatoes when he came through the front door. Cori smiled at him from the stove, where she was sauteing onions. If he had to guess, it was probably for the green beans she had on the platter off to the side.

"Oh, sweetheart, if you knew how beautiful you are to my stomach right now." He patted his stomach, and she giggled.

"I knew you only loved me for my cookbook."

He chuckled and limped over on his cane. He was in exquisite pain, but the series of shots he received that morning were making him numb enough to deal with it. "Hardly," he murmured before kissing her forehead. "How are you doing?" He squeezed her slightly in a sideways hug.

"My back hurts, my feet hurt, and I think the baby has dropped—since I can't seem to not waddle when I walk."

He chuckled and kissed her on the temple. "I meant since Ethan left. Are you mad at me?"

She sucked in a deep breath that made him dread the answer that was to follow. "No." He drew back and looked at her to see if she was just placating him. "I'm just unhappy now."

"I'm sorry, Cori. You know if I could have sent anyone else, I would have. Did you make all this food just for us?"

She knitted her brow and laughed. "Of course not, I made extra for our house guest."

"House guest? Is Belus coming for dinner?"

Cori frowned. "Oh shit, I keep forgetting to ask him. No, I made all this for Duke."

"Duke?" Danato grimaced. "Why would you invite him for dinner?"

"I didn't," Cori said, putting all her attention back on her onions.

"Who did?" Danato put enough depth in his voice to make her head dip further.

"Ethan did," Duke answered as he clambered down the stairs, reaching the main floor. "Good evening, sir." He stopped midway to the island, apparently waiting for Danato to respond.

"Duke," Danato said civilly as he moved around Cori to meet him. "Would you mind telling me what you were doing upstairs?" Danato settled in beside the stools at the end of the island and waited for him to answer. The stand-off was poised, but so far nothing had prompted drawing guns.

"I was unpacking my things, sir."

Until that.

"Excuse me?" Danato smiled, but the amusement he found in the scenario was in Duke's audacity. "I don't recall inviting you into my home."

"You didn't, sir," Duke said with surprising bravado. "Ethan assigned me to look after Cori."

Danato took a step forward that should have sent Duke running. He was either braver than Danato had ever given him credit for, or he was just that devoted to Ethan. "Walk me through this, Duke, because right now my interpretation is getting a little blurred by my desire to throw you out on your ass." Duke had the good manners to look a little concerned by that statement.

"Ethan was none too pleased about leaving his lovely wife by her lonesome, so I'm going to be staying with y'all for a while, until he gets back."

"And I was not consulted." Danato managed to keep his volume down, even though he was about ready to wring Duke's neck.

"Ethan instructed me to follow his orders above yours, sir." Duke wasn't comfortable saying that out loud, but he stood his ground well enough.

"Tell me, Duke—if you happen to know—why did Ethan think he had the right to usurp my authority?"

"He said that the prison is your supreme province, but as far as his wife is concerned..." Duke trailed off, not willing to say the rest. Danato wasn't entirely surprised that Ethan would pull something like this. He still resented not being able to rush to Cori's rescue when Clark had locked her up in the prison. This was just his way of keeping control of a situation that was out of his hands.

Also, Danato thought that Ethan might have lost faith in his ability to protect Cori. He was doing his best to hide his pain, but it was obvious to everyone that he was not as spry as he once was—if he ever really was during the time they had known him. When push came to shove, if Cori needed to be rushed to the infirmary for labor, he may not have been the best man for the job.

"You aren't suggesting that you share the apartment with Cori?" Danato asked, suddenly thinking back to Duke's unpacking.

"No, sir," Duke snapped, personally offended by the suggestion.

"Danato," Cori scolded him from the table, where she was setting out the last of the food.

"Are you really okay with this?" Danato asked her, seeing that she had not jumped in to fight for her feminine independence.

Cori shrugged at him and scratched her belly. "I don't know. I mean, it's just Duke. It might be nice to have someone to talk to after you fall asleep under your newspaper." She was fidgeting under his gaze. She wanted to let Duke stay, but she didn't want to say so in case it hurt his feelings, which it did, but he understood their concern. He was going to have to accept that he wouldn't be the one she turned to for protection anymore.

"So, if Duke stays"—Danato scrutinized him a moment, before finishing his statement to Cori—"you'll have to keep impressing him with your culinary skills." Cori smiled. "I mean, you can't lose face." Cori shook her head.

Danato waggled his finger for her to come over, and she waddled over and paid her dues in hugs and kisses on his cheek. "Both of you sit down. I just need to wiz, and we can eat," Cori said before waddling off to the bathroom.

"Spoken like a true lady, sweetheart," he called after her, and she waved haphazardly before disappearing into the bathroom.

As soon as she was behind the closed door, Danato grabbed Duke by his shirt and yanked him into a backbend. "Now, Duke, before we can eat, I need to reestablish that I am indeed still your warden."

"Yes, sir." He held Danato's fists, but didn't try to squirm away, except to get purchase for his feet.

"Tonight could have gone a very different way, and we both know it."

"Yes, sir."

"Do you know why it didn't?"

"Because you love Cori more than life itself, and when presented with the option of losing face in front of me or keeping her safe, you'll choose to sacrifice your own ego to protect her," Duke rattled off the explanation like it was memorized just for the occasion. "Sir," he added for good measure.

Danato put him upright again. "In a nutshell, but he forgot to tell you that I would be willing to do as he wishes because I love and respect him as well."

"No, he didn't, sir," Duke murmured.

Danato paused, feeling a stab of pride in his ever-so-smart young protégé. He'd known a day would come when he would feel more gratified by Ethan's contention than aggravated. He just hadn't expected that it would come this soon. He supposed it wasn't so much a change in Ethan that had caused it—since he had long since been on this path—but rather a change in himself. Life was humbling him... in good ways and bad.

10

ORI WASN'T SURE WHEN she had fallen asleep against Danato, but there she was, leaning on the sleeping bear, sleeping herself. She blinked lazily at Duke, who was gently coaxing her out of sleep. "Ma'am, would you like me to escort you upstairs?"

Cori nodded, and Duke very gently guided her legs off the couch and helped her rise to her feet. He looped her arm around his and he didn't flinch at the weight she put on him. She opened her mouth for an endless yawn before she could speak. "You're a good man, Duke."

"Thank you, ma'am," he whispered, despite being out of earshot of Danato.

"I'm sorry I fell asleep." They made it to the first landing. "I really wanted to get to know you better."

"I appreciate that, ma'am, but I'm not much good in a conversation. I'm pretty boring."

"Ethan's fond of you," she mumbled.

"He's a good friend to me, so I'm a good friend back."

They reached the second floor, and Cori stopped. "I'm sorry you got stuck babysitting me." She frowned at him.

He deserved a more respectable duty than guiding his boss's wife to her room.

He shrugged and offered her an equally modest smirk. "I'm not. I babysit demon creatures all day long. Escorting a young lady such as yourself to her quarters is about as pleasant as a man's day can get."

Cori smiled at him. "You are just too damn sweet. Do you have a girl back home?"

"No, ma'am." He shied away from her gaze.

"Well, we are going to have to find you one, before you have a married, pregnant woman swooning like a teenager."

He chuckled and blushed. "Yes, ma'am, I'd appreciate that." Cori moved to open her door, but stopped and turned back to Duke. "Something you need?"

"Umm..." Cori gulped and cleared her throat. She was suddenly without any witty dialogue to make her transition in topics. "Duke, I never... thanked you."

"Really, ma'am, I'm happy to do it."

"No, um, not tonight. I mean..." Cori shrugged. "You probably don't remember, but when I first came to the prison, I had a little run in with some overly friendly men. You stopped it."

"I remember." Duke frowned and shook his head. "It was nothing any respectable man wouldn't have done."

Cori grimaced, feeling tears pushing at her eyes. "That's just it, Duke. It *was* something. I was in a really bad place when I came here. If you wouldn't have helped me that day, showed me that little bit of kindness, I wouldn't have made it, you know?" Cori shrugged.

Duke nodded in understanding and stared down at the floor.

"I'm sorry it's taken this long to offer my gratitude. I just wasn't sure how to thank you for renewing my faith in the human race without making you uncomfortable." Cori chuckled. "Which I don't think I achieved even now."

Duke smiled and looked back up at her. "I reckon that smile is enough reward for my gallantry, but I appreciate you mentioning it. Now you best scoot yourself off to bed, before you make me get teary-eyed."

Cori chuckled and turned back to open her door. She wasn't sure what hit her first, the heat wave, or Duke as he defensively pushed between her and the door. She fell back, partly from his intervention, and partly from the pressure of the explosion. Duke's airborne trip, on the other hand, was entirely from the force of the blast. His short flight landed him harshly against the opposite wall.

"Duke!" she yelled over the roaring fire, but he didn't move. "Danato!" She changed tactics.

She did a quick evaluation of her body parts and determined that, aside from a possible bruise on her hip, she was fine. She tried to move and found her assessment severely lacking, since she hadn't noticed the five-inch piece of wood sticking out of her calf next to her shin. It was cutting off the blood flow, so she'd hardly noticed it.

Flames engulfed the apartment before her, spilling out of the doorway. The inferno that lapped over the ceiling above her wasn't rhythmic like water, it was wild and serpentine. The flames licked down at her, snapped like whips when they reached beyond their limits. Sparks spat out from the tips as they did, showering her in biting embers. This was not a house fire. This was the house.

"DANATO!" Cori screamed at the top of her lungs. She had never been so afraid in her life. This wasn't a monster escaping from captivity. This was her "welcome" mat, trying to tamp her out.

Hands grabbed around her and hoisted her up. She jumped from the sudden touch, but Duke's calming accent informed her in no uncertain terms, "I gotcha, I gotcha." He plodded down the stairs to reach safety, but the fire slithered around the stair railing and all but walled off the remaining descent to the main floor.

"Duke," Cori whimpered.

He backed up, looking up and down for another option. He looked as frightened as she was. He tightened his grip on her and backed into the railing of the first landing. "Hang on," he said before flipping backward over it. By some miracle, he kept hold of her and stuck the landing with little more than a puff of exhalation.

The flames spread and curtained off their passage from the hallway into the living room. There was no smoke—yet another indicator that this was not a real fire—but the heat was tremendous. The flames forced

Duke back, and he shielded himself and her by turning his back. "I don't suppose you have a back door."

"No," Cori answered, all at once realizing how utterly wrong that was. "Danato!" Cori could just make out Danato's frame through the veil over Duke's shoulder. He was standing midway through the combined rooms, staring at the blaze. He looked scared and pained, but he wasn't panicked like she and Duke were. He was speaking. Speaking to the house?

All at once he put his hands together in prayer and she could see him mouth "please." He was begging for their lives. It was already unbearable watching the man that she once thought of as invincible limping in excruciating pain, but now seeing him pleading for her life instead of demanding it...

The blanket of fire parted and Danato stepped into the break, but no further. She presumed that he still suspected the opening to be an indecisive gesture. "Duke!" he yelled and Duke whipped back around and launched through the break in the threat.

Danato was quick behind them, and they were out the door without coats or cares about their belongings left inside.

11

A s soon as Belus's door opened, Danato pushed in with Cori in his arms. He had left Duke to alert the guards of what was happening, and to advise them not to attempt quelling the flames in the burning house. He was reluctant to leave Cori's side, but he could see the situation was beyond simply watching over her.

Belus jumped back, stunned by the sudden upheaval of his evening plans, but not paralyzed by it. He barked at Danato to set her on the couch while he ran to his bathroom. A moment later, he returned with a first aid kit the size of a briefcase. Belus hated infirmary paperwork more than anyone.

"What happened?" He sat down on the coffee table before Cori and laid out alcohol pads and needles.

"The house tried to kill me!" Cori bellowed.

The look Belus gave him was a combination of "I told you so" and "How could you let this happen?" He stowed the accusing look behind his usual hardened exterior and proceeded to cut open Cori's pant leg. He brusquely swabbed the area around the shrapnel.

"Hello?" Cori shrieked. "Isn't anyone shocked that the house tried to kill me?"

"Yes, Cori," Belus said, calmly trying to exert his composure onto her. Danato nearly smirked since he knew this was one time even Belus's cool demeanor and stern looks wouldn't pressure her into silence.

"Why did the house try to kill me?" She smacked her fists into the couch.

"Get her some water, please," Belus instructed him. Danato stepped into the kitchen area just off the entryway, which was much like his own house, only smaller, and pulled a glass from the cupboard for water.

"Forget the water! I want answers!" Cori yelped as Belus injected her with three tiny shots around the wound to numb it.

"Hold still," he griped.

"Bite me!" she yelled.

Belus chose that moment to rip out the five-inch piece of shrapnel from Cori's shin. Danato cringed at the cry that Cori let out and wondered how Belus could stand to be the cause of it. The wound gushed, and Belus pressed gauze against it.

He returned with the water and, despite being so vocally against it before, she took a long drink of it. He looked at Belus, who was only occasionally glancing up at him from his stitch work. He was mad, but he wasn't letting that get in the way of what needed to be done.

"First the elevator, now this," Cori panted over her loss of breath from drinking. "What is going on? Someone tell me the truth for once in my freaking life," she implored both of them, but it was Belus who spoke.

"The house, the elevator, and Danato's office are all manifested by the same being." He threw the information at her like it was nothing of consequence, but her awe-stricken face said otherwise. "The two incidents aren't just related; they are caused by the same entity. You are *officially* in danger, Cori."

"Why?" Her eyes pleaded with no end to their disillusionment. "Why would she try to kill me? I thought I was keeping things tidy," she whimpered thoughtfully, as if she was counting every mismanaged piece of laundry.

Danato shook his head. "Oh, sweetheart, this has nothing to do with tidiness. This is a being of complex emotions, but it can only express it in simple actions. Unfortunately, the slew of emotions she's expressing now is turning violent."

"What is she trying to express?" Cori asked him.

Danato glanced at Belus, but he only shrugged. "It's complicated," he said weakly.

"Complicated?" Cori's eyes screamed, long before she did. "She's tried to kill me twice! Why is she doing this? Ouch!" she yelped as Belus stuck her in the thigh with another needle. "What the hell was that?"

"Sedative," he answered blandly. "I want you to calm down."

"I want answers!"

"We have bigger concerns than your edification!" Belus finally broke and yelled back at her. Despite it being aimed at Cori, Danato knew it was meant for him. "Hold this!"

She growled through clenched teeth and replaced Belus's hand, putting pressure on her calf.

"Outside." Belus pointed to the door and Danato led the way.

"You were right," Danato said as Belus shut the door behind them. "I should have listened to you this afternoon."

"I was just guessing," Belus contested. He paced back and forth, trying to get a grip on the situation as well as his temper. For a change, Danato was too anxious to be mad.

"I need to go back," Danato mumbled.

Belus froze and his jaw clenched tight before he answered. "I know." He rubbed his face peevishly. "What are you going to do?"

"I have no idea, but we have to keep Cori away from her."

"That's going to include the prison now. The proximity to the—"

"She'll have to stay here." Danato didn't offer any exception to the statement.

Belus glanced at his door, no doubt already imagining what odd roommates he and Cori would make. "Short of locking her in, she isn't going to stay. You know that."

Belus looked down to the ground. "Not unless I tell her the truth."

Danato didn't answer right away, and Belus took it as a negative.

"She will never stop asking the questions now. And we won't be able to protect her if she seeks out the answers herself."

Danato felt ill; his past and present were finally colliding. It had been inevitable. He knew it was time to let go of his secrets, but he was going to need help. "Would you tell her?"

Belus's concern faded into indifference, as if he had just shut off his heart for good. "Yeah, I'll tell her."

"You can decide how much she needs to know." Danato walked away. He should have walked back inside and told Cori himself. At the very least, he should have apologized to Belus for being a coward again, but he didn't. Instead, he went back home to have a long talk with his wife.

12

C ORI BANDAGED HER OWN wound while Belus was outside talking to Danato. She had too much experience to wait for nurses. She twisted open a package of pain killers and popped them down her throat with the last of her water.

She stood, grimacing at the pain, but she refused to give in to it. She'd had worse, much worse.

Her head was woozy from the sedative Belus had given her, but she wasn't giving in to that either.

She marched confidently to the door, but it opened before she could make her dramatic exit. Belus came back in and saw her standing. He glanced at her bandage, quickly evaluating it as acceptable before offering her a curious look. "Where do you think you're going?"

"I want answers from Danato."

"He's gone back to the house," he said bitterly.

"What?" Cori took a step forward, but Belus shifted, announcing his intention of stopping her. "He can't go back there, Belus. She... it... that thing wants to hurt me. What makes him think it won't do the same to him?"

"She won't hurt Danato." Belus said it confidently, but she could see part of him was questioning it.

"Why do you say that?"

"She's permanently imprinted on him." Cori scrunched her face in confusion. "Let's not get into that just yet."

"No! No more placating! No more treating me like an outsider! I have a right to know what the hell is going on!"

"You need to calm down, or I'll give you another sedative."

"You need to move before I *make* you move!" Cori fumed.

His brow perked. "Why don't you go ahead and try that, kid? I think we both know that I'm not afraid of you."

Cori clenched her teeth and let out an aggravated growl. "If I weren't pregnant, I would slam you up against a wall."

"I'm not sure you've ruled it out yet," Belus mumbled as he shut the door.

Despite his concern for her temperament, she was already losing steam, either from the sedative, or her hormones were nosediving into a different emotion. "Just tell me what's going on."

"I will," Belus said clearly, and Cori's mouth drifted open in surprise. "I'll explain everything in the morning, I promise, but for now, you're going to bed."

"What, here?" Cori stumbled as she tried to look at his house. The conjoined living room and kitchen reminded her of an apartment more than a house. The furnishings were plush and neutral-toned, but they felt more like props for a model house than anything personal to Belus.

"Easy, kid. Let's get you to bed before you pass out. I have no intention of carrying you anywhere." Belus left the door unmanned, but her desire to escape left with his promise to give her answers.

She followed him to a bedroom adjacent to the bathroom. There appeared to be a third room, but from what she could see, it was being used as an office.

Cori paused in the doorway and looked over the caramel walls accented with sinuous, black, hanging sculptures, and several oversized frames exhibiting unabashed female nudes. The focal point in the room was a king-sized bed with an ebony and gold comforter. The rich décor contradicted the blandness of the rest of the house, but in many ways, this room felt more like Belus than the others.

She was hesitant to enter the room. She had never been across the threshold of Belus's home before tonight, and now, faced with the seclusion of his bedroom, she felt as if she were trespassing.

"You want a nightshirt?" he asked, rummaging through the bottom drawer of an antique chest of drawers. The reddish wood should have clashed with his motif, but it came off as an eclectic pop.

He tossed her a t-shirt that was a few sizes too big for him. She wondered if it belonged to one of his lady friends. "You mean for me to sleep here?" She nodded at his bed.

"It's the only bed." Belus pulled a pair of reading glasses off the nightstand by the bed and hung them on his lapel. She had never seen him use glasses, but she didn't want to bother with unnecessary queries.

"Can't I just sleep on the couch?" she murmured, trying not to sound insulted by his offer.

"No, because I'm not going to sleep just yet, and I don't want to keep you awake." When she didn't move further into the room, he tipped his head sympathetically. "Cori, you're injured, you're pregnant, and I know you are just seconds from passing out, so please, put on that nightshirt and crawl into bed."

He moved past her as she stepped inside. He reached back to shut the door. "Please don't go yet." She knew he had higher priorities, but she wasn't ready to be alone yet. "Please," she added when he didn't acknowledge her plea.

"Holler when you're tucked in," he said before he shut the door.

13

C ORI YAWNED AND SANK down into Belus's bed. The sheets were soft as kittens and the mattress was just supple enough to sink into.

"Comfy?" Belus leaned on the jamb with the door half open. He had a slight smirk on his face, no doubt amused by her bathing in the glory of expensive sheets.

"Mm-hmm." She blinked sleepily. The sedative was taking a strong hold on her brain.

"Okay, stay here, I'll be—"

"Belus." She reached out to him, but let her hand fall. "I'm sorry I yelled at you." He nodded. He either didn't think the apology was necessary, or he didn't want to talk about it. "I was just so scared. I'm trying to understand, and be respectful of Danato's privacy, but I'm just so sick of the secrets."

He moved into the room and sat on the edge of the bed. She rested her fingers on his. "This all has something to do with her, doesn't it?" she asked cautiously. "Olivia."

Belus's eyes flashed up at her, but it wasn't anger, just surprise. He looked back down at her hand and took hold of it. He stroked his thumb hypnotically over the back of her hand. "Yes, this particular 'Once upon a time' does start with Olivia, but we don't have time for all that now. We'll talk tomorrow, okay? Just sleep."

Cori yawned again and giggled. He perked his brow in question to her outburst. "I'm part of a pretty elite club to make it into this bed, aren't I?"

"Cori." He shook his head, scolding her for the inappropriate humor.

"Oh relax, Belus. You know I'm just jealous," she mumbled.

He smiled, and a quiet baritone chuckle vibrated in his chest. "Is that so?"

She smiled back at him, but her feigned flirtation made her think of Ethan, and her playfulness faded. "I wish Ethan was here."

Belus squeezed her hand. "I know, kid. I do too." Cori wasn't sure he thought one way or another about Ethan's presence, but given the situation, it would have been easier on him to have someone to share the burden of fixing this melee.

"Are you going to go help Danato?" Cori asked, barely keeping her eyes open. He nodded at her. "Will you wake me when you get back so I know you're both okay?" He shook his head slowly, without anything to qualify his answer. "Be careful," she murmured. He nodded and lifted her hand to his lips for a kiss before leaving. She wasn't awake long enough to hear the front door close.

14

CORI BOLTED UP OUT of bed when she smelled something burning. "Belus," she whispered into the dark. The room didn't have any windows, so she couldn't tell if it was night or day.

She slipped out of the bed and opened the bedroom door, prepared for nothing and everything. The bright sunlight of the morning streamed in through the high windows surrounding the main room.

"Good morning." Belus smiled warmly at her from the kitchen, where he was making breakfast. She cocked her head to one side, seeing him move deftly around the kitchen that was custom made for his height. "Hungry?" he asked when she didn't offer him any greeting.

She nodded and rubbed the sleep from her eyes. The t-shirt that she was wearing lifted enough to remind her she was being a little too informal. She looked back into the bedroom, but the clothes she had dropped on the floor were gone.

"Bathroom." Belus pointed to the door between the bedroom and the office. She expected to find her clothes piled inside on the hamper, but instead she found a duffel bag filled to the brim with random clothes. As happy as she was to have clean clothes, she realized they were expecting this to be more than just a one-night stand.

Once properly clothed, Cori joined Belus in the kitchen. She sat on a stool across from him and watched him flip pancakes. "How's your leg?"

"Fine." She looked down at the offending area; she had all but forgotten it. There were so many aches and pains from her pregnancy, one more was no different. "Where's Danato?" She looked up, horrified that she hadn't thought to ask sooner.

"He's fine," Belus said, not looking up from his pancakes.

"Is he at the house?" Belus nodded. She took in a sharp breath, trying not to get angry that he wasn't offering her more information. "You promised me the truth."

"You mind if we eat first?" He held up a pancake on his spatula. "Sleepover special." He winked at her, and she smiled.

"Bed *and* breakfast. Careful, you might never get rid of me."

He smiled, but he cleared his throat. "Speaking of that, I'm sure you've guessed, but you can't leave." He frowned and handed her a plate of pancakes after adding a few sausages.

She took the plate and started buttering her pancakes more vigorously than necessary. "How long?" He didn't answer, which meant he didn't know. Cori scoffed and dropped her knife on her plate, letting it clank loudly. "Can I even go to work?"

"You can go to the greenhouse, but anywhere else you'll need to be escorted."

"What about the bubble? I have crops to harvest."

Belus's eyes widened nearly unperceivably, but she was getting better at reading his subtle social cues. "I don't think that's wise either."

"Why is she doing this? Why is she so mad at me?"

"Short answer… because she's jealous."

"Of what?" she said, dumping far more syrup on her pancakes than any human should consume.

Belus looked at her, but didn't answer. She must have been missing something obvious. Her pregnant brain was leaving her moody and a little dimwitted. Then she caught on. Only one thing had changed in the last eight months. The house was jealous that she was pregnant.

Cori touched her belly and acknowledged the scrutinizing gaze that Belus was giving her. She wanted to ask a hundred questions, but since her pancakes looked so good, she took a different direction with her mouth.

15

CORI TOOK HER PLATE to the sink and immediately started to fill the basin with soapy water. Belus smiled at her from his stool against the island. "You don't have to do that. My house has no rules for tidiness."

She glanced back at him. "Habit. Besides, I know you're probably uncomfortable having me here to begin with, so I don't want to make this any harder."

His brow dipped, and he took in a steadying breath. "Don't try to discern my feelings or opinions, Cori, please. I don't usually like your blunted interpretation." She continued to gather up the dishes, unsure of whether an apology was necessary or if she even wanted to offer one.

"When you first came here, you looked like her daughter." Cori glanced back to verify that he was talking about Olivia. His glassy-eyed reminiscence answered her question. "You were a little shorter, your hair was longer, similar facial structure, but I think it was your anger that brought back more memories. Olivia was feisty." Belus smiled. "She had to be. Danato was pretty full of himself back then."

Cori wanted to get to the heart of the issue, but since Belus was the one with all the answers, she didn't try to rush him. She got the sense that this was the first time in many years that he had spoken about her.

"I worried that Danato was trying to replace Olivia with you, but it soon became clear that he had more paternal feelings for you." Cori cringed, remembering the kiss Danato had given her in her wish reality. She imagined that, a little older and with shorter hair, she looked even more like his Olivia. "Little did I know that would be worse." Belus winked at her, and she smiled.

"Was she really a prisoner?" Cori asked, trying to steer him back to the main topic.

"Yes, she was a very talented telepath, and as per her aforementioned feistiness, she got in trouble with a few high-end political figures. Her prison sentence was as much an exile as a punishment."

"How long ago was that? I mean, when she arrived."

"Oh, about ten years now." Cori quickly calculated that Olivia had died less than three years after she came to the prison. "She arrived in a piss-poor mood and was demanding to speak to whomever was in charge. Danato, naturally, was more than happy to oblige her and had she been a rodent-faced troll, he might have succeeded in knocking her down a peg or two, but instead they just went head-to-head in an argument that lasted nearly an hour.

"I actually had time to grab coffee and come back. By that time the volume had come down, and the guards no longer had to hold her back."

"What were they arguing about?"

"She was insistent that it was within her rights to utilize her God-given skills to *help* in war negotiations. She was one of those geopolitical, world-peace-or-bust type of women—American, of course. She was actually training to be a lawyer when her abilities came on full-strength. The trauma of it threw her off track for a few years, until she decided that being a human lie detector would come in handy for a news reporter."

"Oh, no," Cori said, already imagining what damage a telepath could do to someone's reputation when they had a camera crew backing them up.

"Oh, yes." Belus nodded in agreement. "She started out simple, uncovering a few criminal operations here and there, but she started to realize that chopping off the head of the weed doesn't guarantee that it's going to die. She moved up to corrupt businessmen and lazy politicians until eventually on live television she all but accused a very rich man of pouring funding into an undercover nonmilitary-sanctioned project in Russia." Belus peeked up to see if she understood him. As her mouth dropped, his smirk grew.

"Olivia found out about the prison."

"Yes, she did. Unfortunately, what she didn't account for was that the man she was accusing was only one of many rich and connected men responsible for keeping the prison a secret. He laughed off her accusations, but within two hours of the interview, she was captured, placed on a plane, and shipped here indefinitely. The cover story back home was she was fired and sued into submission."

"So, she arrived here, fresh from capture, spouting about the rights of an American citizen, while Danato basically told her she no longer had any rights," Cori summed up.

"Obviously that went over about as well as a brick on a little toe."

Cori drained the sink and left her towel to dry on the stove handle. She leaned over the slightly too short island propped up on her palms. "I assume that fight led to some mixed feelings that eventually blossomed into love."

Belus shook his head. "No, I believe that after that fight, they did truly hate each other. Much like your first introduction to the prison, she found the idea of *indefinite* a little too consuming. She hated Danato because he represented a forever that she didn't choose."

"You mean she wasn't the Zen, accommodating woman that I was when I arrived?"

Belus looked like he was trying to glare at her, but the grin he couldn't quite keep control of ruined it. "No, kid, she wasn't all rainbows and bumper sticker t-shirts like you," he said, nodding to her 70s floral design t-shirt that said, *Pick your nose, not a fight*. She laughed at his disapproving head shake.

"What happened in the days, weeks, and months following that fight?"

"I fell in love with her," he said casually, as if it was no more an admission than leaving the toilet seat up.

16

C ORI CLEARED HER THROAT and followed Belus to the couch. He sat on one end and she on the other. She tucked her bare feet under her and sat facing him. "Were you two...? I mean... how close...?"

"No, it wasn't like that. At first, I was just the guy to ask questions, so she didn't have to interact with Danato. Then our conversations extended beyond the walls of this prison. It was a revelation to me to be able to speak to someone about something new. No offense to Danato, but when two people spend a majority of their lives in the same place together, the quality of conversation wanes... a lot."

Cori chuckled. She had struggled with that as well. Feeding new life into the dinner conversation usually involved reading more, and since she wasn't an avid reader, she had to get creative.

"Did you ever tell her that you loved her?"

"I had only begun to realize that I was feeling more toward her than a mutual respect. That's when we had an escape. It was a simple mistake, but one that almost cost her her life. Unencumbered by metal hinges, our beloved ork ripped off the door to her cell and attacked her. He had only just begun to beat her senseless when Danato arrived and offered a little quid pro quo."

"I don't remember any ork," Cori murmured.

"That's because Danato killed him. It only took a few blows to the head. Orks aren't quite as thick-headed as one might think. He didn't really mean to kill him, but he never was a big fan of seeing a woman hurt." Belus eyed her carefully. "She had been with us nearly a year, but that was her first taste of our bizarre world. She realized we weren't just a bunch of mad scientists creating hybridized animals. She was finally scared.

"She was torn up pretty bad, so Danato carried her to the infirmary. I saw her clinging to him and I knew... He saved her life. That was going to be hard to compete with."

Cori frowned. "I'm sorry."

"Don't be." He shook his head indifferently. "We had a wonderful relationship, it was just platonic."

"Danato and Olivia started to fall in love. You can spare me the details."

"I'm not sure I have many. I only know what Olivia told me and, frankly, that was enough to get Danato and me into a buck fight or two. He was envious of our friendship, and no matter how many times I vowed my loyalty as a friend to him, he just didn't like it."

Cori nodded, remembering Belus explain why he was keeping such a distance between them. Danato would have been wounded deeply if he thought Cori was getting too attached to Belus.

"Within a few more months, they were married. It was against every protocol imaginable, but I didn't fight letting her out to move in with him. I moved out, into this place, to give them privacy. They lived happily ever after for about a year. They were trying to have children, but it was proving difficult." Belus paused, staring down at the coffee table. When he looked back up, his story renewed. "Then the radio arrived."

17

CORI VAGUELY REMEMBERED ETHAN telling her about the radio that helped them discern her from the other transmorphs. What was very memorable was how viciously Belus had destroyed the device.

"It's hard to say if the house created it. It should have been outside of its abilities. Creating music, I mean. I still suspect that it was planted by someone, but who and how are so dizzyingly complex that I've stopped asking the questions." He paused, possibly thinking over those questions once again. "She didn't know. She picked it up to move it and it played a delightful song she hadn't heard in years. She hadn't heard any music in months, so she was thrilled. She danced and laughed, and when Danato came home and saw the radio, he threw it against the wall, shattering it."

"But I thought you used it to help me when I was trapped in the transmorph."

"We did. I was very surprised to see it. To my knowledge, the scraps had been thrown into the incinerator. I was most unhappy to see it again. I'll be furious if it returns a third time."

"What happened to Olivia?"

"Nothing... so far as we could tell. Life continued as normal. Olivia still couldn't get pregnant, so they did some tests." Belus frowned. "Everything came back blank."

"No problems."

"No, no results. The pap and blood tests showed nothing. They might as well have been testing water. The ultrasound showed up as a blank white image. It was being blocked by something. Olivia denied knowing anything, and at the time I don't think she did know, which made every decision that much harder."

Belus stood up and paced for a moment. Cori already knew how this story ended, but it didn't mean it wouldn't be hard to hear the second time. "You couldn't extract the entity?"

He frowned and shook his head. "By the time we figured it out, it was already entrenched. Removal was not an option and believe me, we entertained far more options than we ever thought we would."

"Couldn't you have just left it be?" She waited for him to glare at her, but he didn't offer any response. He was barely in the room with her at all. "I mean, if it wasn't hurting her, couldn't she just be a host or something?"

He looked at her blankly and shook his head. "Olivia was long gone by the time we knew, Cori. Her body was alive, but all independent brain function had stopped. She wasn't just a host; she was a shell. The sickest part of all of it was that the entity duplicated her mind so perfectly that she didn't know any different. Right up until the moment I raised my gun to shoot her, she was still pleading to me that she *was* Olivia."

18

CORI HADN'T EXPECTED THE sniffling, tearful hiccups that wracked her body, but she couldn't fathom what it would be like for Danato to lose his spouse and Belus to have to kill his friend. It was just too much for her hormone-addled brain to take.

"I'm sorry," she apologized, trying to calm herself down. Belus brought her some water, and she sipped it. He took a seat beside her and waited for her to settle.

"The part of the entity that was Olivia, or played at being Olivia, is still a part of its cognizance. Her base emotions and desires were retained and have become the foundation for her impulses. Olivia loved and cared for Danato. In that sense, the house is still her, but that couldn't be further from the truth. Like Danato said, the creature itself is complex, but it can only express itself in simple ways. That's why if you don't take care of your home, it will retaliate with little punishments."

"Is that why Danato's room is so unadorned and cold? A punishment for his part in... everything?"

Belus thought about that. "At first, maybe, but the house also reflects your mood and penchants. I imagine

Danato hasn't been interested in decorating his bedroom in quite some time."

"You think that my pregnancy has unburied Olivia's core emotions?"

"That's my first theory." Belus nodded and motioned to her rounded belly. "This is something she could never give Danato, and albeit exterior to his bloodline, you are achieving just that."

"If she loved Danato, she should be happy for him," Cori tried to rationalize.

"Right, because love always wins over jealousy." He smirked. "This being isn't in any way, shape or form human, but it is an emotional being. It will not act logically or morally; it will simply react."

"Why would you allow such a volatile creature into the prison?"

Belus chuckled and squeezed her leg as he got up. "I'm going to put on some coffee. Do you prefer tea?"

She furrowed her brow and opened her mouth to object, but then realized she didn't have anywhere to go, so she might as well take advantage of Belus's hospitality. "Do you have decaf?"

19

"Yeah, she's okay." Belus looked up at her through the office door. She had been easing her way toward the room since the phone rang. She knew it was Danato on the other end, but she also knew he wouldn't stay on the line long. "She knows the bulk of it. How did things go after I left? ... Well, that's better than nothing, I guess... What do you want me to do? ... I'm already doing that. What else? ... Yes, she understands that... Do you want to talk to her?"

Cori perked up and took a long step into the doorway. Belus frowned at the response on the other end, and she cringed.

"Danato," Belus said, turning slightly, "she just needs to hear your voice."

Belus got the answer he wanted and handed her the phone. She jumped over and pressed the receiver to her ear. "Danato?" she said, sitting down in Belus's desk chair.

"Hi, sweetheart," Danato said on the other end, and she broke into tears. His voice felt like a lifeline to the real world. She was grateful for Belus's kindness, but without Danato or Ethan, she still felt displaced.

"Hi," she managed to squeak back at him. She heard the door to the office shut as Belus left them to speak in private.

"How are you?" he asked with the weight of a thousand apologies lingering on the threshold.

"Scared and mad," she whimpered.

"I'm not going to let anything happen to you."

"I'm not scared for me. I'm scared for you," she scolded. "Why didn't you tell me any of this?"

"A hundred reasons that don't make sense right now."

"When can I leave here?" Cori picked up a pencil off the desk and rolled it through her fingers.

"We are trying to get her to settle down, so I need you out of sight for a while. Then we can appease her."

"Appease her?"

"Yes, our common interests must be balanced."

"When are you coming back?" She pulled open the top drawer of Belus's desk and slipped the pencil into the long slot meant for it. Along with various writing instruments was a pile of ten gold rings, including her wedding ring.

"I'll come see you tonight. Please listen to Belus."

"Okay," Cori said, distracted by the shiny diamond that she missed more than she could have thought possible. "I love you."

"I love you too, Cori." The phone clicked off, but no dial tone took its place.

Cori picked up one of the gold bands and stared at it. She was glad that they didn't have any unnatural pull on her, but nevertheless she couldn't help but wonder if she would be safer with them on.

She put down the ring, hung up the phone, and left Belus's office just as she found it.

20

"Everything okay?" Belus said, bringing a tray of coffee and cookies over to the coffee table as she came out of the office.

"No, but it's not any worse than it was before I got on the phone. Are those cookies?"

"Mmm," Belus answered through his first sip of coffee. "I hear pregnancy gives women an appetite."

Cori slunk over to the couch and took a seat. They were on the opposite sides from where they started. "I'm surprised you're letting me have cookies," she said, snatching one off the plate before he could second-guess it. It wasn't store-bought, so Belus must have had cooking skills beyond breakfast food.

"First off, I have never been opposed to letting a woman eat." She giggled through her cookie. "Second, you are nearly to the end. I doubt cookies will hurt you. And thirdly, I think you've earned a cookie."

Cori grabbed another after she washed down her first with her coffee. Belus had made something fancy with cream and sugar already in it, so it wasn't nearly as distasteful as she'd expected it to be. She noticed Belus was drinking plain black coffee.

"Aren't you going to have any?" she asked, looking at the plate of cookies.

He shook his head slightly. "I'm not much for sweets."

"Why do you…?" She trailed off, realizing she probably already knew the answer to her question. "Danato said he would stop by tonight."

Belus looked down at his coffee. "Back to your earlier question…" He shifted, so he was facing her more and she did likewise, drawing her feet up to get more comfortable. "We refer to this entity as a she for various reasons, but the designation is no more accurate than saying he, it, or they. She isn't a corporeal being and never has been. She is simply an energy that exerts her presence through the manipulation of matter."

He must have sensed that he was losing her because he set down his coffee cup so he could utilize his hand gestures properly—because that was going to help her understand the biochemistry of a nonorganic being.

"Okay, take, for example, your baby." Cori looked at her stomach. So far, it wasn't a baby. It was just a bulge that poked her in the rib cage occasionally. "You are growing a human being unconsciously via intricate cell division that was programmed into your DNA since the dawn of man. You eat food in order to sustain that process."

"I'm with you so far." Cori chomped down on another cookie.

"Now, imagine if you could consciously grow a baby without the fixed construct of the DNA blueprint. Imagine if you could grow something other than a human baby."

"Eww." She winced, thinking of a horror movie plot.

"No... you don't understand... this is a metaphor." He scooted a little closer. She had never seen him quite this enthusiastic about anything. "I'm saying you could manipulate the cells and the DNA. You could create a kitten, or a... spleen, I don't know. The point is that the female of the species has the unique ability to create brand new life that didn't exist before."

"I had a little help... well, not little," she added.

"Cori," Belus scoffed and laughed. "Can you focus, please? This is kind of interesting stuff."

"Sorry. Okay, so this creature is similar to me, because it can create life."

"No... well, no. Remember, she isn't corporeal, so she uses her energy to manipulate matter. Like your body divides cells to grow a baby, the creature divides matter to build and create objects, like the house."

"Doesn't dividing matter create nuclear energy?"

"Atoms are basically composed of three main ingredients: protons, neutrons, and electrons. Depending on how they are combined, that determines the element. She simply splits them and rearranges them how she wants them. She seems to have no trouble with metal, plastic, and brick, but so far she has never made any living organic materials."

"So, we can't install her in the Enterprise food replicators yet."

"No," he said quickly. "I believe that one of the reasons she targeted Olivia was because she wanted to be a part of creating a new life. It's something that she can't do. My second theory regarding your attack is more concerning than my first. I think she wants to experience the birth of your child."

"But that doesn't fit, because she was trying to kill me."

Belus pressed his lips into a flat line and nodded. "I hope that's what she was doing."

"You would prefer that?"

"Yes, Cori. We can protect you and repair you, but once she gets inside of your mind, we can't do anything to help you. She's like the hermit crab of psychics."

"But as long as I don't have any electronics, I should be safe."

"What about what Cleos said? Your mind is vulnerable. You have gaps that beg to be filled. I can't guarantee your safety with basic protocols."

Cori stood up abruptly and put down her coffee. "I'm putting my rings back on," she said flatly, and waited for Belus to object.

21

B ELUS STARED AT HER, momentarily baffled. He glanced at the office before hardening his gaze on her. "Are you *asking* for my permission?" he asked, not hiding his irritation at her *request*.

"Yes, sir," she mumbled.

"Mmm, a 'sir' even. You are earnest, aren't you?" His ire softened, and he picked up his coffee for a painstakingly slow drink. "Why didn't you just take them out of the drawer when you found them?"

"Because you told me not to wear them." Cori bit back her lips, hoping that was the right answer.

"Interesting. And if I tell you I still don't want you to wear them?"

She shrugged. "Then I will spend the remainder of the day trying to convince you in the most annoying ways possible."

"And if that doesn't work?" He narrowed his eyes at her, double-dog daring her to challenge his authority.

She sighed and flopped back on the couch. "Then nothing." She hated conceding to his authority when she so vehemently disagreed with him, but she needed Belus to trust her more than she needed to trust him.

After a short pause, Belus moved into the office and collected the rings from the drawer. He returned to the couch and dumped the fistful of rings on the cushion between them. "Did it ever occur to you to ask me if you could have the rings back?"

"Would you have said yes?"

"No," she huffed. "But that's when you would give me a reason to change my mind."

Cori looked down at the rings. He wasn't offering them yet, just displaying them. She needed to choose her words carefully. "These rings prevented me from losing my memory after a wish relocation. I'm not sure how powerful our house creature is, but the genie was referred to as god-like. If I'm going to be in danger, I think I should have the right to defend myself by any means necessary."

"I have two concerns. Firstly, Ethan is not here to take them off. Secondly, your emotions are very erratic right now. I don't want to get zapped every time you get pissed off."

"I guess you'll just have to call Ethan back if you need them off. And in regard to you getting zapped, just stop pissing me off." She pinched back her smile, waiting to see if he was going to be amused or not.

He gave her a smile, but it quickly faded. "I don't like complicating things, but I do agree with your logic." She reached for the rings, but he put his hand out over them.

"You understand this doesn't change anything. You can't go back to the house unless one of us is with you."

"I know." She took his hand in hers and squeezed it. "I promise. I won't."

"Okay." He relaxed back on the couch and she slipped her rings on. He checked his watch.

Cori smiled, slipping her diamond ring back on her finger. Belus tipped his head at her. "I missed that one." She wiggled her ring finger.

His mouth tipped in amusement. "How about a walk before lunch?"

"Yes, please," Cori said, ready for an activity outside of her new confinement.

22

Cori and Belus stopped at what was formerly the guardhouse. The scattered remnants of the wooden structure were already blending into the surrounding landscaping. "I didn't even know lightning could do this," she murmured, kicking the upturned soil that now scarred the courtyard.

Belus looked down at it as well. "Metallic ores…" He trailed off. "Efrat has a good deal more power than I realized."

"Does that mean you can't help him?"

"No, despite the immensity of it, he still uses his own internal energy to distribute the power. Efrat may be a very key factor in this prison someday. If we can rein in his temper tantrums and get him to focus."

Cori nodded in agreement. "He's just very bitter. His life has been stolen from him."

"Yes, I know, Cori, but just like you and Ethan did, he needs to embrace this new life."

"It's not the same, Belus." Cori wasn't sure why she was defending him, perhaps because he wasn't there to do it himself. "He didn't just lose his friends and family and home; he lost himself. I still remember what he was like before all this. He was like Daniel: a loyal friend, flirtatious to a fault."

Belus nodded. "Yes, but what you don't recognize is that Daniel was once like he is now: hostile and petulant. I got through to Daniel. I don't think I'll have trouble with Efrat."

"What do you mean that Efrat may be a very key factor?"

Belus nodded to her home in the distance. It was on the southwest edge of the compound, looking ominous—if that was possible. "Her." He started walking again, and Cori followed. "We didn't bring her here, the house entity. She is a schism in time, space, whatever. Technically, I don't think that she is supposed to exist at all." Belus paused in thought.

"About two centuries ago, she was discovered. Her power at that time was limited. Her manifestations were simply the duplication of small objects. Hikers would fall asleep with one backpack and wake up with two. One tent turned into two. It was myth more than anything, until one young man, Roland Latham—our founder, if you will—got the idea to duplicate diamonds."

"Diamonds?" Cori said, immediately wondering why she wasn't covered in them, if the house could duplicate them.

"She duplicated the look of it, but for all intents and purposes, it was glass. She didn't understand what he wanted. He wanted the exact mineral replicated, and to her, *looks like a diamond* was good enough, and I imagine took up a great deal less energy to make. It was a disappointment, but it was the first step in understanding that she was intelligent, and not just a phantasm miracle."

"So he didn't get super rich?"

"No, he did. He just had to do it the long way. He duplicated household goods and tools. He was an excellent salesman. When he purchased his first automobile, he thought that his production would skyrocket since he could make faster and more frequent trips, but of course, the creature had limited energy. Can't make a baby without cookies." Belus nodded to her belly, and she instinctively started petting her bulbous front.

"He didn't start making real progress until about ten years later. It was during a lightning storm one night that she duplicated his car... 300 times. He woke up in a parking lot." Belus paused to let her react to that number.

"That's why you think Efrat can help us."

Belus shrugged, not willing to commit to his theory yet. "That was when he realized electricity was the key. She needs energy to do what she does."

"You mean like the time bubble? Wait, does she...?" Cori saw the tiniest smirk on Belus's face. "She's the entity that controls the time bubble too?"

Belus rocked his hand back and forth. "To some extent, she *is* the time bubble. You see, when this place was originally built, it was meant to be a factory. They built the building around her. At that time, the edges of the bubble were in constant flux, and far from identifiable. Considering that stepping through the bubble puts you in an entirely different place, you can imagine how long the construction process took.

"Over the years of feeding the bubble with energy, she has offered us more exhibitions of her power: the elevators, the office, the house. I imagine they would have continued to increase her feed, if they hadn't discovered in the 1920s that she can inhabit minds. Some connection between artificial sound waves and brain waves, but we really don't understand it all that well. In 1923, the first moratorium was placed on electronic media devices. That, of course, didn't mean everyone was going to listen, though.

"It took a few decades and a few deaths, but they finally figured her out. She's an explorer. She's in a fixed position, peeking through a hole into this world, and she desperately wants to interact with us, but since we are organic, she can't do it the way she wants to. She doesn't copy things anymore. That parlor trick is old hat to her. She creates new surroundings based on what she discerns from us. She is perceptive to a fault."

Cori hadn't realized it, but they had gravitated toward the house. She doubted the house would come alive and eat her, but she was very reluctant to get any closer. Belus stared at the house for a long moment before turning back to head home.

"You seem fascinated by her," Cori commented after they were back behind the prison.

"She communicates with us empathically. Strong emotions she understands, but it's hard to communicate to her the small ones. She doesn't understand when she's doing something wrong until it's already done. Somehow Danato has to express to her that she can't hurt you."

"How do we do that?"

Belus frowned. "I have one idea, but Danato isn't going to like it."

23

"Absolutely not," Danato grumbled across the small table from Belus. Cori looked between them, as did Marissa—a rather young, attractive nurse with a robust hourglass figure, who didn't get the message that her dinner date was canceled. She would have been more than happy to have left without dinner, but Cori insisted she stay, much to Belus's dismay.

"So, Cori's moving in indefinitely, then," Belus suggested.

Marissa looked up sharply, apparently dismayed by that idea. Cori found a sudden need to itch her nose, which conveniently covered the growing smile on her face.

"No." Danato glared at Belus for forcing him into a corner with reverse psychology.

Belus was just as frustrated by the conversation. Cori knew they were both trying to protect her, but Danato's instincts were to squirrel her away, while Belus's were to face the problem head on. Danato was usually brave enough to take action, but the threat against her was making him freeze.

"So, what, abandon the house altogether? She won't find that insulting as hell." Belus violently scooped another helping of mashed potatoes onto his plate, but didn't touch them.

Cori wanted to mention that she didn't want to give up the house, but at some point, she had become unnecessary to the conversation. "How long have you been seeing Belus?" She smiled warmly at Marissa and stuffed her mouth with grilled chicken and mango salsa.

"Oh, we aren't..." Marissa stammered, not sure what to say regarding their relationship.

"Cori," Belus cautioned her quietly, but she just shrugged.

"We can find another way," Danato continued. "I don't want Cori back in that house, with or without me."

"Instead, you'll just wallow in misery there by yourself as punishment?" Belus cut his chicken gruffly. "Just like before?"

"She just needs to settle down!" Danato opened the gate on volume.

"She needs to see that in Ethan's absence, Cori belongs to you!"

"Excuse me!" Cori added to the volume.

"It's empathic interpretation, Cori," Belus defended. "It's not literal."

"What makes you think she cares about that?" Danato snarled. "It's not like she doesn't see that I love Cori."

"She doesn't *see*, Danato, she only feels. She feels what you feel around Cori, and I know it's not all love."

"What does that mean?" Cori volleyed the question between them. Marissa tried to sink deeper into her chair.

"It's not what you think, Cori," Danato assured her.

"What do I think? I don't know what to think," Cori pitched in frustration.

"She feels the love," Belus clarified, "but she also feels the sadness, and the pain, and the guilt. It's a package deal."

Cori dropped her fork. Apparently, Belus wasn't the only one put off by her similarity to Olivia. "That's it. I'm going to shave my head and get a face tattoo."

"It's not like that, Cori!" Danato insisted.

"Neither one of you can stand looking at me because you see *her*."

"Cori, don't be melodramatic!" Belus said sharply, before Danato could defend himself. "Danato, you need to take her back there. She won't hurt her with you around."

"Why wouldn't she?" Danato asked.

"Because she loves you! Whether it be Olivia's memories or your years in that house, she is devoted to you. You're the only one she caters to."

"I thought you said the house was jealous of me?" Cori interrupted. "Won't that make her madder?"

"That is a possibility," Belus admitted.

"And a risk I'm not willing to take!" Danato slammed his fist into the table.

"Maybe I am!" Cori yelled back at him and he stared at her in awe. She had stayed quiet long enough. "What is your plan, Danato? Tell me you have some other way to communicate with a non-corporeal being."

"I want to give her time," Danato reiterated. He was clenching his jaw, trying not to raise his voice at her.

"You want to avoid the confrontation," Belus murmured. Danato jumped from his chair, and Cori was up right after him.

"Stop!" She pressed her hand to his chest and she could feel his heart thumping. "He's right." Danato's eyes widened at the betrayal. "Look, Danato, if this was a year ago, I would give you the benefit of the doubt, but since I told you about my pregnancy, you've gone from elated to forlorn."

Cori glanced back at Belus. "Theory number three. I get that this must be bittersweet for you. I understand firsthand how you can love someone and resent them at the same time, but maybe the house can't comprehend those differentiating emotions. Maybe all she feels is how many awful memories I'm dredging backup for you. Maybe she is just trying to protect you."

Danato looked at Belus with an unspoken question.

Belus shrugged. "That makes sense."

Danato looked down at her hand pressing on his chest and scooped it up. "You may be right on, Cori. In which case," he bowed his head slightly to Belus, "taking you back with me might help her understand."

Cori let out a sigh of relief and hugged Danato. He leaned in close to her ear. "I do not resent you, sweetheart." She gave him a somber smile and nodded as she pulled away.

"When do we..." Cori sat back down in her seat, and Danato followed. "...do that?"

"Why don't we at least finish our meal?" Belus suggested with a hint of displeasure.

"Not that I would mind sleeping in your bed another night." Cori bit back her smile as Marissa choked on her water.

Belus shook his head, fully exasperated. "You can take her back whenever you're ready, Danato."

Danato smiled slightly, finding some amusement in her joke. "With pleasure."

24

"I'M SORRY I HAVE to put you through this," Danato said as they walked through the door to the house. Belus and Cori agreed that there was no time like the present to work toward an understanding with the house.

Belus, along with a team of men, waited outside the house with axes, just in case there was trouble and they had to force their way in. No one had bothered informing them that a rescue attempt would be futile if the house retaliated, but they had put Cori at ease and that was enough of a reason to bring them.

Danato wasn't as confident that the house would treat him with any special care, but since he was able to convince her to release Cori the first time around, he hoped Belus was right about that as well.

"I'm not sorry." Cori gripped his hand. "I only wish you had been honest with me about your past to begin with."

"I know it was foolhardy and dangerous, but..." They stopped between the table and the couch and waited for the house to respond to Cori's presence. "I barely kept my sanity through it the first time. Reliving it wasn't appealing to me."

"I understand that, but you can't expect pain like that to just go away." She turned to face him. "You loved Olivia."

Danato felt a pang of heartache at hearing Cori say her name. The lights flickered, and he glanced around. Cori did the same. "Go on, sweetheart," he urged her. "Say what you want to say."

"I love Ethan, and if he died, I would be beside myself with sorrow, but..." The temperature in the room skyrocketed, and Cori shifted uncomfortably. He gripped her hand and drew her in a little closer. "...I would tell my children how wonderful he was, not hide him from them."

Danato knew the pain she was inducing was fueling the house, but he needed her to continue. It was the only way the house would understand the complexity of his love for Cori.

"You must have good memories of Olivia. You should be able to share them with us so we can know her."

The tears rolling down his face seemed to spring from nowhere, but he didn't wipe them away. He let the emotion overtake him. The grief, the pain, the sorrow. That was when the kitchen erupted in a burst of fire.

Danato pulled Cori away from the tentacle flames and sheltered her under his body, blocking the force of the blast that sent glass raining onto them. "No!" he yelled over the din of crackling flames and inhuman creaks from the house. "Don't hurt her!"

The heat on his back eased, and he looked up. The entire house had shifted slightly, making it appear malformed and offset. The flames of the fire twisted and writhed in a tornadic form at the base of the stairs.

"What is she doing?" Cori clutched him tightly.

From the whirlwind of fire, a body formed. It was only a flame shell, hollow on the inside, but it represented a human form as well as a shadow did. The figure pointed accusingly at Cori, sending tendrils of fire toward her.

Danato pulled her back behind him and the reaching attack retracted. "No! Don't hurt her!" He pushed every thought into the anger he felt at anyone trying to hurt Cori.

The figure stepped forward, tipping its head back and forth. It appeared to be trying to see around him to see Cori. The creature threw its fists to the ceiling, and the rafters cracked, sending the roof down on them.

After a shower of drywall, one of the rafters collapsed above them. The brace was directly above Cori and on its way to crush her. She moved, but a tendril that Danato couldn't stop tripped her footing.

He flung himself over her just as the thick metal landed. He would have been lucky to survive the massive impact, but it never hit.

He leaned over Cori, and she hyperventilated and clutched her stomach protectively. The tears in her eyes were enough to make him regret coming there, let alone the scratches on her face and hands.

He glanced back at the beam, which had conveniently or intentionally gotten hung up on the table. The fire shadow behind him looked like a bobble head, trying to impress upon Danato its confusion.

Danato touched Cori's cheek, wiping away a tear and smudging her with dirt at the same time. "Are you okay?"

"Are you?" She sniffled, glancing back at their enemy's face.

"I've had better days." He smirked, and she laughed tearfully.

"I don't think this is working," she said. "She's just getting angry at you for protecting me."

"Yes, she's frustrated." He brushed her hair away from her eyes.

"Ouch!"

"What's wrong?" Danato searched her for broken limbs and shrapnel wounds.

"The baby's kicking me. Adding punishment to misery, are you?" she scolded her belly.

"May I?" Danato looked her over, not sure what was kosher.

"Now?" Cori glanced back at the creature. Danato smiled, and she gleaned his purpose. She grabbed his hand and pressed it to where the child had previously poked her.

He frowned and shook his head. "I can't feel anything."

"Poke it," she said, glancing at the creature, which, as Danato hoped, was still watching the scene play out.

"Really?" he asked, surprised that she would approve. She nodded. He pushed in on her stomach and bumped into something that could have been her rib, except that it pushed back against him. "What?" He looked up at her and she smiled. "Was that a foot? It just kicked me." She nodded, and he poked at her again.

The tiny body inside seemed perturbed by his intrusion and pushed back against Cori's stomach to reposition away from him. He laughed abruptly and for a moment forgot the mortal danger they were faced with. "Oh, Cori, I can't wait to meet your baby."

"I'm kind of interested in getting to know it, too." She smiled.

Danato moved from under the beam and helped Cori out, as well. He took her hand and marched forward, no longer afraid of the imagery of humanity before him. Cori dragged behind him, not wanting to get any closer.

He stopped face to *face* with the projection. "Do you feel that?" he asked, booming his voice through the room. "You will not hurt her! She *and* her baby are everything to me." He pressed his hand to his chest. "I would sooner rip apart this entire prison and leave you alone in this tundra than risk her life! Do you understand?" Danato pulled Cori close and crushed her to his chest. She pushed him away slightly, but once she realized the body of flame wouldn't hurt her, she relaxed against him. He leaned down and kissed her forehead.

The head of the projection weaved back and forth, trying to imitate looking between them. After the quiet observation, the head seemed to bow and the entire creation disappeared. The house creaked and groaned as the metal and glass re-manifested itself in proper order.

25

C ORI WOKE THE NEXT morning in her own bed, in her own home, and she smiled. The house seemed to have forgiven her for inadvertently causing Danato so much pain, but neither she nor Danato was willing to take the chance that they were wrong.

Cori snuck through the salon doors of her bedroom and past the sleeping cowboy on her couch. She wasn't sure Ethan would approve of another man staying in their apartment while he was away, but since Duke had been entrusted with her safety, she figured it wasn't too far from his permission.

When she stepped back out of the bathroom, Duke was up, dressed, and at attention. Last night's sheets and blankets were neatly piled at the end of the couch. "Ma'am." He nodded shyly at her. She was still in her maternity night gown, which might as well have been an old lady's housedress.

"Good morning, Duke." She smiled at him. "You could have slept longer."

"No, ma'am, I think it's best if I head into work. Danato wouldn't approve of me being late, especially this morning. Should I wait for you?"

"Ah?" Cori looked around at her room. Everything looked fine. There didn't seem to be any indication that the house had ill will toward her. "I think I'll be fine. I still have my rings if I need to fight my way out the front door. Thank you for staying last night. I really do appreciate it."

"Yes, ma'am, I didn't mind at all." He blushed. "Doing my duty, that is," he amended, and Cori tried not to let him see her delight at his discomfort.

"Would you just let Danato know that I've survived the night?"

"Yes, ma'am." Duke ran out, happily dismissed.

Cori shook her head in amusement and leisurely dressed for work. Since she was nearly ready to pop, her duties were reduced significantly, but someone—most likely Belus—had given Danato the bright idea that even a pregnant woman could fill out paperwork. For the last six months, she had been spending most of her time procuring carpal tunnel syndrome.

After dressing, she headed to the kitchen for a light snack to ease her stomach into the real breakfast which wouldn't be for another hour. She chewed on a granola bar and sipped on a small glass of milk.

The feeling of eyes watching her uneased her, and she looked around to see if anyone was home. She knew it was probably just the house, *observing* her, but it felt strange.

Not threatening, but invasive nonetheless. Something had changed.

She heard whispers all around her, but as soon as she turned, they stopped. She felt a burning sensation in her hands, and she looked down. Her rings were glowing brightly, brighter than they ever had.

"Oh, shit," Cori hissed and ran toward the front door. She yanked on the doorknob, but it wouldn't budge. She braced her foot and pulled hard on it.

The knob broke, and she fell back, landing on her back. She reached instinctively to feel her belly, but the blossoming baby bump was completely gone. She screamed down at her slender blue-jean-and-t-shirt-toting body.

"What the hell's wrong with you?" Cleos snapped from above her.

She stopped screaming and looked up at him and the many other disapproving faces staring down at her from Cleos's perpetual dinner party. She gasped with enlightenment, then cussed loud and long.

26

CORI SPILLED A TORRENT of cuss words while Cleos followed her, sipping on his liquor. She searched for a door or window she could escape through. "What is wrong with you?" he snarled.

She pushed a kissing couple apart and checked behind the bar for a magical Alice in Wonderland-style escape route. "The stupid house is trying to take over my mind."

"The house," he said flatly, gazing at her through hooded eyes.

"Yes! The house! Are you going to help me get out of here or not?"

"Out of where, Cori? This is my trophy room; the only way you get out of it is if you go to another part of my mind, and believe me, if I let you do that you can forget about making friends with Cleos again."

Cori shoved her face into his. "I already have," she seethed. She expected him to glare right back at her, but he smiled broadly.

"Oh, what a fabulous trophy you would make."

"Stop it! This is serious!"

"I'm always serious," he said, walking around her to pour himself another drink.

"Shit!" Cori slammed her fists down on the bar and Cleos watched her with curious fascination. "Cleos, if she gets in, she won't get back out. I have to wake up!"

"Corinthia." He clicked his tongue. "What makes you think she isn't already in?"

"My rings." Cori raised her hands. The rings were still glowing even in this interpretation of things. She wondered why the baby didn't transfer, but she supposed it had a separate consciousness that wouldn't follow her. "They're stopping her... or at least trying to. How the hell did she get inside my mind? I wasn't listening to anything electronic."

Cori blanched and looked at Cleos. He tipped his head, interested in her deduction. "The vacancy. My unconscious is here." She motioned to his so-called trophy room, aka dinner party for douchebags. "You told me that I would be vulnerable to psychics. That empathic bitch just settled into the floodplain of my brain."

"It's good that you're here, then."

"That makes no sense," Cori grumbled in frustration. "If I wasn't here, she couldn't be there."

"I meant for me. I enjoy having you." He perked his brow.

"Seriously?" Her voice turned low and cold. "Do you hate me so much that all you can do is joke while the rest of my mind dies?"

His forehead crinkled in confusion. "Did he tell you he hates you?"

"I don't have time to discuss your petulant emotional evasion. I need help. Do you remember what that is?"

"Okay." Cleos nodded and raised his hand for her to leave the bar area ahead of him. "Let's sit down and see what we can do to fix this."

Cori took a seat on the couch near the fireplace, and he sat beside her. Several partygoers approached her, only to give her disgusted looks. She balled her fists tightly, ready to pick a fight with anyone that so much as rolled their eyes at her.

"Easy, Corinthia." Cleos rested his hand on her fist, and she looked at him. "Why is the house inhabiting your mind?"

"I don't know exactly. She was trying to kill me, but Belus thought she might actually want to take me over so she could experience the birth of my child. It's something that she could never experience as a non-corporeal being. Damn it! We all had it right, just at the wrong time."

"It is possible that staying here is the only way that you can preserve your mind."

"I'm not staying here to be your trophy, Cleos. I'm mad as hell and I want back in my own mind to kick her out."

Cleos smiled and tucked a hair behind her ear, which to her knowledge wasn't necessarily out of place. "I can try to help you, but..." He licked his lips, seemingly nervous. "A shared unconsciousness is one thing. A shared consciousness is very, very, dangerous."

"*Everything* is dangerous!" Cori shook her hands at the heavens. She jumped up, unable to contain her anger—baby or not, the hormones were still along for the ride. "The prison is dangerous, the inmates are dangerous, the whole freaking world is dangerous and I'm about to put a newborn baby into that world, so for the love of whatever you hold dear, *help me*!"

Cleos stood and approached her, just as the lights in the room flickered and somewhere a door slammed open. He tossed his drink haphazardly into the fireplace, making the flames erupt momentarily.

He pulled her close to him, clutching her hip tightly. She would have pulled away, but the stomping footsteps parting the crowd terrified her into submission. The sea of party goers peeled, revealing... Cleos. He was a mirror image of the one standing next to her, except that this one was enraged.

"Oh, holy shit, what the hell is this?" Cori whispered to the Cleos next to her.

"That, my dear, is danger," he said, gleaming with amusement.

27

"I TOLD YOU TO stay out of my mind!" the newcomer, Cleos, yelled, making the room shake.

Cori took a step back, that her friendly Cleos joined her in. "What's going on?" she whispered to him.

"This is my conscious mind." He waved his hand, displaying the irate version of himself. "You so thoughtfully announced your presence like a booming cannon, so here he is to kick you out. That is what you wanted, isn't it?" He smiled innocently at her.

The enraged Cleos flipped the couch with a mere sweep of his hand. Cori clutched tighter to her safer Cleos, but with another wave of his hand, he was launched into the distance. Cori stumbled from the sudden change in her balance.

"Cleos?" She backed away. "Is that you? The real you?"

"Yes." He glowered. "What are you doing here?"

"I'm under attack."

"Clearly!" He narrowed his eyes and dove for her.

She side-stepped him and pulled an innocent woman between them. She peeked from behind the woman's bouffant hair. "Not you! My mind, my conscious mind, is under attack by the creature that created the house. She's using the vacancy created by my unconscious to slip me on like a slipper."

He tipped his head. "How invasive of her." His voice sang with sarcasm.

Cori pushed aside the whimpering woman she was using as a shield and faced Cleos, like a... not whimpering woman. "I'm not in the mood for your heartless digs. It is not my choice to be here. As far as I'm concerned, this is all just an accident."

"You purposely entered my mind!"

"I didn't know what I was doing! Doesn't ignorance count for anything?" He opened his mouth to respond, but he said nothing. She took her opportunity while he was stumped for a comeback. "If you want to destroy our friendship to make it easier to leave me behind, go ahead, but it isn't going to change what's happening right now."

"She has a point." The other Cleos commented from behind them. He sat contently in a leather tufted chair smoking a pipe.

"You shut up!" Cleos groused at him.

"I need your help or I am going to die. Danato had to order his wife's death because this thing got in her head. The only thing protecting me right now is my rings, and possibly being here."

"If you weren't here, you wouldn't be here," he snarled with the same dizzying logic she had earlier. He paced back and forth past his other self before coming to a conclusion. By the look on his face, he didn't like it.

28

DANATO TAPPED HIS PENCIL on the desk and checked the clock on the wall. Cori was late—later than usual. Duke had popped in to inform him that all was well, and she would be in shortly, but that had been a half-hour ago.

She knew better than not to check in with him before doing anything else. He picked up the phone and dialed for his house. The phone rang several times. On the eighth ring, he hung up the phone, grabbed his cane, and marched out of his office, ignoring the searing pain in his leg.

Halfway to the house, he could see the fireplace smoking. It didn't usually light unless someone was home. He hoped Cori had simply fallen asleep, or at worst, had fallen and couldn't get to the phone. He prayed that was the worst that had happened.

He shoved open the front door, and it slammed against the wall with a crack. The downstairs was dark apart from the fire in the hearth. Cori was sitting on the couch watching the fire. She turned her head serenely, unsurprised by his entrance, and smiled soothingly at him.

"Danato. Welcome home, darling," she said, raising the glass of wine in her hand.

"Cori?" He stared at her, trying not to believe what he already knew to be true.

"Why do you look so frightened? Is everything all right?" Cori slipped off the couch, revealing a tight red wrap dress. Her hair was in an up-do and the makeup plastering her face was all wrong for her. She looked older. She looked like Olivia. "Darling, shut the door. You're letting the cold in."

"Who are you?" Danato covered his eyes, not wanting to look at her. He could feel the wetness from his tears, though he hadn't even come to terms with what he was seeing yet.

"It's me, Danato. Cori." She was coming closer, but he didn't want to look. She closed the door behind him and touched his arm. "Please, let's sit together and have a drink. Like we used to."

Danato put down his hand and looked at her. "Cori hates wine."

"No, I love wine," she insisted. "We always used to drink it, by the fire."

"No, *Olivia* loved wine. I used to drink it with *her* by the fire." Danato's voice grated as anger overtook his fear. "If you don't release her, I will starve you out."

"I don't know what you're saying."

"Yes, you do." Danato took a step away from her and circled to the coffee table. He picked up the wineglass she was drinking from and shattered it in the fireplace. "Alcohol is bad for the baby. If you were Cori, you would know that. Olivia is dead, so you can't be her either. Who are you? *What* are you? Why don't we just cut all the bullshit and get to the point once and for all? You have Cori's mind and body. You should be able to communicate with me well enough to explain yourself."

Cori tipped her head back and forth, examining Danato just like the fire projection did the night before. "Doesn't this make you happy?"

Danato shook his head slowly. "No."

Cori moved closer to him, facing off with him between the couch and coffee table. "Does this make you happy?" Cori untied the wrap dress and revealed sexy, red lingerie underneath. Danato looked away, shaking his head.

"No."

"But you love her," she rationalized.

Danato pulled the dress ties from her hands and rewrapped the dress around her. "Not like that," he stated carefully.

"I thought you loved Olivia, but you destroyed her. Will you destroy Cori as well?"

Danato looked down at the floor. "If you don't leave her, I will have to." He caught sight of the glowing rings on her hands. They were fighting to protect her, but they weren't keeping the entity out. He hoped it wasn't too late to help her.

Cori shook her head. "I was everything that Olivia was. Why couldn't you love me the way you loved her?"

"Is that what you want?" Danato narrowed his eyes on Cori, trying to read between the blank-faced expression and the tone in her voice. "Do you want me to love you?"

Cori tipped her head in thought. "Yes. I want to experience love. I want to feel love."

"You *do* feel my love. I loved Olivia and I love Cori. They are different forms of love, but both very powerful. You must feel that from me. You must sense my draw to them."

"Yes, I feel your love toward them, but I do not experience their love toward you. I want to... *be* in love. I do not understand this emotion. I understand happy, sad, angry, and jealous, but I do not understand love."

"It isn't a singular emotion that you feel in the moment. It is a condition, so to speak."

"It is a sickness?" Cori asked, tipping her head again.

"It is a connection, an imaginary tie that draws one's attention repeatedly back to that person. It opens you up, leaving you vulnerable to joy and pain."

"Is that why you destroyed Olivia? Were you defending yourself against pain?" Danato sat down on the couch and looked into the fire. Cori sat down next to him, intent on receiving an answer.

"I destroyed Olivia because you are a creature with great power, and you hurt people when you take a body over."

"No pain." Cori touched her own cheek, as if she was consoling herself.

"I mean emotional pain. You are taking away the person I love."

"I am an *exact* replica."

"So are twins, but as they develop, they deviate from each other. Life experience changes everyone. You can never duplicate who Cori would become."

"That is irrelevant. You don't know who she will become."

"It's relevant, because I know you aren't her. I only love Cori, and the fact that you can't reciprocate that emotion should be proof enough that you are an inadequate replica."

Cori turned away, absorbing that information. Danato had a half hope that it would be enough for the entity to release her, but it faded when she smiled. "Her mind is strong. She is very angry. She wants me to let her go as well, but I won't. I believe I can experience love when this child is born." Cori petted her belly tenderly. "All human mothers love their offspring unconditionally. If I experience this, then I will know love. I will feel love."

Danato frowned. Cori wasn't due for another month. That would be too long. Even if the being was satisfied with the experience, she wasn't likely to give up Cori's body.

"If you don't leave her, I will destroy her," Danato threatened.

"No, you won't. You couldn't kill Olivia. You won't kill Cori. You definitely won't risk the baby. You love this child, and you haven't even met it. That I find very interesting."

"I find it interesting that your nose is bleeding." Danato smirked. Cori touched her nose, revealing the blood that Danato was seeing. "What's the matter, *darling*? Is she fighting harder than you expected?"

29

"This is going to hurt him, isn't it?" Cori asked Cleos, who was content to lean against the fire and watch the other Cleos meditate in preparation for the coming battle. He was sitting on the leather couch that had unceremoniously returned to its original position when no one was looking.

"Oh yes. I can't say I'll feel much, though, so I'm not really concerned."

Cori frowned at him. "You're kind of an ass, aren't you?"

He shrugged. "Yes, but I'm fun at parties." He winked, and she held back her smile for the most part.

"It won't kill him?" she asked.

Cleos waggled his head. "It's always a possibility, but as the central core of his ego, I can't admit to any shortcomings in strength or ability, because I'm awesome."

Cori moved to the meditating Cleos and sat beside him. His frown told her he knew she was there. "If this is too dangerous, you don't have to do it."

His eyes fluttered open, giving her the usual glare. She wondered if he would ever look at her with the same flirtatious, mischievous gaze he used to. She would never have guessed that she would miss it. "What happened to, 'Cleos, help me?'"

"I want your help, but not at the expense of your life."

He grimaced. "What do you care?"

"I'm not the one trying to abolish this friendship. You are! Plus, I am not an asshole! I actually give a damn about you. I don't know why. Between you and Efrat, I should be put off making friends for the rest of my life, but somehow I still keep fighting to find that sliver of hope. And you know what I figured out, thanks to Efrat? It's not about you, it's about me. I am a good person, and I will fight to find good in everyone, no matter what."

"Even Gypsy?"

Cori blanched and lost her train of thought. "How do you...?" She gave up the question. Cleos knew everything about everything. "Whatever. She was a bitch. I don't blame her for that. I just blame her for being a psychopath. Can we get back on topic?"

"Certainly," he agreed, but she could see the slight amusement in his eyes. He had gotten his stab in. He would be content for a while. "Are you ready for this?"

"No. What are we doing... exactly?"

"Her mind is in your mind, and your mind is in mine; so, by the law of distribution, she is in my mind." He smirked.

"But she's really powerful."

"Yes, but only part of her mental capacity is inside your mind. We just need to introduce her to me, so I can educate her on proper etiquette, and to stay the hell away from my friends."

"Is that what we are?" Cori asked before she could stop herself.

Cleos's enthusiasm dimmed, and she instantly regretted drawing attention to the verbal slip-up. "First, we'll see if we can use the rings to our advantage. No matter what happens, you need to let me keep control. This is going to get messy, and my mind is not someplace you want to get lost in. Understand?"

"Yes." She nodded abjectly.

He reached out his hands, and she took them, not questioning anything more. The room faded out like dimming lights at the end of Act 1. In the darkness, she could hear a conversation. It was muffled, but she sensed it was Danato and her, or rather, *her*.

"Cleos?" she spoke, and the words echoed.

"Shhh!" She felt the hush more than heard it. "Stay calm and open your eyes." Cori opened her eyes and found herself standing on a small wooden pedestrian bridge. There was no water to speak of, but in and around her were images that if she focused on would become clearer. "Don't worry about that," Cleos said from one end of the bridge. She moved toward him, but he put up a finger. She stopped instantly.

"Do you know how vast my mind is?"

"As vast as your ego?" she said automatically, without thinking if it would anger him. A slight smile played over his lips, but it faded into something that might have been sadness, but it was probably just annoyance.

"It is the key characteristic that separates readers from collectors. It's what makes us do what we do. I can house thousands of minds inside of me. Hundreds of thousands if I just take a pinch. Once in a while, I find a mind that appeals to me. There is no rhyme or reason. I'm just drawn to it. You, my dear, are one of those minds. It's a dangerous temptation putting your unconscious and my unconscious together. What should happen if they decided to run away together?"

"What *would* happen?" Cori asked quietly.

"They can't," he said flatly, like she had just ruined his metaphor with logic. "I'm just trying to impress upon you that we really need to fix this connection. However, since it is available to us now… I'm going to use it to my advantage, but… for the record, I'm only doing it because your house creature is bound to have some invigorating memories for me."

"I don't believe you." Cori stared blankly at him. "It's not the only reason." His response was nothing but cold, inquisitive eyes. "If it makes it easier on you, though, I'll pretend. Help me on this *and* stop intentionally trying to hurt me, and I'll give up. I'll leave you be. Whether I owe you that is still up for debate, but I'll do it, because I…"

Cori couldn't say the words. She tried to think about ways to skirt around it, but there was no point. He was listening to her, but only to watch her writhe. She wanted to express her sincerity, but not to the point of diminishing herself. If this was what he really wanted, then in gratitude for all the help he had been over the last few years, she would release him from any obligations of friendship.

"The connection between mind and body," Cleos continued when it was clear her performance was done, "for someone such as yourself is profound. I may meander in and out of my own mind like it is a real physical place. You, however, are very connected with your body. Even now, as you stand here, you are not fully here. Your conscious self is fighting very hard to get control back. While she is handcuffed to your body and being body-slammed by a superior intellect, you—your unconscious self—are remarkably free to help her."

"How?" Cleos pointed to the far end of the bridge opposite him. A light sparkled at the end of it, like sun through water. Cori started to walk toward it, but he hissed behind her. "What do I do?"

"You calm down, and then you close your eyes, and reach out to me and to yourself."

Cori didn't bother asking, 'how' again, since she was likely to get the same answer. She did as he asked and literally extended herself to and fro. He didn't laugh at her, so it must have been a reasonable, albeit metaphorical, approach.

"No matter what, Cori, you come no closer to me and no closer to her. Just stay in the middle. You are my bridge to her, to you, and to your body. I will do the rest, but be prepared; you don't have the easy job."

C ori could feel the pull from both directions. The moment she slipped forward, she pulled back, and then did it all again; fighting the gravity of her body and the mental draw from Cleos. She hadn't expected physical pain, but since she was two horses away from being quartered, something was bound to hurt.

She screamed and pulled back on both ends. Cleos was saying something encouraging, so she must have been on the right track. As near as she could tell, she was either trying to draw Cleos closer to her or *her* closer to Cleos. Either way, she was moving mountains with her mind.

She felt white-hot stinging around her fingers, and she was certain that the rings were about to sear into her hands. A thought had been at the back of her mind, but it suddenly jumped forward to scare her. She worried that the rings might someday adhere to her hands permanently.

She lost focus and the imaginary mountains snapped back. She was about to give up entirely when she heard Danato. It was low and distant, but he was calling to her, begging her to keep trying. She must have been affecting her body somehow.

She pressed on, pulling her arms nearly out of socket before the weight moved. It occurred to her that the weight couldn't be real and it was just her mind's way of translating the energy it was taking to do this task, but of course, that didn't make it any easier.

"Cleos?" she ground out as the two forces were nearly touching.

"You're doing everything right, just a little more. Once I get access to your mind, three things are going to happen." His voice was so soothing, it took all her concentration not to let go and lie down for a nap. "Your rings are going to absorb my gift, just as they did before. You are going to get ricocheted back into my mind—remember, don't get lost. Then I'm going to start devouring every last inch of that bitch I can get to." The disdain in his voice was only slightly less than when he talked about his photophobic neighbors.

Cori's hands touched and a flash from her rings blinded her even through her eyelids. All three things happened as he said they would. What he didn't mention was that it would feel like a rollercoaster coming to a full stop mid dive.

31

"WHAT IS THIS?" CORI looked at the blood on her hand from her nose and looked around like she might see the invisible force causing it.

"Come on, Cori, fight! Come back to me!"

"How is she doing this?" Cori stood and walked away as if to find a place to hide, but she only made it to the fireplace. "She isn't strong enough to fight me."

"She doesn't have to be. She just has to be stubborn, clever, and lucky as hell, and yes, she is all that."

"How can you choose her over me?" Cori returned to him, kneeling before him, her hands touching his chest. "I do everything for you. I provide you with a house. I protect you. You haven't even begun to see what I can do. My powers are limited only to my energy; I could build you a city."

"And what would I do with a city? Fill it with the things you create and stare at them. I am truly honored to have a home from you, and I appreciate the cage you have provided for our wizards, but this arrangement is mutual. We feed you energy, you provide for us. You are overstepping your boundaries by taking the minds of my people."

"They are superfluous."

"Not to me!" Danato saw her flinch, and she drew back away from him. He wondered whether it was *her* he was affecting, or if some part of Cori was still awake enough to feel the boom of his voice. "We are not playthings. We are not research opportunities. We are not interchangeable. And we are certainly not expendable." She tipped her head, taking in the statements, cataloging them, and shoving them in the outgoing pile. This wasn't working.

"Did you make that baby?" Danato stood and approached her.

Belus and many men before him had surmised that this entity was childlike. A child with great power, but nevertheless, a sentient being coming to terms with new emotions through each and every encounter. It wasn't a matter of logic. It was a matter of established rules. He had to find a moral boundary that even she didn't want to cross.

"I am not the creator of flesh." She stepped away, saying the statement with undeserved pride.

"You didn't make it, but you want to keep it."

"No, I want to love it. I want to feel love."

"Why would you love something you didn't make? You can't. A mother loves her child because she created it.

You created this house. You are proud of that creation and, as such, you have expectations for how we treat it."

"Yes," she said, looking over the house.

"I would no more break down the walls of this house than I would burn a work of art. I respect what *you* have created. It is beautiful, valuable, and purposeful." Cori raised her chin, absorbing the compliments without an ounce of humility. "I expect you to respect what I have created as well." Her face pinched, not understanding. "I have created the family that resides in this home. They are my masterpiece, and you are desecrating it."

"I am a replica." Her voice pitched into a whine.

"But I cannot love you, and neither will Ethan. That is the masterpiece you are ruining: the love that has been created here."

"I only wanted to be a part of it."

"You are. You have provided the canvas."

Cori's eyes blossomed, delighted by that declaration. Her shoulders rolled back, and she stood a little taller. She was flattered.

"Please." Danato stepped closer to her and took her hands in his. "Give her back to me."

Her head twisted awkwardly, and she grimaced. "She is mine. She was open. I like it here."

Danato wasn't familiar with children, but he guessed this was the irrational tantrum stage. He should have been terrified for his Cori, but between the rings, her undeniable luck, and the blood coming from Cori's eyes, he knew this fight was far from over.

"Then we will have to decide on a punishment for your disrespect of my belongings."

Before Cori could snarl a response, her body convulsed forward. Danato held her up while she panted and groaned. "Noooooo!" Her eyes were still open, but she scrunched her face in pain. She slipped to the floor and Danato followed her, holding her, waiting. "This can't be!"

"Oh, I think it can." Danato laughed despite the seriousness of the situation. "Please, sweetheart, come back to me."

The lights flickered, and the fire flared hot enough to warrant him pulling her away from it. For several minutes, she floundered in his arms, groaning and whining about her current predicament. Danato wiped away the blood on her face and shouted for his Cori to return.

When Cori's body went still, he gasped and opened his mouth to scream, but her eyes fluttered open a second later. She boomeranged her eyes from him to the surroundings.

"Cori?" It was a question, but he was also begging.

She smiled slightly before rolling on her side and puking. He laughed and pulled her hair back to let her get it all out.

32

"THE DECISION IS FINAL, Cori," Danato said diplomatically when they had reached the loading dock. His eyes were still red from their tearful reunion and she knew he hated sending her away as much as she hated going, but the house was—for lack of a more charitable word—pissed.

"I don't want to leave." Cori looked at Belus, who was standing next to Danato with his arms crossed, staring at the floor. He hadn't said much since she and Cleos had explained their side of things. She wasn't sure if he was being contemplative, or if he was hiding more emotion than he was sharing. Depending on what that emotion was, she might be just as happy with his silent dismissal.

Cleos, however, was watching her with predatory intent from behind Danato, just inside the door. She had barely remembered her cerebral interaction with him, but it only took a touch to raise the unconscious memories to the surface. He had saved her life, but it didn't seem to be out of benevolence or any altruism deeper than the avoidance of tainting his soul's resume. As she had promised him inside his mind, she kept the conversation on task, and kept her eye contact to a minimum—a concession that apparently didn't apply to him.

The dock manager was frantically trying to get things in order. He was unhappy that his shipment of non-goods was going to be put behind schedule because of her inconvenient need to flee for her life. He was such a jerk.

"Can't I just hide out?" she whispered, so no one else heard her pleading.

Danato shook his head. "She needs time to get over this. I can't risk her trying to get into your head again. Until you two figure out how to fix that," Danato glanced back at Cleos, but he didn't even afford him a glance, since it would disrupt his deadlock stare at her, "you're going to need to be extra careful. Right now, that's coming in the form of an impromptu vacation."

"What if she doesn't get over this?"

"She will," Cleos said, and she was forced to look at him, per proper conversation etiquette. "I've gathered a lot of information from her memories. She's a very extemporaneous creature. She isn't capable of long-term revenge plots. It's comparable to you burning your hand on a hot kettle. In the heat of the moment, you might yell and cuss at it, or even risk hurting your hand again just to throw it at a wall. But your anger would dissipate long before the pain, and the pain would be gone long before the mark of the burn."

Cleos was immobile as he spoke, and at one point, she thought they weren't talking about the creature anymore.

She wanted so badly to ask, but she had promised, and she was determined to keep that promise.

"Why can't I just go see Ethan?" she asked suddenly, breaking the connection. Danato glanced at Belus. It was a familiar tactic, but she hated that it was always being used to team up against her. "Please tell me you aren't afraid that we'll run off together. Danato, this is my home. A home I can barely stand leaving now."

"You're a distraction, sweetheart. I know you want to be with Ethan, but if he can provide even a sliver of knowledge about the dragons, we need to let him devote his time to that. I love you both very much, and it pains me more than you know to be without either of you. Besides, traveling that far in your condition is less than desirable."

"How long?" Cori looked at Cleos for the answer.

He shrugged and smiled. "I'll let you know." Once again, she wasn't sure if he was answering about the topic at hand or something else.

"We'll give it a week, Cori," Danato answered for him. "I want you back here before the baby comes. If necessary, we'll bunk you up with Belus again." Danato sounded serious, but his eyes were glittering with delight. He must have gotten an earful from Belus about her impromptu stay. She glanced at Belus, but he wasn't reacting to anything.

"I'll fill her in," Belus finally said.

She wasn't sure what there was to *fill in*. She wasn't always the brightest bulb, but the "get out" had been pretty clear with or without pictures. She could only assume it had something to do with the private conversation she had been dismissed from prior to their announcement of her relocation.

Danato pulled her into a restrained hug, so he didn't hurt the baby. When they split, he touched her belly. He was past the point of asking for permission, and she didn't mind. It was nice to observe his excitement. "I'll miss you both," he looked up at her, and she saw him swallow, "very much."

She mouthed 'I love you'—not to conceal it from anyone, but rather to keep it sacred. He mouthed it back and drew away from her. He nodded to Belus and turned to face Cleos.

Cleos finally drew his eyes away from her and looked over Danato. His eyes settled on his cane. "I can still help you, Danato."

For a moment, Danato seemed to consider it, but then he laughed and grabbed him by the shoulder, less than gently ushering him out the door. Neither one of them looked back.

She turned to say something to Belus, but he was already on the raised level of the dock behind her. His sudden looming height made her jump. "Geez, Belus."

"I've *called* ahead to Sophie. She will make sure Daniel is there to meet you."

"Daniel?" She didn't mean to make a face, but Belus was less than pleased with her placing any insult on his protégé's name. "I just mean... I thought maybe I could stay with Jordan."

"No," Belus said firmly, and she started to ask why. "Because I want you with Daniel. Just in case."

"Just in case of what?" Her eyes flickered over his, looking for the invisible threat no one told her about.

"Just in case you go into early labor."

"Oh. Really? What's Daniel going to do that Jordan can't? She can drive, can't she?"

"Cori..." His voice was loaded with threat, but she couldn't mind him since she didn't understand his reasoning.

"Belus," she said right back, giving an exasperated shrug.

"I want Daniel to attend to you, if you should go into early labor."

"You mean actually deliver the baby? Belus, he's my husband's best friend, and that is a very intimate experience." He didn't waver. "Belus!" She pointed to her bulbous belly. "This isn't your decision. I'll just go to a hospital *if* it comes to that."

She could sense his ire rising, but instead of blowing up, he kneeled down before her, bringing himself face to face with her. "Cori, I need you to trust me on this. Daniel has been privy to many births. He has saved your life more than once. I trust him implicitly and I wouldn't have agreed to you leaving if it wasn't for that contention."

Cori's mouth dropped open. She couldn't imagine how that argument went with Danato. Daniel had begun to earn Danato's respect, but it was a hard road. Their relationship wasn't quite ready for trusting him with Cori's life, or her child's. On the other side, though, Belus was the one who was fighting for her to stay, and the only person he did trust with her life was Daniel.

Oh, to be a fly on that wall.

"Belus." Cori glanced around the room, looking for the argument that wouldn't disrespect Belus's authority or incapacitate her claim to adulthood.

"Cori." He spoke her name softly. It was his concern driving his insistence rather than his desire to have her compliance.

She still wanted to say no, but the part of her that wanted to keep Belus on her good side won out against the part of her that didn't want Daniel to be her stand-in gynecologist. "Fine," she conceded. "I'll do as you advise, but I want a big-ass gold star for this in your book."

"What do you mean, kid? You *only* have gold stars in my book." He smirked.

33

E THAN PEEKED OUT THE window of the horse-drawn carriage. It reminded him of the one he had ridden in the night Danato rescued him into slavery, albeit a little rickety. The desert scenery was remarkable, but after 36 hours of planes, trains, and vehicles loosely described as transportation, he wasn't as captivated by the distant rugged mountain landscape as he should have been.

He was more than disappointed to find out that his rendezvous with Annette would not take place in Beijing or Hong Kong, but rather in the province of Xinjiang. Naturally, the area was undeveloped, underpopulated, and deceptively cold. His guide and driver, who barely spoke English, was fluent enough to warn him that the desert they were traversing was known by many names, among which were "The Desert of Death" and "The Point of No Return." So much for his vacation disguised as a business trip.

The coach came to a halt, and Ethan stepped out to stretch his legs. The driver looked down at him and nodded forward, ahead of his horses. Ethan stepped around the horses and found a young man leaning against a dune buggy playing a hand-held game.

He was notably Chinese, but his subdued features hinted at a mixed parentage. His short ebony hair was spiked in a faux-hawk, and he wore a red and black NASCAR jacket. He hit his hand-held game, frowning at the results of his concentrated efforts.

Ethan grabbed his bag from the carriage and met with him. He was a little shorter than Cori, but it was hard to say if that was a weakness for him or not. Ethan stared down at him as he continued to achieve his high score, despite the surrendering sunlight.

"Just a second," the young man drawled distractedly, twisting his lips in concentration.

Ethan might have been sympathetic to his gaming goals had he not been running on six hours of interrupted, uncomfortable sleep. "Now," he said simply, implying as much motivation as he could into the word.

"Yeah, I just need to—"

Ethan placed his hand over the game screen and squeezed tightly. The plastic started to crack, and the gamer looked up at him in shocked awe.

"Okay, okay! Please don't break it! It's the only one I have," the boy pleaded with honest distress. Ethan let go of the game and the boy immediately shut it off, frowning at the crack in the plastic casing. He stuck it in his back pocket without any further complaint. "Sorry, I just... I'm

Levi. Like the jeans." Levi stuck out his hand for Ethan to shake.

"Ethan." Ethan took his stiff hand in his, pressing just enough to declare his presence as someone of importance, but not enough to be a dick. He had already peacocked enough for one day.

Levi glanced down at their joined hands before his eyes flickered over Ethan's face. Ethan retracted his hand and Levi motioned to his vehicle. "We have to take the next few miles by dune buggy, if that's okay. The horses don't do as well in the softer sand." Levi smacked the roll bar, looking over the vehicle proudly.

Although they were probably similar in age, Ethan wondered if he had ever been that young: jubilant admiration for toys, short attention span, and easily intimidated. "And if it's not okay?" he asked, unable to resist making the boy's nervous smile fade.

"Oh... um... well, I guess I could go back and fetch a camel." Levi looked at his watch. "Gets even colder after sunset," he mumbled to himself. "I should bring some furs along."

"Levi," Ethan interrupted, "I was being flippant. The dune buggy is fine."

"Oh, right, yeah, sure." He looked at Ethan's bag and reached for it. "Oh, here, I can load that up."

Ethan removed the strap from his shoulder and Levi strapped the bag in despite the vehicle not being designed to carry luggage. The two-seater buggy looked like a frame-only car, but with significantly smaller wheels and engine. The two plastic seats afforded comfortable seating, but Ethan was already imagining the pelting sting of wind and sand.

"Nice wheels. How fast does it go?" Ethan asked, more to ease Levi into a conversation he knew he would enjoy.

"Thanks, it comes with the job, but I reworked the engine so I kind of get dibs on it." Levi once again patted the vehicle like it was his loyal pet. "Max is usually 50-60 for this style, but the terrain doesn't allow for much more than 35-40. I always wanted to get it out on the dry bed of the basin, but... well, you probably know how that goes. No drawing attention," Levi said through clenched teeth.

"Yeah, I know about that." Ethan rounded the vehicle to get in the passenger's side.

"Did you want to give her a go? Drive, I mean?" Levi's brow perked with the offer.

"I wouldn't dream of depriving you of the pleasure."

"Oh, no, man—er—sir, I drive it all the time. I don't mind."

Ethan chose to ignore the sir, since he had probably inadvertently demanded the respect with his braggart introduction. He looked over the mechanics of the vehicle. He rarely got to drive at the prison, and his experience prior to those walls was limited as well.

"I wouldn't want to wreck it for you," Ethan said humbly, but he was already moving back around.

"Go ahead. I'll just fix it up again. No skin off my back. I like hanging out with grease and wheels all day."

Ethan smiled at the image of Levi under a car, smeared in oil. It reminded him of Cori in her greenhouse, smudged with dirt from head to toe. He had yet to be away two full days, but his heart clenched at the thought of her so far away.

"In that case, I'd be honored." Ethan climbed in and Levi clapped his hands together and jumped into the passenger side. "How do I...?" He searched for the ignition.

"Right here, sir." Levi pointed it out as he handed him a pair of goggles. "You should probably fasten your seat belt. Annette will have my head if she knew I'd put you in any danger."

Ethan dutifully clasped his restraining belt after he started the engine. He couldn't imagine the beautiful, grandmotherly Annette ever being angry at anyone, but she wielded the power of the earth like a book of matches. She was probably best kept on one's good side.

34

THIRTY MINUTES LATER, ETHAN pulled into the grass hut village Levi had pointed out to him. The seemingly abandoned village was at the base of the mountain line, just before the ground started to elevate exponentially. Levi gave him a throat-slashing signal, and Ethan cut the engine.

"Tell me this isn't it." Ethan looked over the half-dozen structures with unhidden disgust. He was by no means spoiled, but he had hoped solid walls would be part of his lodging.

"No, but I should probably take over from here; the road gets kind of obscure after this."

Ethan nodded, not bothering to ask the definition of that. They switched seats, and Levi checked that Ethan's bag was secure before smiling at him and starting the engine. Ethan knew that smile meant he was in for something special and/or terrifying, but he just strapped himself in tightly and resisted the urge to question him about it.

The dune buggy took off fast, and Ethan smirked as Levi glanced over at him. He didn't want to give him the satisfaction of being surprised. Past the primitive structures, but before the mountain line, was a gorge. Ethan couldn't tell how deep it was, but its length spanned miles, disappearing in the distance.

Levi geared up to the alleged 50 miles per hour that Ethan had not come close to on the sandy dunes. The gorge barreled at them in fast forward, and Ethan couldn't help but grip the roll bar. He glanced at Levi and, as he suspected, he was smiling—whether from the thrill of speeding, or Ethan's discomfort, was unclear.

The depth of the gorge was still indistinct, but the width that expanded before them revealed to Ethan that jumping the gorge was impossible. At the speed they were going, a sudden turn would likely roll the vehicle. He knew Levi was only teasing him with the display, but they were quickly running out of reasonable braking distance and Ethan's patience for the cockiness would end sooner than that.

"Trust me," Levi said, losing his smirk. He must have sensed Ethan's irritation, or at least predicted it.

Ethan wasn't sure why he should trust him, and he was just as baffled that he did trust him, but he relaxed back into his seat, arms down, and let the impending cavernous fall come to him without objection or intervention.

At the gorge edge, Ethan's heart leaped into his throat and he made a concerted effort to keep his eyes open. However this was going to work, he wanted to see it for himself. Whether he believed it after the fact was up to his brain.

The dune buggy left the solid ground of the desert and glided, without so much as a bump, onto the thin air over the gorge. Like distracted cartoon characters, they were following the imaginary line that would break if they acknowledged it.

Ethan dared to look down and found the gorge to be several stories deep. Perhaps not as deep as his imagination would have guessed, but by no means a fall they could survive. He expected to see a hidden road invisible to the casual observer, but he saw nothing. If they were on a road, it was made of the clearest glass ever created.

When they arrived on the other side, a shimmer rippled through his vision, temporarily interrupting all conscious thought except the obvious "what the fuck" that never seemed to leave one's mind, no matter how disoriented one became.

"I can't see," Ethan said, blinking his eyes furiously, trying to get the damned shimmer off his retinas.

"I know," Levi said. "It will pass. Just try to keep calm."

The dune buggy hit a couple of bumps and abruptly descended downhill, sending butterflies from Ethan's stomach to the back of his neck. "What the hell?"

"Sorry, the entrance goes under the walls."

"What walls?" Ethan said sarcastically. "I can't see a flipping thing." He should have been used to the enigmatic disposition of everyone even remotely involved with Danato, but being blinded to protect the entrance of this top-secret location was going too far.

"Yeah, me neither; sucks, doesn't it?"

"What?" Ethan looked over at Levi, though he couldn't actually see him. "You're blind too?" Ethan had just assumed that the magical barrier was intended for strangers and that Levi would be immune. "But you're driving."

"It's okay, man—sir, I've driven it like a hundred times. I'm the errand boy. I could do it with my eyes closed." Levi chuckled, amused by his own joke. Ethan was about to snap at him, but shook off the unnecessary anger and joined him in the humor of things. At least they were surrounded by roll bars.

As if the outside wasn't cold enough, the decline brought them into a damper coolness. Ethan still couldn't see, but he smelled earth and moisture. He could only assume that their tunnel was taking them into the mountain.

Occasionally, the tires would hit the rumble bars and Levi would adjust his course, but for the most part, the ride went without interruption. Ethan didn't bother trying to fill the silence with conversation since Levi obviously needed to concentrate, but a minute passed, and he wondered how far into the mountain they were going.

Before he could ask, the reflective echo of the dune buggy engine ceased, and the air warmed. He could see the flicker of firelight through his blindness, and hear the echoing voices of men directing Levi to slow and park.

"Now what?" Ethan asked after the engine shut off. He probably sounded like an impatient child asking, "are we there yet?" but he couldn't help feeling vulnerable without his eyesight.

"Adrianna?" Levi called out. "There you are," he said, sounding relieved. "You mind doing your magic voodoo for me and my friend?" After a short pause, "Perfect, thank you. That's Ethan Pierce, Annette's *special* guest. Sir, the lady about to touch you is Adrianna Levinson. Don't... um... just let her do her thing."

Ethan was already questioning the designation *special*, so he didn't really have time to read between the lines of Levi's statement. Gentle hands grasped his biceps, willing him forward. He leaned with them, and two small soft kisses were placed on each of his eyelids.

Almost instantly, the smear of fairy dust clouding his vision dissipated to reveal a woman, perhaps in her twenties, standing before him in what looked to be pajamas. From the soft sweet kisses, he had expected her to be a beautiful, luminous woman, but his cleared vision revealed a gaunt, pale-skinned girl with long, ragged, deep russet hair that hadn't seen a brush in days. Her sharp nose might have been considered cute, if her cheekbones weren't demanding to be noticed right along with it.

Adrianna's wide eyes stared at him like a wild animal, fearful of every movement they saw. Though her discomfort at his gaze was obvious, he couldn't help but stare into the one part of her that was undeniably beautiful without reproach. Her gray-rimmed irises faded to a pale green at her pupil, making the color negotiable depending on the lighting.

He could feel an instant draw to her. It was not a physical attraction, but rather emotional. He wanted to envelop her in warm, loving arms, feed her a mammoth cheeseburger, and whisper endearing, paternalistic praises in her ear.

Ethan wasn't aware that he had reached out to her until she sprang back away from him. He was certain he was thinking only of shaking her hand for an introduction, but he was mortified to make her flee. "I'm sorry, I..." He looked down at his hand, wondering why it had caused so much confusion in her eyes. He hadn't even attempted to stand up.

"Ah, that's okay, sir," Levi assured him, but he was still racing around the vehicle to break up the situation. "I think that's good, Adrianna. Run ahead and tell Annette that Ethan is here?" Levi crossed his arms tightly over his chest as he spoke to the girl. "I was just going to give him a little tour first." The girl turned slowly, leaving them in her periphery until the last possible second, and then she was gone, leaving only an unnatural breeze from her sudden exit.

Ethan finally noticed the huge fire-lit room. It was vast and empty except for the vehicles it held. The only activity was a few men who had directed them into the gigantic parking garage. There were dozens of exit paths. Two twelve-foot hunchback giants guarded the one they had come through. They regarded Ethan enough to memorize his face, but that was the extent of their interest.

"Who are they?" Ethan nodded to them.

"Our resident guard dogs, Gog and Magog. They're harmless as long as you don't call them by the wrong name."

Ethan scanned over the similar beastly faces and scruffy hair. "Which one is which?" he asked, in case he needed to address one or the other.

Levi cleared his throat and ushered him toward one of the exit paths. "I have no idea," he mumbled, giving the giants a furtive glance.

35

"SO WHAT'S HER STORY?" Ethan asked once they were in the tunnel. Levi's lantern was the only light separating them from the level of pitch black that can only be experienced inside a cave.

"Adrianna?" he asked, as if he was surprised Ethan had even remembered the girl from five minutes ago. "She's sort of... well, nuts, I guess."

"Care to elaborate on that?"

"Not really. Do you know much about Greek mythology?"

"I'm sure I have a few entries left in my memory."

"Do you remember the furies?" Levi asked.

"They were spirits of punishment for evildoers."

"They were?" Levi stopped and crinkled his nose. "Huh, I guess I need to catch up on my mythology. Well, I can't say she does that, but she definitely could if she wanted to." He started walking again, shouldering the strap on Ethan's bag a little higher.

"I can carry that, you know. You don't have to be my bellhop."

"No, it's okay, I don't mind. It's kind of what I do. In addition to being an errand boy, I also moonlight as a personal assistant, maid, and a sacrificial lamb."

"Excuse me?" Ethan asked as the tunnel opened into another fire-lit room. "You're kidding, right?"

"Not really." Levi shrugged. "I mean, they don't kill me or anything, but sometimes a ceremony requires a representative sacrifice, like blood or something. I usually don't remember it, anyway. Up this way."

Levi led him up a set of carved stone stairs minus the safety rail. The room was lined with two stories of at least a dozen arched openings sheathed by curtains. After they ascended to the top level, Levi slipped through the curtain of one.

Ethan followed him into what turned out to be his quarters for his stay. The single room had a bed and wood table that served to hold a lantern, water pitcher, and basin. Levi dumped his bag on the bed and raised his arms to the room.

"It's not much but, it's..." He shrugged, giving up on the positive end to that statement. "We don't have plumbing, so you just have to use the basin to wash up as needed. There's a chamber pot under your bed for evening... emergencies. It's gross, but walking around at night is discouraged for newbies. Plus, it's like a five-minute walk to the toilet."

Ethan nodded. It wasn't quite the solid walls that he was looking for, but three out of four wasn't too bad.

Levi stepped through the curtain again and pointed to the matching curtain on the opposite open balcony path. "That's my room over there, so if you need anything, just down these stairs and up the opposite ones. We usually just rustle the curtain to knock."

"They all look the same." Ethan frowned, wondering how he would even remember which one was his, let alone Levi's.

"The floor." Levi scraped his foot over the number three, chiseled into the rock.

"Don't worry, sir, I'm pretty much going to be on you like glue while you're here. Designated personal assistant, remember?"

"I think you should call me Ethan, Levi."

"Annette wouldn't like that. She has old-school ideals about titles and shit—stuff."

Ethan smiled. "You can call me whatever you want when she's around then, but rest assured, I have plenty of people at home to boost my ego with proper addresses."

"Okay, Ethan." Levi tried the name on. He probably was more comfortable calling him sir, but at some point, the title stopped being respectful and started being detached.

36

A FTER A QUICK TOUR of the bathhouse, which offered a natural water source that they heated for proper showers and relaxing baths, Ethan cheered up about the quality of his vacation. The hotel may have sucked, but at least they had a hot tub.

The next stop was a room big enough to fit a two-story house and its adjacent neighbors. There were three openings apart from the door they had just come through. The openings were at least garage-door sized, and Ethan knew without asking that they were for dragons.

The center of the room held an ornate stage carved into the rock several steps above the surrounding floor. An altar of sorts, he assumed. The multiple concentric circles carved into it coalesced in the middle. Annette was standing in the center of the altar with her hands raised to the heavens—or at least where the heavens would have been had they not been standing under a mountain.

Her tall, slender, yet muscular figure was as he remembered it. Instead of jeans and a t-shirt, she wore a red robe. Her blond spiky hair had grown out in the front enough to tuck behind her ears, but the back was still a short, immobilized frenzy.

Adrianna was off to one side of the altar, kneeling on a mat. She might have been meditating, sleeping, or doing yoga; whichever it was, she was impossibly still. "Why can't you touch her?" he asked Levi.

"Who?" he asked.

"Adrianna."

"Adrianna?" he asked with the same surprised confusion in his voice as he had the last time the subject of her came up. "She has a knack for reading people, but only the bad stuff. She..." Levi glanced surreptitiously over at Annette. "She got the wrong mix, and now she's... messed up."

"Messed up how?" Ethan asked, lowering his voice to match Levi's concern for Annette's ears.

"She was supposed to get the yin and yang, but she just got the... actually, that's a bad analogy. She was supposed to get the whole garden, but she just got the dirt."

"What does that mean?"

"It means she's broken," Annette interrupted as she walked over. She gave Levi a faint glare before smiling broadly at Ethan. "Ethan." She pressed her hands to his cheeks. He could sense she was resisting pinching them.

"Hello, Annette, it's good to see you again."

"Oh, you sweet boy. Had I only stayed a little longer that day... my goodness, I would have boxed you up and taken you with me. So, I suppose it was better I hadn't stayed."

Ethan gripped her hands, drawing them down from his face. "I know this is a very important visit, Annette, but I must be honest about my displeasure with your timing. My wife is eight months pregnant, and I have not been given a timeline for my stay."

"Oh, I see, I'm sorry. The timeline is dependent on several things, but of course my invitation is only that: an invitation. You are not my prisoner. If you wish to leave this instant, I will understand."

Ethan chuckled and released her hands. "I appreciate the offer, but I am ready to pass out. I would at least like to eat, sleep, and bathe, and not necessarily in that order."

"Of course. How about food first? Levi will take care of you. We can talk tomorrow when you are properly rested. Perhaps you can stay a few days or even a week. I just need enough time to determine if the dragon's blood does what you said it did. Not that I don't believe you, but it is known to have hallucinogenic effects." She pouted and he couldn't help but smile, since he knew she was probably hoping it wasn't the latter.

"I'm rather curious myself. Don't worry, I've come all this way. We might as well check. Besides, Danato would rip me in half if he knew I didn't cooperate."

"I hope you know how proud he is of the man you've become."

"I think I do, but it's nice to hear."

"Adrianna!" Annette hollered and whipped around to look for the girl, but she was right behind her. "Why don't you go with them?" She looked back at Ethan. "You don't mind a tag-along, do you?"

"Not at all." Ethan nodded to Adrianna.

"I do," Levi mumbled under his breath.

"Ungrateful..." Annette's eyes flared, but she shook away the anger. "She is mute, but she is not dumb. As I'm sure Levi has told you, she is not as affectionate as this old woman, so just respect her space, and none of you have to be uncomfortable." Annette leaned in and kissed Ethan on the cheek. "Thank you, so much." She turned and left before Levi could further object to the tag-along aspect of the evening.

37

"Eat!" Levi scolded Adrianna as if she was an obnoxious child throwing her food instead of eating it. They were in a small kitchen that looked like it had been copied from a medieval castle. With several fires burning for the stone ovens, the room was toasty warm, making Ethan drift off even as he ate. Levi's sharp command lifted his lids again.

"Why are you yelling at her?" Ethan questioned Levi across from him. Adrianna was sitting next to Levi, though a good distance away. Her small serving of stew hadn't lost more than two bites.

Levi looked at him sheepishly and shrugged. "Look at her." He sighed. "She never freaking eats."

Adrianna pushed the bowl away. Levi glanced at Ethan. Levi probably wanted to scold her again, but didn't want to do it in front of him. Instead, he pushed the bowl gently back to her. "Please," he said gently, "one more bite."

She stared at him a moment, before sticking her fingers in the bowl and pulling out a hunk of meat that she popped into her mouth and chewed. She spread her arms for her accomplished magic trick.

"Congratulations, maybe for your next feat you can figure out that the brush bristles go against the hair."

Adrianna frowned and smacked her bowl into his lap. She moved herself farther down the table away from them and lowered her head onto her arms, effectively giving herself a timeout. Levi griped as he wiped the remainder of her food off his pants.

"What's that all about? You seem like a pretty even-tempered guy, Levi."

"Yeah, I guess it's just... I don't know." He looked down at Adrianna. He grimaced, revealing the guilt he felt for what he had said. "She doesn't talk, she barely listens. Look, I'm not trying to be an ass, but sometimes hurting someone's feelings is what it takes to get them to listen to you. I'm a one-man intervention."

"What exactly are you trying to get her to do?"

"I don't know." Levi rubbed his forehead. "Be human again, I guess."

"When did she stop?"

"The incident," Levi air-quoted, "happened before I was ever in this gig. I hear stories about the beautiful Russian princess with the voice of a songbird, the one all the men were in love with, but all I see is a malnourished brat." Levi said it loud enough for her to hear, but she didn't move.

"Princess?"

"Yeah, I don't know if it's really true. What I do know is that her mute-ism is selective." Adrianna peeked up at him, and Levi gave her a wry smile. "Just like her hearing." She set her head back down, ignoring him again.

"How did she get here?"

"She was selected by Annette to be her apprentice. She wanted someone to learn her craft and carry it on for future generations."

"Familiar story, just a different job. What happened? Why is she like a wild animal?"

"Because she is." Levi rolled his eyes. "Don't get me wrong, the girl's got mad skills. She is amazing to watch." Adrianna's head moved slightly to uncover her ear, probably to hear the conversation better. "The stuff that goes down here is like a rehearsal for future performances. Annette goes all over the world for rituals, blessings, and a bunch of odds-and-ends house calls for people who like to use earth magic like toilet paper."

"I thought you guys just dealt in dragon blood?"

"Dragon blood is like fertilizer to earth magic, or maybe it's the seed. Anyway, both are pretty intense on their own, but together you can do some pretty nifty stuff."

"Like what?"

"Grow an entire field of crops overnight. Undo the damage of a forest fire in weeks instead of years."

"Mostly farm work?" Ethan tried not to sound disappointed.

"No, but that's the stuff I've witnessed. I don't always remember the rituals. When they are particularly high-energy rituals, that's when I get to play sacrificial lamb."

"Why you?" Ethan interrupted before he forgot.

"I don't know. She says I'm worthy. I'm not a virgin, so I don't know exactly what that means, but I guess it just means that I have a good heart. At least I hope that's what it means."

"How did she talk you into blood-letting for crops?"

"She didn't." Levi shook his head and ducked his eyes shyly. "The first time I ever did it, I... sort of volunteered. It was the energy of the spell, and I suppose that means it wasn't my choice, but I wasn't scared, and Adrianna was so..." Levi looked to Adrianna, and she slowly turned her head to look at him. For a moment, Ethan thought he saw something more than conflict between them. "The rituals are very intense," Levi said, turning back to Ethan. "If Annette allows it, you should observe one."

"I was present when she took the dragon's blood. That was pretty impressive."

"You haven't seen nothing yet." Levi smirked. "You want to take a soak before you head to bed?"

Ethan wanted to say no, but he figured he should let his food settle before he went completely supine for several hours.

38

LIKE MOST PUBLIC BATH houses, Ethan was required to shower prior to entering the hot-tub-style water baths. Clad in one-size-fits-all drawstring swimwear, he slipped into the bath and immediately yawned.

When he opened his eyes again, Adrianna was standing across the bath from him, looking uneasy. She was in what looked like night clothes: a long flaring top and tight shorts that could have doubled as underwear. The scant clothing showed off her thin arms and legs that by some men's standards might have been attractive, but Ethan was in agreement with Levi that she was much too skinny.

Ethan was about to ask if she wanted to come in when Levi yelled behind him. "Cannonball!" Levi splashed into the short pool, making water go everywhere. When he bobbed back up, he whipped his wet hair around like a dog, splashing Adrianna intentionally, and consequently, Ethan. "Woo! I hate living in a cave, but this makes it almost worth the vitamin D shots."

Levi was far more muscular than Ethan would have presumed. His compact body was lean enough to show a six-pack without much effort, but his arm definition was as much from strength as lack of fat. He wondered if that was natural or if Annette had snuck him a few dragon shakes to build him up to be a better bellhop.

"Are you coming in, tag-along?" Levi propped his hands on his hips while Adrianna dipped her toe in at the edge of the water. "Come on, just jump in." Adrianna pressed down on her shirt, as if she was afraid that it would bubble up and float off the minute she jumped in. Which, given the loose design, was entirely possible. "Here." Levi stuck out his pinky and moved to the edge of the pool. "I won't give you a hand, but I'll give you a pinky. You can step down onto the seat and wade in."

Adrianna looked at him sadly.

"I'll be fine. Just think your happy thoughts." He wiggled his pinky.

Adrianna tentatively reached out her hand, deciding as she went how to grab his finger. When there seemed no way to do it without bending his finger back uncomfortably. Despite his previous moratorium on hand holding, he opened his hand and offered the full support of his palm. She paused, looking at him fearfully.

"Come on. Don't be shy."

She rested her hand on his and stepped down into the pool. When she let go, she looked to Levi for an answer she hadn't put a question to.

"Not bad. I don't feel like bashing my head into a wall. Maybe you're getting better at this."

She smiled, and he smiled back. He turned away from her to join Ethan against the wall and his face winced into something akin to pain. It was unclear what kind of pain, so Ethan decided not to get into that conversation with Adrianna present.

When Levi was situated an arm's length away, he reached over and nudged Ethan. "Check this out. Hey, Addy, do the thing for Ethan." She blushed and shook her head. Levi laughed. "What's wrong? Ethan's a good guy, he won't tell."

Ethan glanced between them, trying to discern if this was going to be an inappropriate display.

Levi leaned down into the water and blew bubbles into the water. When he came back up shrugging in mock surprise, Addy, as he called her, smiled at him. "Come on, just a few."

Adrianna caved to his badgering and leaned forward to blow bubbles in the water. However, instead of a few blubbering quakes in front of her mouth, the entire tub erupted into tumultuous foaming, bubbling water.

"Holy hell..." Ethan looked at Levi for an explanation.

"I told you she was amazing." Levi smiled and settled back into his spot for a nap.

Ethan did the same, but he noticed Adrianna moved to a spot nearer to Levi. He assumed she didn't want to be close to a complete stranger, but given the expanse of the pool bath, she didn't have to be near either of them.

Despite her reluctance to touch Levi, she still preferred to be nearer to him than not.

39

Daniel couldn't help but watch her fall apart beneath him. Sometimes it felt like it was the only time he saw the real Nevia. She wasn't trying to be stoic or brave. She was just embracing life and the wonderful privileges of the human reproductive system.

He'd told himself he wouldn't do this again. He'd been telling himself that for six months. At first, the arguments between him, her, and Heaton were enough to cool his attraction to her, but eventually she made a move on him he couldn't deny. Since then, at least once a month, she made her intentions clear and brought his desires reluctantly to a simmer again.

Every time he thought he understood what she wanted, she threw him off again. He had depended on her to be open and honest about their social relationship and shy about their physical relationship, but now it seemed to be the opposite. He was the one who had to bring up the uncomfortable discussions about the future and what potential they had together if sex was the only thing drawing them to each other. She was the one evading the question and insisting he not think too hard about it.

As a result, he was feeling more and more like a booty call. At one time, that type of relationship would have been ideal, but now he resented it. He didn't mind the part where he was being used for sex. The part that turned him off was that one day she would find a more appropriate man to walk down the aisle with and have children with and...

"What's wrong?" Nevia asked breathlessly beneath him. He hadn't realized he had stopped.

"You good?" he asked, distantly aware of how callous it sounded.

"Sure, but you didn't..." He was off her before she could finish the sentence. It was true, but he didn't care. His mind was stuck on the image of standing in the back of a big beautiful church while she gave herself—body, heart, and contractual obligation—to another man. The idea was enough to shut down his libido completely.

He slipped on his pants and went into the kitchen for a beer. He decided on a soda. He didn't need to dull this moment. He needed to embrace it. Maybe this was the pain he needed to help him say no to her.

Nevia stepped into the kitchen, wrapping herself in a silk robe that she had *accidentally* left in his bathroom. She also *accidentally* left her toothbrush and hairbrush, and she probably didn't even know that he knew about her *special* compact stuffed in the back of his bathroom drawer. Preparations for impromptu sleepovers weren't quite the long-term outlook for their relationship that he wanted.

"Daniel?" She stayed away from him, which meant that he probably looked mad as hell. He wasn't trying to, and he didn't want her to be afraid of him, but, nevertheless she knew his boundaries pretty well. She usually just trampled on them, but this was different. This wasn't frustrated relationship anger, this was hurt anger, and she couldn't distract him from it with sex. This might actually have to be... discussed.

"Do you want me to go?" she asked, crossing her arms self-consciously.

"Do you want to go?" he said without a thought about how insolent he sounded. He wished he could smell her emotions as easily as she could his.

She held his gaze for a moment, but then looked down at the floor. "I... want..." she stammered.

Before she could articulate what she wanted, there was a sharp rap at the door. Daniel brushed past her and opened the door. Heaton was on the other side. He took a quick note of Daniel's bare chest, bare feet, and Nevia stepping around the corner in a robe. The scolding, disappointed "dude" was implied, but not said. Instead, he nodded at her cordially and stepped inside.

Heaton was the one person who had gotten the full report on everything that was happening between him and Nevia. Daniel had expected that Heaton's coming out—to him—would somehow benefit him with yogi-level relationship advice, but the only contribution he had after the beans were spilled was: "Stop sleeping with her." It seemed to be the general consensus that the only way to figure out if a relationship could stand on more than sex was to stop having sex. It made sense, but that was easier said than done. Other than that sage advice, Heaton had been trying to stay out of it. Which was also easier said than done, since they all worked together.

"What's up?" Daniel said, slumping down on his newly delivered couch. He still had his bed in the living room, but only because he had been too lazy to move it. For reasons opposing his previous agendas, he was seeing the advantages of having a separate room for his bed.

"Just got a call from Sophie. Something's gone amuck with Danato's house. It tried to take over Cori's mind."

"Feck." Daniel scooted to the edge of the couch, suddenly uncomfortable with being comfortable.

"How did that happen?" Nevia closed the gap between them, sitting down on the arm of the couch beside him. It felt strangely intimate, like he should place his hand on her back to stroke it, but he didn't know if that was what she wanted, or if she just wanted to sit... right beside him.

Heaton noted the move. He seemed just as surprised by it, but didn't let it distract his purpose, which, judging by his tone, was important. "I didn't get the specifics, but Cori is on her way here. Danato wants you to watch over her while the house settles down."

"Me?" Daniel asked. "He specifically asked for me?"

"According to Sophie, you are the designated baby-mama-sitter. All other priorities are being back-logged."

"Feck. What does Ethan think about this?"

"Ethan is in Asia, and apparently isn't going to be back soon."

"Oh. What's he—?"

"I don't know." Heaton looked at Nevia. "We are effectively on vacation until further notice. I was thinking this might be a good opportunity for you to visit your family in America if you want."

Nevia stared blankly at him. "Are you trying to get rid of me?"

Heaton glanced at Daniel. He was about to stick his foot in his mouth and was looking for opposition, but Daniel didn't really care one way or another. "No, of course not, but we've all been working pretty hard. It might be nice to get a break from each other. Clear our heads."

"My head isn't foggy," she said dismissively. "I think I'll head out." She looked back at Daniel. "Call me when she gets in." He nodded. It was all he could do. The night had just taken a turn for the worse. Not only was he having relationship drama, he was about to add a hormonal pregnant woman to his life.

Nevia slipped on her pants, sans panties—which Daniel noticed went in her pocket. She didn't bother leaving the room to slip off her robe and put on her t-shirt. The half-turn that prevented Heaton from seeing everything—not that he cared—afforded Daniel a glimpse of her pert, ever-alert nipples. He bit the inside of his cheek in hopes that the pain would keep him from remembering that he had yet to satisfy himself.

After Nevia had collected her things, she slipped out the door. Part of him wanted her to kiss him goodbye, but that was only the part that wanted more than a kiss.

"You know she does it on purpose," Heaton said, stalking back in from the kitchen with a beer for both of them. *Now* was the time for beer.

"I love you, man," he said before he took a wistfully long draw from the bottle. Heaton smirked and shook his head. Daniel wasn't entirely comfortable with his best friend being gay, but he also didn't want to be the guy that thought their sexuality had anything to do with why they were friends. He was still working on a happy medium between friendly ridicule for his hair and clothes and the drunken familial love declarations.

"I know you do," Heaton said before chugging half his beer.

"What does she do on purpose?" Daniel asked after he had quenched his thirst.

"That." He nodded to the bed. "She lures you back in with sex. A little goes a long way with you right now. The minute you stop giving her puppy-dog eyes, she's on you. Hell, dude, I know you're getting laid before you do."

"I can see it coming." Daniel cleared his throat. "She's going to just shag me until her future husband comes along, and then I'll be the shit on her boot that she just needs to scrape off." He shifted, unable to find a good position. "Feck, why can't she just get it over with? We are so doomed. She knows it; I know it."

"Have you talked about it?"

"I've tried. It either results in an argument or sex, usually both. I can't get enough traction on this relationship to even start it, let alone end it."

"Maybe she feels the same way. Maybe she's just trying to remind herself why you began this in the first place."

"It began because I met the one woman in the world that actually wanted a one-night stand. She started this, and now I don't want to end it, but..." Daniel stopped and drank his beer. He'd already told Heaton this. He needed to just tell Nevia that he loved her, and if she wasn't interested in more than just shagging, then to leave him alone. It just hurt too bad to be *with* her, and not really *be* with her.

"Daniel, don't get caught up in the end of the story before you've finished the first chapters. Maybe you just need to give her a reason to hang around, instead of demanding that she not leave."

Daniel glanced at the door, wondering if it was too late to ask her to come back. "When's Cori getting in?"

"Later tonight. Here are the instructions." Heaton handed him a paper with the details of her arrival in impeccable handwriting. His handwriting should have been the first clue to his sexuality.

"Wait, aren't you coming with me?"

Heaton shrugged. "Sorry, I'm effectively on vacation, and I'm going to use it."

"Where are you going?"

"I was thinking France." Heaton pursed his lips in thought.

"Why France?"

Heaton grinned. "Frenchmen." Daniel groaned. Gay humor was funny, but only when the participant wasn't actually gay. "Come on, let's move this bed."

"Excuse me? It's going to take more than one beer for that." Daniel scoffed.

"We need to finish your redecorating project. I'm not sure Ethan would mind you watching over Cori, but he definitely won't approve of you two sleeping in the same room, even if it is the living room."

Daniel grimaced, knowing how true that was. He put down his beer and started dismantling the last vestiges of his bachelor pad.

40

C ORI STEPPED OFF THE train and headed to the gates. She was exhausted, sore from too much bumpy transportation, and nervous about what the coming days would hold for her. When she caught sight of Daniel and Nevia, she could see that he looked irritated. She was so caught up in her own misfortune it hadn't occurred to her that her visit was probably a huge inconvenience to him.

She slowed her approach to re-adjust the duffel bag on her shoulder. It was beyond heavy. She hadn't packed it, so it was bound to contain a good number of things she didn't need, and probably couldn't even fit into.

"Cori." Daniel caught sight of her and came over. He was beaming ear to ear, but she knew it was probably a forced smile. "You look brilliant." He paused to look over her rounded belly and smiled even wider, if that were possible.

"I'm sorry about—"

Daniel wrapped his arms under her and lifted her with his hug. He was careful not to compress her belly, which was a contortionist feat on top of the already herculean task of lifting her. He set her back down and frowned. "What is all this about? Are you in trouble?"

"Aren't I always?" she joked as Nevia approached. They nodded politely to each other, but Nevia did not share in the delight that Daniel was offering her arrival.

"Come on. Let's get you back to my flat so you can rest." He wrapped an arm around her in a sideways hug, only slightly interrupted by Nevia pulling her duffle bag off her shoulder to carry it. Cori noticed a slight exchange of looks before Nevia lagged back behind them.

On the ride home, Daniel attempted to make small talk, but she was more content to peer out the window at the world she had given up to be at the prison. She never would have imagined her former life could feel so strange to her. So empty.

"I'm really sorry about all this. Belus was very insistent I stay with you," Cori reiterated as Daniel opened the door for her to his flat. He kept it open for Nevia, and again Cori caught a look between them. Whatever animosity she was observing may not have been solely from her impromptu visit.

"I'm always happy to help a friend," he said, closing the door. She gave him a shy smile.

"I'm sure Belus appreciates your help."

He stepped behind her and pressed his hand to her back, and leaned over her shoulder. "I meant *you*, silly."

"Oh." She blushed, mostly from embarrassment at not assuming that he considered her a friend, but also because his infectious, flirtatious smile was making her feel bashful. "Sorry."

He chuckled and patted her back. "Don't worry, my personality grows on you. You're still about two weeks away from being madly in love with me. I guess we should be glad you're only staying for a week, huh?"

Cori snorted at his audacity, but she couldn't hide her smile. As borderline as their relationship was, she couldn't help but find amusement in his "always on" charm. However, contrary to his speculations, she estimated that the amusement would wane if she had to spend more than a week with him.

"You must be bushed," he observed as he headed into the kitchen just off the living room. "Do you want something to eat or would you rather just sleep?" he called back to her. Cori looked over the living room. It was cleaner than she had expected. The plush couch and chairs surrounding the coffee table looked brand new. She hoped he hadn't gone through the effort of buying new furniture for her visit. Then again, if the furniture had been too embarrassing to share with the public, perhaps that was for the best.

Nevia had already made herself at home on the couch and was reading a fashion magazine. She didn't look happy, but Cori didn't know her well enough to judge her demeanor.

"Cori?" Daniel popped back out of the kitchen and she shook herself out of her thoughts.

"Um... I don't know." The tears were as much a surprise as they were unwelcome. She had never been the tough, composed woman that Nevia was, but to be a completely blubbering mess was beyond mortifying.

"Hey." Daniel came directly to her and pulled her into a hug she could barely move in, much less push away from. They were the wrong arms, in the wrong living room, in the wrong country, but they would have to do for the moment.

"I'm sorry. I promise I'm usually not such a mess," she mumbled into his shoulder.

"It's okay, Cori, I'm not judging you. I know you miss Ethan."

Just the mention of his name made Cori weep harder. Daniel rubbed her back and directed her to sit on the couch. Nevia stood up and walked to the kitchen. Cori heard her putting water on for tea.

After the immediate necessity of coddling wore off, Daniel reached forward for something on the coffee table and she heard a distant, familiar click. In a moment, voices filled the room. Cori snapped up and looked over at the cause of the noise. The flat screen television glowed from the partial kitchen wall.

She laughed and looked at Daniel. He was amused, but a little baffled. He had probably intended to balance out her awkward emotional breakdown with a little background noise, but he'd actually just opened a different can of worms.

A flood of thoughts came to Cori as she thought about the shows she might catch up on, or the movies she hadn't seen, or the *music* she hadn't heard. All thoughts of her exhaustion went out the window in exchange for a night filled with rare treats.

Cori gasped and put her hand on Daniel's chest in earnest. Given his lack of adherence to proper button height, she ended up being skin to skin with him, but she was too excited to care. "Can we go dancing?"

He grinned and patted her hand. She probably looked like a child asking to go to the zoo. "Are you serious? Now?" He checked his watch, and she looked him over, waiting for his decision. He shook his head in amusement. "Alright, Mrs. Pierce, dancing it is."

She squealed and ran over to her bag to dig out something that might be worthy of a club. Nothing was worthy, but with her being pregnant, no one was going to criticize her stretchy pants as long as they covered her.

"Dancing?" Nevia asked from the kitchen.

"Aye, I think I'll take her to that new club that keeps plastering its advertisements to my windshield."

"I'll join you," she said to Daniel.

"I don't need a chaperone," Daniel said sharply.

"I do," Cori answered cheerfully, before a bitter fight could break out. She was already uncomfortable enough without being in the middle of relationship issues. Plus, she didn't want to hang out alone with Daniel. "The more the merrier, right?" Cori looked between the two of them, hoping they would both absorb her excitement and get happy. Daniel scuttled off to his room and Nevia ducked back into the kitchen.

Close enough.

41

C ORI HOLLERED THE MINUTE she got into the dance club. No one could hear her over the loud thump of the music, but it wasn't so much to announce herself as a release of the pent-up energy that had been pooling in her stomach on the ride over.

She started gyrating to the rhythm even before the bouncer had checked their IDs. To her surprise, Danato had supplied her with a fake ID. She wasn't entirely certain what would happen if someone found out she was alive and well and living in a secret prison on the Kola Peninsula, but she imagined the higher-ups would frown on it.

Daniel wrapped his arm around her waist—as far as it would go—and directed her inside. The bar took up the whole back half of the club and it was on a different level, so you could still see the band and the mosh pit below. Rather than taking her down below where she could dance, he moved her to the bar.

She thought she would have to remind him she wasn't drinking when he ordered two beers, but he added a Coke. When he dragged the beers and soda off the bar, he handed her the soda. "I want to dance!" she yelled so he could hear her.

"I know." He grinned at her and handed Nevia the other beer. "We need to case the place first," he hollered back.

Cori sipped her soda and looked to Nevia for the answer, but she was already in work mode, scanning the dancers for... whatever. "Why?"

"Because we are on the Council of the Moon's shit list." He put his arm around her again and directed her away from the bar so the desperately sober people could get their drunk on. He tucked her into the corner railing that bordered the back of the designated bar area and the stairs leading to the dance pit. She noted that his position leaning on the rail behind her essentially locked her in, but since the night was going to be filled with unintentional groping—and some not so unintentional—she wouldn't get particular about how he protected her.

"They still mad at Jordan?" Cori looked around for Nevia, but she was gone. She was concerned by that, but Daniel shifted and nodded to where she had moved to scan over the bar crowd. She was resting against the railing like she was waiting to be hit on, but her eyes were darting between faces, and as certain people passed by, she leaned forward to sniff them.

"We've had a few close calls. There's a shitload of uproar going on in the werewolf community." Daniel eased closer so the mention of werewolves didn't get noticed by anyone. "Nevia may have started this, but she wasn't the only person ready to take up arms to fight for it. Right now, the Council is too damn busy fighting their own kind to mess with us, but we aren't going to assume that there isn't a battle left for us."

"You would have preferred staying home." Cori pinched her lips and raised her brow, offering him an opening to wrap up their night, if he thought it was necessary.

"No, I'm enjoying your enthusiasm. Your wish is my command."

"Oh, don't say that." Cori laughed, and he chuckled.

"Seems okay," Nevia said, rejoining them. "I can't get a clear scent on anything, but it smells human, for the most part."

"For the most part?" Daniel asked.

"Yeah, for the most part," Nevia snapped. "You know I'm useless in these places."

Cori quailed at the tension between them. She felt like she was looking at a divorced couple rather than an intimate one. She wondered if Ethan and she had quarreled that much before they had finally given in to their relationship.

"She wants to dance." He looked over the crowd. "She's not going alone, if you're not sure."

"Then I'll dance with her."

"You don't have your gun," he said, and she tipped her head in disbelief. He furrowed his brow. "Do you?"

He looked around to see if anyone was watching them. Nevia did the same before tugging up on her pants to reveal the gun strapped to her ankle. Daniel smiled at her, and Cori could see that if she weren't there, he might have pulled Nevia in for a heated kiss. As it was, Nevia's chest rose slightly and her lips parted in preparation for just that event. Indifferent to her invitation, however, Daniel turned away, shattering the connection in an instant.

"I'll take her." He pulled Cori's soda from her and left it on a table with his beer, which he emptied with a final swig. "Watch the crowd. I don't want any surprises." He snapped the order before taking Cori's hand and dragging her out of the corner.

She didn't catch Nevia's face before they left, but judging by the brooding expression Cori could see from the dance floor, she was probably hurt. "You wanted to dance, let's dance," Daniel murmured in her ear and he started moving to the quick beat.

He stayed close to her, but didn't insist that they dance together. Her center of gravity was off since the last time she'd danced, but it was easy to find a pace with the thumping that was bringing life to her legs.

Before long, she found herself twisting and whipping her hair like she was a teenager. She knew she was getting a few looks from the other dancers because she was pregnant, but somehow Daniel's constant backup seemed to ease everyone's concerns that she was out to get laid. If anything, they were probably supposing she was trying to put herself into labor.

Eventually, Cori felt comfortable enough to do a little grinding with Daniel, but they both made sure they kept themselves at a prudish distance. Still, she couldn't help but do a few moves that should have been reserved for Ethan.

Daniel shook his head and smiled. "You're going to get me in trouble." He held her hand while she sinuated her body down to a crouch and then brought it back up slowly. She turned around and rolled her shoulders against him so she could lean into his ear.

"With Ethan or Jordan?" She pulled away and smiled a knowing smile, and he glanced to where Nevia was looking on. If she was watching, she wasn't likely to appreciate Cori's zeal for dance, but Cori also knew that jealousy was a great aphrodisiac.

"I don't know that she cares. I'm just her booty call."

Cori raised her arms and shimmied back to him like a standing lap dancer—close, but not too close. "That's bullshit," she said matter-of-factly, and he narrowed his eyes at her. She shifted so he couldn't intimidate her with his eyes. "She wants to be with you. She's just confused and scared."

"I'm not interested in your analysis of the last couple of hours."

Cori shifted back to face him, leveling her own glare at him. "It's not an analysis. She told me."

Daniel's eyes flickered over hers and his mouth dropped open. The music slowed enough to warrant more proximity, and he drew her hands up around his neck. "She said she wants to be with me?" He rested his hands on her hips with barely any pressure.

"She wants to be with a man that she can be proud of. One that she can introduce to her family and not have them wonder what the hell she's doing with her life."

"I thought she didn't care about what her family thought." Daniel glanced back at Nevia. Cori wasn't sure if he had caught her eye, but he didn't look back for a long moment. "Does she... love me?"

"She didn't know. This is all very new to her, Daniel. I told her to be persistent and patient. I told her an emotional relationship was going to be new for you, too."

Daniel looked her over. She wasn't sure if the intensity in his gaze was angry or staid. She had apparently crossed a line by making assumptions about his personality. "I'm glad he married you," he said abruptly. The sober respect lingered in his eyes for a moment, and then it was gone. "It's a good thing, too, because I'd be more than happy to steal you away." He winked at her, putting on his best flirtatious smirk.

Cori laughed. She knew this was as close to a heartfelt moment as she was probably going to get with Daniel. "Baby and all, huh?" She leaned back, pushing her stomach into his.

His smirk shifted from flirtatious to mischievous and he leaned into her ear. "That's part of the draw."

Cori finally caught a glimpse of Nevia, looking over the scene dutifully. She was a hard woman to pinpoint, but Cori could see the pain on her face. She was only standing guard out of duty. If not for that, she would have stormed out and walked home. She felt guilty, but that only meant the ingredients in her love spell were just right.

"Dance with her," Cori said, motioning to Nevia with her eyes only.

Daniel shook his head. "I'm not leaving you alone."

"I'll stand by the bar. You can watch me the whole time."

Daniel glanced anxiously to Nevia. She could tell he really wanted to get his hands on her, but he didn't like the idea of leaving her alone.

"Daniel," she said conspiratorially and drew her hand in front of his face. She lit a small flame in her hand and extinguished it just as quick. The expression on his face was priceless, a combination of fear and pride and *what the hell*! "Remember, I'm not without my defenses." She smiled and raised her brow.

"Mmm-mm-mmm, you are just a piñata of *with benefits*." He grinned and let her lead the way back to the bar.

42

D ANIEL BYPASSED CORI ON the way to the bar and slipped a twenty into her hand in case she wanted another Coke. When he reached Nevia, he didn't bother asking her to dance or even hold out his hand as a gentlemanly request. He just grabbed her wrist and pulled her along.

On their way back through, he noticed the concern on Cori's face for his perceived irritation. He winked at her to let her know he was only faking it.

Unable to detect his lie, Nevia was immediately concerned by his abrupt change in behavior. She probably would have pulled her firearm if she hadn't seen that Cori was safely ensconced at the bar, ordering a drink. "What's wrong with you?"

He didn't answer. He just pulled her through the crowd onto the dance floor. The band was still playing a slower beat, so he pulled her into a tight embrace. She struggled to get control of the situation, but he didn't let her. He clamped his arm around her back, pressing her into his chest.

She looked up at him with annoyed and confused eyes, but when she saw his somber expression, she relaxed against him. He eased his grip, letting her move more freely. As he did, she moved her hands up his chest and around his neck. He had never been this close to her without being in bed with her. It was strange how something almost sexual could be more intimate than sex.

He shifted with the music, and she followed his movements without hesitation. He wasn't sure what she was thinking, but he assumed she was wetting her lips in preparation for a kiss. He held off, letting the dance be the foreplay.

He bent her back in a rotating dip, wondering if he could get away with drawing his finger down her neck into her cleavage. When he brought her back up, she shifted her stance so her thigh was pressing harder into his crotch. He smirked and leaned down to her ear. "Did you find something you like?" he asked playfully.

"Someone, anyway," she responded and sucked his earlobe. The tantalizing pleasure sent shivers through his body.

"Have I mentioned I love that you aren't shy?"

"Not lately," she whispered and swirled her tongue along the outside of his ear.

"If you don't stop, I'm going to have to shag you in the bathroom of this place."

"How about right here?" she whispered and bit his earlobe hard. He yanked her back and kissed her hard, shoving his tongue in her mouth. He expected her to pull back, but she just sucked his tongue and drew him closer.

Eventually, he needed to breathe, so he pulled away. "Feck, woman, I have no control over myself with you."

"Is that a bad thing?"

"No, but it makes me feel powerless. You make me feel powerless."

"I know how you feel," she said earnestly, drawing back slightly.

"What do you want from me, Nevia? I'll give you anything, but I can't give you my heart until I know for sure." Her eyes flitted over his, shocked by his honesty. Or perhaps she was terrified. For once, they couldn't just fall into a bed to avoid having this discussion. "Don't tell me you don't know either, because you've had plenty of time to think about it."

"I..." Her voice cracked, and she looked like she might cry if she spoke. He had only seen her shed a tear or two once, and that was only because she had been significantly startled. Like she always said, she didn't wear fear well. "Where's Cori?" Her eyes darted to the bar behind them, and for a moment he didn't fall for the distraction, but when she didn't find her right away, he whipped around to join the search.

43

C ORI LEFT THE BATHROOM, happy to have released the sudden pressure on her bladder via the baby tap-dancing to the music. It didn't surprise her that the vibration had woken him/her up, but it impressed her that the pokes were almost going in tempo with the beat. Perhaps her baby was as fond of music as she was.

She made it back to her frilly drink that was overloaded with enough fruit to make it look like a small gift basket. After a satisfying sip of the sweet virgin beverage, Daniel approached from behind her, startling her with his tone. "Where the hell did you go?"

She choked on her cocktail and shrugged. "I had to pee." His jaw clenched tight, and he looked almost ready to pout. "Daniel, I have to pee. I was only gone a minute. I figured you guys would be making out for a while."

He flushed and looked at his feet. "Yeah, we were having a moment."

"And where is the lucky other half of that moment?"

"Looking for you." He glanced around the room for her, but he didn't seem to find her. Cori joined him in looking around, but she didn't see her either.

"She probably went to check the restroom," Cori suggested, grabbing his hand. "She's smart like that."

"Yeah," he answered, squeezing her hand back before he let go and sat down across from her. "I shouldn't worry so much. She's tougher with a gun than most of the men I know." He gave her a small proud smile, and she smiled back at him.

The band stopped suddenly, and there was a tap on the microphone. "Attention, patrons," a tall lanky woman with muscular arms and thighs peeking from her black satin dress said into the microphone, "we have a *special* request for all the animal lovers out tonight. Enjoy." She smiled mischievously and left the stage.

The band returned to their posts and the lead singer howled into the microphone. There was a slight growl at the end of his howl that sounded unintentional. "Who's that I see walking in this bar?" The singer talk-sang the first line. "Why, it's little red riding hood." He proceeded to sing the "Sham and the Pharaohs" song with a good deal better drum backup than the original. *"Hey there little red riding hood... You are sure looking good... You're everything... a big bad wolf could want."*

Daniel shot up out of his chair. "Feck!" He grabbed her hand and dragged her to the door before she could ask what was going on. "Go to the car and lock yourself in!" He shoved the keys into her hand and ushered her to the door.

"I'm not leaving you. What's wrong?" she asked, frantically looking for the threat. Even as she asked, she felt the danger like hot breath on her back. Two bouncers corralled the door before they could leave, staring at both of them with extreme interest. One of them licked their lower lip at her and she nearly blasted him with her rings for the insult, but she remembered she was supposed to be incognito.

"Werewolves, Cori. That song is for me. They have Nevia," Daniel said, still scanning the crowd.

"Then let's get her back." She ushered him back into the club.

"This was a trap," he said, lost in thought. "They've been plastering advertisements on my car for months. Holy shit, Cori, I've walked all of us into a fecking werewolf den."

Cori could see the panic taking over his judgment, but for some reason, a den of werewolves couldn't scare her more than being brain-raped by her own house. "You!" Cori yelled to the doorman, that wasn't licking his lips at her. "Come here!"

He stepped forward and rested his big beefy arms on each of their shoulders. She could see the glint of anger starting to take over Daniel's panic. "What can I help you with, little ones?" His voice sounded deep and hollow, like his voice box was echoing in his chest.

"Where is Nevia Jordan?"

He laughed. "With my boss."

"Yeah, and I bet your boss wants to watch us squirm on the line a while before you take us to her, but frankly I've had a really bad third trimester so I'm not in the mood to play the game by your rules."

"What makes you think you have a choice?" He brought his face close to hers, baring his big, bright white teeth, accented by the lengthy, sizeable canines. Werewolves weren't predacious in human form, but she wouldn't be surprised if he could take a bite out of her with ease.

"These." She waved her rings in front of his face before pressing her hand to his cheek. He yelled as her super-heated hand imprinted on his face. The lip-licker behind him jumped forward to help, but one look from Daniel slammed him into the wall. He shook his head at the man, and he begrudgingly kept his distance.

"Now." Cori cooled her hand as her new buddy kneeled down, cradling his face. "I can either keep manhandling you, drawing the attention of all these profitable drinkers. *Or* I could burn this place to the ground. *Or* you could do as you're told, and take me to Jordan and your boss!"

The werewolf looked up at her with murder in his eyes, but just to be sure they understood each other, she bloomed a fireball in her hand. The shock on his face contorted into the standard angry pout of someone who knows they are outwitted and outgunned. He stood and marched down to the dance floor. Cori and Daniel presumed they should follow.

Daniel leaned over to her as they walked. "Would it ruin the moment if I commented on how cool that just was?"

"I think we're due some back-slapping for our awesomeness," she answered, and he grinned.

44

DANIEL EXPECTED TWEEDLE-DICKHEAD TO take them to some seedy back office, but instead, he led them out the back door to the alley. It was a closed off alley, designed for unloading truck supplies for the entire building. The cool wet air—compounded by the smell of dead fish—made for an appropriate ambiance for his first meet-and-greet with the queen bitch since Nevia incited a coup.

"Frederique," Daniel said cordially to the tall blonde blocking the exit to the alley. He was amazed at how put together she looked for a street fight. Although, he imagined she had no idea what night he might arrive on. "Nice to see you again," he lied, eyeing her back up.

The two fem-wolves backing her up were shorter and stouter than her, but they did look ready for a fight. The jeans and t-shirts they wore were even matching, and now that he thought about it, they were probably the roadies for the band. As if on track with his mental thought process, several more people exited the club, joining them in the alley. It was the band—obviously not just on a smoke break—and the other bouncer.

"Where's Jordan?" Cori asked boldly. Her fortitude impressed Daniel, but he wondered if her hormones were clouding her judgment a little. They were, in fact, in trouble.

"You can't even imagine how thrilled I am that you're here, Cori," Frederique shrilled. "I never dreamed that I would have any chance of exacting any revenge on Ethan for his part in this fracas of political upheaval. Seeing you makes all the months of baiting Daniel here worth it."

"Don't you mean baiting Nevia?" Daniel asked, remembering that it was his car that the ads were on, not hers.

"No, Daniel, this was also a fortuitous event. I was only hoping to lure you in to offer you a chance to save her life. The fact that she is here now for me to bring home the point is just a cherry on my already bursting cake."

"Seriously," Daniel scoffed, drawing in closer to Cori. "I'm just not into you. Get over it." Everyone behind him laughed, and he got the sense it wasn't because of his levity.

"Daniel, I'm offering you a position of employment. I am struggling to keep control of my empire and I need strong supporters. My sister has already turned so many of my allies against me that I am forced to seek partnerships... external to my race. I am not proud of this, but many of my followers believe in the traditions that we have upheld for so many years, and they don't want to change. So, we will do whatever it takes."

"Where is she?" Daniel asked, ignoring almost everything she said.

She pointed up, and he saw Nevia hanging from a noose four stories up. She wasn't choking since the noose was holding her by the back of the neck, but he imagined she might need some chiropractic adjustments later. Her mouth was gagged, and though she wasn't struggling much, he could see she was trying to get a view of what was happening below.

"Damn it, Frederique, just let her go! She's just a stupid, obstinate little girl! She's just a hippy fighting wars with a picket line."

"From that height, she'll die on impact. Unless, of course, you have something to offer me in exchange for her."

"I have something to offer," Cori snapped.

Before Daniel could stop her, Cori's hand erupted in electricity that threaded out at Frederique. The fem-wolf convulsed from the shock, but the bouncer who'd brought them out quickly elbowed Cori in the stomach, stopping the attack.

She gasped and collapsed. Daniel caught her and eased her down. Cori held her pregnant belly and struggled to breathe. He could see she was angry, but he hadn't realized she was still up for a fight until he saw her hands frosting over with ice.

"Don't," he whispered, "please." She didn't seem to like that answer since it was her baby that had taken the brunt of the hit, but she kept her hands to herself.

Daniel stood and eyed the burned man. He was more than happy to seek retribution on Cori any way he could. "Touch her again and I'll end you," Daniel said evenly, but the man only chuckled at his cockiness. Little did he know, he wasn't being cocky.

Once upon a time, Daniel would have obliterated every last one of them to protect his friends, but along the road of learning to heal people, he had realized that he wasn't as evil as he'd once thought. He was starting to believe he could be the hero. Unfortunately, with his power, villain and hero were too damn close to call.

"Frederique, what exactly do you want?"

Frederique ripped her glaring eyes from Cori. She seemed undamaged by the electrical offense. "I *want* to kill your little chippie, but short of that, I am willing to accept your submission." Above them, Nevia tried to say something, but her mouth was crammed with too much cloth.

"I join you to fight your sister, and Nevia goes on unharmed?"

Frederique stepped forward and shrugged. "Unharmed would require further negotiation, but I would be willing to offer... unscarred for free." She waved her hand like a magic wand, bestowing the option generously.

Daniel narrowed his gaze at her. "And if I refuse?"

Her smile grew and dropped. "Then *I* end *you*. *All of you*."

"I won't let that happen," he said, shaking his head apologetically.

"I understand you are very powerful Daniel, but there are..." She recounted the men and women surrounding him. "...nine of us."

He frowned at the number, which made her smile since she didn't understand why the number bothered him. "I'm not sure that will matter, but you can give it a go."

"I thought you might say that, so I added a tenth." Frederique pointed up and a rifle toting fem-wolf looked down at him from her perch above Nevia. Her gun was pointed right at him.

Daniel was capable of taking out bullets and people with nothing more than a look, but four different angles and the speed of bullets did put a question in his mind. He glanced at Nevia and she tapped her leg. He dipped his brow slightly, and she tugged on her pant leg. They hadn't bothered searching her. She was still armed, and her hands weren't bound tightly enough to prevent her from reaching her gun if she lifted her leg. She might be able to get a decent angle to fire below her if she could crane her head enough to fire aimlessly at the dog pack behind him. Maybe he wouldn't have to kill everyone after all.

"Still not convinced?" Frederique asked, seeing him considering the battle, anyway. "My, but you are confident. Okay, my final offer for your submission." She waved her hand and her two roadies pulled handguns.

He sighed, seeing no way out without killing or risking being killed. At the very least, he could kill half of them before he got a bullet in his face or a knife in his back. If he knew Cori or her talents better, then he might have been able to trust her to back him up, but he just couldn't depend on that.

"Daniel, what is your choice?" Frederique asked, and Cori stood up beside him.

"His answer is no!" Cori insisted. Her hands trickled with electricity. It reached out to the surrounding fire escapes, dancing off the metal. Burned Face tried to get close to her, but the power snapping off her was enough to back both of them away.

Her power increased, and the roadies struggled to maintain a grip on their weapons. "She's magnetized," one of them groused, and fired an errant shot that nearly hit Nevia.

Daniel could see everything playing out, but in the end, he would still be forced to kill someone. Werewolves were fun to bat around, but they were just too tough to surrender without a significant show of force. Frederique had seen him flex his muscles a time or two, but she still hadn't seen the feature presentation. She didn't know what he could really do to her if she pissed him off enough.

He raised his hand to point at Burned Face, who was angling to give Cori a kidney shot. "I... will... end... you," he repeated more fervently. "All of you need to back off or this battle for the throne will be done tonight."

"Still too damn cocky for your own good, Daniel." Frederique shook her head, disappointed and impressed at the same time.

"Did someone call for cocky?" A tall brunette with a slicked back ponytail, dressed head to toe in black, ambled across the street side of the alley. She paused behind Frederique's bodyguards to light a cigarette. "Because I am the queen of cock."

The heavy gun hanging from her shoulder strap wasn't offering much of a threat. However, the six men that rounded the corner after her, aiming their red-dot scopes on the fem-wolf and her arm candy, were rather impressive—especially since they were all targeting the vulnerable points Nevia had educated Heaton and him about.

"What the hell are you doing here?" Cori asked. She had apparently stolen the line from Frederique, because nearly everyone gave her a befuddled glance, including the brunette. Despite the surprise change in focus, the brunette was more than happy to answer her question... after a drag from her cigarette.

"I am your hero." She splayed her arms and almost bowed.

"The hell you are!" Cori hissed, losing focus on her power.

The brunette seemed just as surprised by her animosity as Daniel was. Her eyes narrowed to focus on her face, but her curiosity went unfulfilled.

"Grace," Frederique said flatly, offering a belated greeting that also served to get her back on task.

"Frederique," Grace said, drawing her eyes slowly back to her. "You know, I really wanted to just let you have this one. I mean the girl strung up by the neck." She motioned to Nevia. "This young mother with electrodes stuck up her ass. And who can forget Mr. Machismo with his empty threats?" Daniel scowled at her evaluation, but she didn't flinch. "I honestly wanted to see you put them in their place, because your work is so beautiful to watch. The torture, the verbal repartee—I mean, between you and Angelina Jolie, I wish I was a fucking lesbian."

"I feel the same way about you, Grace," Frederique said cheerfully. "Although I think my fantasies of eating you go a completely different direction."

Grace laughed heartily. "That's good, I like that. How about we just call tonight a win, lose, or get-kicked-in-the-balls kind of night? You walk back into your club and I escort these fine..." Grace glanced up at Nevia hanging limply by her neck, "...*Kayan* trainees back to their homes."

"We could do that. Or I could finish what I started with you last month," Frederique retorted.

"Oh, baby, you're making me so hot. I would love to have you straddling me again, but I'm not sure you've fully healed from that long, hard, exploding-tipped bullet I put in your side. Do you still feel it... inside you?"

"I could crush you," Frederique whispered, stepping closer to her. Instead of cringing like most people did, she stepped forward and met her face to face. Grace was a good couple of inches shorter than her, but they were otherwise well matched.

"Go ahead," Grace said a little more seriously. "I just need to be able to label your death self-defense." She air-quoted before resting her right hand on her gun and drawing it forward. Frederique was so focused on the movement of the gun, she probably didn't even notice Grace's left hand gripping the nearly invisible black hilt strapped to her thigh.

"One of these days, I'm going to teach you a lesson," Frederique sneered.

Grace smiled. "Will it be a *hard* lesson?"

"You're disgusting," she hissed and backed away. Grace found great pleasure in winning that standoff. Unfortunately, her cleverness was short-lived since she wasn't the only one concealing a knife.

45

CORI COULDN'T BELIEVE WHAT she was seeing. The woman that she had killed six months ago, in an alternate reality, was standing before her in full military garb, smoking a cigarette in the face of a fem-wolf. *Balls of steel* didn't quite sum up her audacity. She really was a psychopath.

Cori saw the knife, but she didn't know whose side she should be on. In theory, Frederique was an evil bitch, but she wasn't sure that Gypsy and her cronies were any better. Had she had more time to think about it, she might have tried out that "enemy of my enemy" baloney, but the instant Frederique buried a knife into Gypsy's shoulder, all hell broke loose.

Guns fired, and werewolves charged from every angle. Cori raised her shield again and bullets audibly *plinked* as they hit the surrounding walls. Behind her, Daniel held off the other werewolves. One man gave a strangled cry for several seconds before he landed somewhere to her right. She could only presume it was the one who had sucker punched her.

Nevia had somehow managed to get her gun out and was shooting rather blindly at Frederique and her roadies, who were bloody with gunshots but still fighting. Cori was frustrated that she couldn't do more, but then she supposed she could. She released her shield, hoping that Daniel would cover her, and she stomped forward.

Daniel called after her, but she continued without regard for her safety... or her baby's—which she had momentarily forgotten about. This was apparently revenge, or maybe she just figured she owed Daniel, but nothing would have stopped her.

She reached the first fem-wolf roadie and pinched her neck. It was an entirely Spock move, but that was the only part of her body she could easily grip. The woman tanked forward, instantly asleep, knocking over her assailant. She reached over to the second, but she already saw her coming and lunged at her.

Before she could topple Cori, she flew back from an unseen force. Cori didn't even bother checking where Daniel was. He had her back; that was all that mattered. Frederique saw her coming and threw down her beaten victim to face off with her.

Cori's hands glinted with the ice that had freshly formed on them. Frederique grabbed her neck, and she latched onto her. She didn't try to pry her fingers off, since that was pointless. She let vengeance seep through from her diluted memories of Hirem.

The ice didn't just form around Frederique's arms. It settled in deep—liquid nitrogen deep. Frederique grunted and groaned, but eventually she pulled her arms back. She stared down at the frozen skin that was darkening even as she stood there.

"What *are* you?" She looked her over, disgusted.

"I'm..." Cori lost her name for a moment. She stepped back, floundering in her own mind. She hoped that was just an after-effect of focusing her energy from a memory, but it concerned her.

"She's my new best friend," Gypsy said from behind her, before a knife whipped through the air at Frederique. She was too caught up in her frostbitten arms to defend herself, and the blade went right into her eye.

Frederique's animalistic roar vibrated through Cori's body like deep bass from a passing car. The sound was a call to war, and the gunfire increased. Frederique dove at both of them, but there was nothing to do to stop it. Heat, ice, and electricity were going to be useless against this feral rage.

Gypsy pushed her down out of the way just as Frederique reached her. Gypsy went head-to-head with her, or rather, nose to elbow. Frederique's pursuit resulted in a cracked nose and a nearly shattered ulna.

Further infuriated by the offense of humans actually defending themselves, Frederique picked up Gypsy and threw her into the first available wall.

The fem-wolf came back for Cori, but even the electricity she shot at her seemed ineffectual against her wounded fury.

Before she could reach her, Frederique's body jolted back, airborne. Other bodies took flight, and the racket of gunfire lessened. Taking its place was the audible sound of joints cracking, tendons popping, and Frederique's screams.

46

D ANIEL COULD SEE CORI was going for the heart of the problem. He admired her spirit, but he couldn't help but think he should have reminded her that werewolves are unfathomably relentless. He kept one eye on her progress so he could help her. He, meanwhile, was struggling to keep the band off his back. Every time he knocked a werewolf out of his path, one was just returning from their flight. Fighting werewolves non-lethally was an exhaustive pursuit. Even if he could fight them off now, they would wear him down. Eventually he was going to make a mistake and despite the awesome power in his purview, he was still vulnerable to fists.

When he saw the battle was about to turn sour, he gave in. He directed his deepest anger back at his opponents. Most of them were still coming back to attack, but a few were passed out. The level of power he was emanating didn't offer the luxury of discerning between self-defense and murder. He would be lucky not to put a hole in the brick wall behind them.

The dust cloud that burst into the air was a mix of disintegrated body and water vapor. It plowed through the line of werewolves like a slow-motion grenade. Their lives ended with a few horrified thoughts of pain and regret that were given to Daniel on a platter. Their contribution to his mind was small, but they would be enough to haunt his nightmares for months and years to come.

When he was finished with all of them, he turned his attention to helping Cori with Frederique. She was surrounded, so he couldn't offer a full-scale disintegration attack. Instead, he focused on a turbulent back and forth. It wasn't a new extension of his power, but it was one he hadn't used in many years. It utilized both spectrums of his power, similar to his impacting bursts, but on a far smaller scale, and with far more power. Without exaggeration, he started ripping the fem-wolf apart slowly, one and every atom at a time.

Frederique screamed as he made his slow approach. She had not felt this before. She had not known this was part of his resume. No one knew about this except Danato, Belus, and Heaton. It was, after all, what put him in prison.

The men in black surrounding Frederique backed away, unwilling to stand near her as the pain racked her body on a cellular level. He wasn't even preparing to kill her. This was pure pain, and it was all in revenge. There was no permissible reason to cause anyone this much agony, except to destroy their will to live.

Without the ability to beg for death, Frederique sank to the ground, cowering beneath him. Her face and body contorted under his will. Her bowels released, and yet he still racked her body with pain. He couldn't let it go. This was the part of himself that he hated. This was the part of himself that didn't deserve to be outside of a cell.

He might have held her there until her heart gave in, but a sharp pain in the back of his head put him down with surprising speed.

47

"Sorry, hero, had to put you down." Gypsy pressed a cold compress to the back of Daniel's neck as he woke. Cori stood back with Nevia, watching him stir. She wasn't sure what to do. She wanted to see if he was okay, but she was terrified. Daniel was such a powerful man, and his devotion to his friends was endless, but it was humbling to see the proof of it powdered all over the alley and on the face of the shattered woman who was now receiving aid from the same people who were trying to put her down.

Daniel looked around at everyone before settling on Gypsy. She didn't offer him any explanation for her care and he didn't question it either. "Is she alive?" he asked, not really out of concern, but just clarification.

"Yeah, but I think that might have been a mistake on your part," she said, pulling another cigarette out of her pack with her lips. She offered him one, but he only took the lighter from her pack so he could light her cigarette. "Mmm, a gentleman, I didn't expect that."

Daniel chuckled as he put the lighter back. He probably figured she didn't know him well enough yet to assess that. "Who are you?"

Gypsy took a long drag of her cigarette and blew it out before she offered a smile. "That's confidential." She winked. "Who are you?"

"That's confidential." He winked back.

She shook her head, still holding her amused smirk. "Your name is Daniel McGrath. You're a former resident of an underground prison in Russia that houses dangerous supernatural creatures. You are currently employed as a bounty hunter for that same institution. A pretty good one, I'm told."

"Holy shit," he answered.

"How do you know that?" Cori asked.

Gypsy turned and looked her over. "It's classified."

"Are you military or private?" Nevia asked.

"It's... class-i-fied." Gypsy's constant smirk didn't waver even as she took another drag. "I am sorry about tonight. I wasn't prepared for so many werewolves. We are used to dealing with two or three. You three must be pretty important. How did you three get involved with her?"

"It's classified," Cori retorted sarcastically.

"You got a problem with me, mama bear, or what? You've been on my ass since I got here, and since I've established that we are the good guys, I think I deserve a pass on the sniping."

"You haven't established anything, Gypsy, but if you must know, I have a problem with psychopaths."

The woman stood, leaving Daniel to hold his own ice pack, which he promptly tossed away. Cori's rings flared with current, but she didn't release it. Gypsy stood before her, taking note of the hair-raising energy she was producing. "Gypsy?" She wrinkled her nose, trying the name on.

"Gypsy Grace, as I knew you, or Grace Gypsum, as the rest of the world knows you, former cancer nurse from New York. You quit to join the military, which I can only assume brought you to this assignment." Cori looked her over critically in case she thought she had cornered the market on swagger.

Gypsy cocked her head to one side and nodded introspectively. "Gypsy, I like that," she said, neither acknowledging nor denying Cori's dissertation on her. "I don't suppose I could get your name."

"Cori Reiger. What, you don't have a file on me?" Cori asked sarcastically.

"Not yet. You are familiar, though."

"My mother was one of your patients."

"Mmm." Gypsy sucked down her last drag and flicked the butt down the alley. "No, that isn't it. I think I remember you from the back of a milk carton."

"That's enough." Daniel stood. "Do you need something from us, or can we go?"

Gypsy held her gaze on Cori for a long moment before she turned to answer Daniel. "Fair warning, Daniel McGrath, Frederique is already an unstable werewolf. She won't take kindly to me taking her eye, but she knows she can beat me in a fight. What's really going to get under her skin is you. She doesn't like to lose."

"I could take care of that now, if you like," Daniel said without a hint of amusement.

Gypsy's eyes danced over him, evaluating him in a whole new way. "I bet you could."

Nevia shifted beside her, stepping closer to Daniel. "Unfortunately, my job isn't to kill, just subdue when necessary."

"Are you sure you don't want to give me a hint about what your other job duties are, or who has hired you?" he asked.

"Oh, I definitely want to. I like telling secrets, but my boss is very..." She took in a deep breath looking for the word, or just adding emphasis to it. "...perceptive. The best I can do is give you my card. Should you ever need assistance..." She pulled a black card from her pocket and handed it to Daniel with two fingers. Daniel gripped the card firmly, but didn't pull it from her grasp until he had given her a leveling stare that she didn't flinch at. "Good to meet you, Mr. McGrath." She glanced at Nevia, who was creeping closer to Daniel the longer the conversation went on. Nevia wasn't fully glaring at her, but the impassive look gave Gypsy pause. She glanced at Cori, but only found a full-on glare.

She snorted and shook her head. "Fuck, this has been a weird night," she mumbled as she walked away.

"Come on." Daniel put his arm around Cori and Nevia and ushered them forward. "Let's get one of you ladies into my bed, maybe both."

48

ETHAN DIDN'T REMEMBER WALKING back to his room after the bath, but nonetheless he awoke there. Stumbling out of his room, he found his way back to what he thought was the kitchen. Instead, he found the altar room again.

Adrianna and Annette were in the center of the altar, kneeling facing one another. Annette held a vial of what Ethan could only assume was dragon's blood between her praying hands. Adrianna sandwiched her hands with her own.

The chant being spoken was quiet, but Ethan could hear a whisper of it from Adrianna. Levi had mentioned that her mute-ism was selective. He could only assume the magic surrounding the ceremony offered exception to whatever damage forbade her speech.

There was no doubt of the power behind the magic. Just stepping into the room, Ethan felt compelled. Compelled to leave or stay, he wasn't sure, so in the end he just stood stalk still and watched.

When the chant was over, the women slumped back and let their heads fall to look at the stalactites on the ceiling. They seemed to be relishing the tantalizing effect of the magic they had just created.

"Ethan," Annette said even before her head turned to look at him. "How did you sleep?"

"Like a bat in a cave. What time is it?"

"It's time to find out if you have been chosen by the goddess Earth to commune with the dragons."

"So, breakfast is out?"

After a quick debriefing—in more ways than one—Ethan found himself standing on the altar awaiting further interrogation. He knew the details of the magical process were important, but he wasn't sure why he had to be naked. He kept his hands crossed before him for some propriety, but it didn't keep Levi from snickering at his misfortune. He wasn't participating in the ceremony, but Annette insisted he observe, so he perched himself on a rocky outcropping nearby.

"Is this really necessary?" Ethan asked again when Annette came over to sprinkle salt around him. "Can't I just take the blood and see what happens?"

"I'm sorry, Ethan. I know this is uncomfortable for you, but once the ceremony starts, you won't care about anything as trivial as clothes." Even as he opened his mouth to protest, Annette slipped off her red robe, revealing her own naked body. He immediately looked up to keep from ogling her. "It's all right, Ethan, it's not really my body; you may look if it pleases you."

"Why do you change your image?" he asked, looking over her face only.

"I would like to say it's because the power of a woman's will is stronger when her youth and beauty are close at hand, but the truth is I'm vain and I just want to be pretty again." Annette laughed heartily and motioned for Adrianna to approach.

As Adrianna neared Ethan, she removed her robe as well. He kept his chin high, focusing on Levi in his enviously clothed state. Levi's eyes lingered on Adrianna momentarily before looking down at his feet. He could only assume that her emaciated body was still a source of uneasiness for him. He wondered why, if she was so powerful, she didn't disguise her image as Annette did.

"Let's begin," was all that preceded the deep heat that passed between the two women and through him.

The power rippling between them lured him to his knees, and they followed his movements, embracing him as he fell forward. He could feel hands and arms pressing against him, holding him and caressing him.

The whispers of sweet, angelic voices offered him sympathy, but no release from the will being pressed against him. He lifted his head to look at his oppressors, to beg for a cool breeze or a short nap.

Annette's sweet face looked old and worn, a window into her true image. She pinched her eyes shut, and her thin lips moved in time with the chant he could no longer hear. He turned to face Adrianna and found her cheeks full and rosy. Her hair draped over her shoulders in smooth, heavy waves. Diverging from his personal decency, he glanced over her body and found the frame to be properly portioned and hydrated.

Ethan wondered if an extraction of Adrianna's essence created Annette's youth. He didn't believe that Annette would be so vain as to cripple another's youth to retain her own, but he couldn't rule out the perils that came with power, especially when that power was as strong as the Earth itself.

49

ETHAN SHOVELED IN SPOONFUL after spoonful of porridge until he was panting from not breathing. He had never been so hungry, nor had he been so energized. Had he been home with his wife, he would have known exactly what to do with this energy, but here he would have to find less pleasurable ways to burn it.

Adrianna stared at him from the opposite side of the long table. He glanced up occasionally to see if she was still looking at him. When she didn't stop, he looked at Levi, who had joined him in a bowl, albeit with less enthusiasm. "Why is she looking at me like that?"

Levi looked down at Adrianna and waved. "He's fine! Go away!" She frowned and crossed her arms, indicating that she was there to stay. "That particular ritual was essentially an interview of your soul."

"What does that mean?"

"They gave you a teaspoon of the power they possess. They want to see how you react to it. Do you feel like ransacking a village?" He smiled.

Ethan chuckled. "No, but I wouldn't mind fighting a dragon." When he glanced up at Adrianna, she frowned.

"I take it that's the wrong answer. Unfortunately, my first choice of playmate is several thousand kilometers away." Adrianna's frown lessened, and she finally looked away.

"Are you ready, Ethan?" Annette asked, entering the kitchen.

"What now?"

"Time for the blood." She smiled, but it faded fast. "Come along, all of you." She left the doorway again, and Ethan looked at Levi.

"She doesn't seem as excited as she was before," Ethan said.

"She's been searching for a way to commune with the dragons... all her life. If you are able to speak with them, then her life's goal will have been achieved... by someone else." Levi stood and headed out. As he did, Adrianna stood to follow him.

Ethan stood quickly and blocked her way. Her eyes widened, revealing the fearful wild animal inside her. He raised his hands in surrender.

"I'm not going to touch you. I just want to ask you something."

She looked longingly at the door behind him, but she took a step back and waited for him to ask his question.

"During the ritual, I saw... you looked different. I just wanted to ask you if Annette's powers were harming you in any way." Her face scrunched with confusion. "Annette looks much younger than she should and, forgive me, but you look very weary. Is her power hurting you in any way?"

Her eyes flickered over his, and she relaxed, looking at the floor. A hint of a smile crossed her lips before she shook her head.

"Are you sure? I will withhold my cooperation if you need help."

She offered a full smile and moved closer to him. She raised her hands slowly and pressed them to his face. He resisted the urge to pull away and let her imbue him with a warm fuzzy feeling that he assumed was a nonverbal thank you for his offering. Intentionally or otherwise, it reminded him that Adrianna was not weak-willed and was in no danger of being taken advantage of.

50

T HE DRAGON STARED ETHAN down as she ate from the large haystack Annette had brought in for her. The altar seemed an odd place for a snack, but Ethan reminded himself that she viewed these creatures as godlike.

After an hour of waiting for the beast to enlighten him with endless knowledge, he was wondering if this particular dragon was more likely to be able to commune with a cow. The constant chewing and the occasional gas did not seem like signs of intelligence to him, but more a commentary on quality of life versus longevity of life.

Ethan finally gave up concentrating and moved back to sit with Levi on the rock outcropping. Annette was more than disappointed, but she was giving up hope, too. She turned to Adrianna beside her and motioned for her to put the dragon back. She nodded and guided the dragon with an unseen lure to one of the large cave tunnels, where it disappeared into the darkness.

"Thank you for trying, Ethan," Annette said, nearly on the verge of tears. "I won't hold you any longer. You may arrange your departure as you see fit. Levi will take care of everything. Please send my love to Danato." Annette left with no further instruction.

"Is she going to be okay?" Ethan asked Levi.

"She probably just wants to mope. I think she was hoping to make you her new apprentice. You know, one she couldn't break." Levi nodded to Adrianna as she joined them, returning from her duty. She caught the last of his statement and pinched his overhanging leg through his pants. "Hey, it's true. I've heard the rumors."

She shook her head.

"Lies, are they?" Levi crossed his arms. "Then tell me what really happened."

Ethan expected her to hit him or pinch him again, but she smiled and peeked toward the door. When she was satisfied no one would walk in and interrupt them, she placed her hands out for both of them to take. He looked at Levi, who was smiling and shaking his head.

"Oh, no, I don't like this. She's smiling; she never smiles. This is where the bat-shit crazy part comes in." She tilted her head, raising an eyebrow at him, double-dog daring him to take her hand. "Are you sure you aren't going to hurt us?" She shrugged.

Ethan reached his hand out over hers, but waited to grab it until Levi joined him. "You did ask her to tell you."

"You're a bad, bad wiccan, Addy. Bad. I don't know what you're about to do, but if you get me in trouble, I am blaming all of it on you."

She wiggled her finger, demanding his hand, and he reached out to her. At once, they took her hands and were transported... nowhere.

The altar remained unchanged in the center of the room, and they were still sitting on the outcropped ledge. Adrianna, however, was gone.

"I can't wait, Annette." Adrianna entered the room, with Annette trailing behind her. They were both in ceremonial robes and they both looked young and vibrant.

"What the...?" Levi gasped at seeing Adrianna enter.

The women paid no heed to them and stepped onto the altar.

"Will I be as strong as you?" Adrianna asked, pulling her hair back behind her shoulders. Although there was no way to determine if she was from royalty, her accent did hint at a Russian birth.

"Stronger," Annette said. "I am just a catalyst for the earth magic. The earth magic will be at your fingertips." Annette smiled. "I've never met anyone with an aura as strong as yours, Adrianna. I think the world would bend for you if you asked it to."

Adrianna laughed, and Ethan could see Levi's mouth drop. If he rarely saw her smile, then he must have never heard her laugh.

"I think your flattery is a little self-serving. If I turn out to be that influential, then you will have to take all the credit in creating me."

"Hmm, that I will." Annette kneeled down in the center of the altar. "I think if your heart weren't so pure, I wouldn't even attempt this, but you are good, Adrianna. I trust you will do great things with what I am about to offer you."

"I hope so." Adrianna kneeled before her and lowered her head abjectly.

"I will draw the power of the earth to you. You just need to open yourself to her. When you are overwhelmed, simply shut your mind and I will stop. I don't know how much you can handle."

Adrianna nodded, and Annette placed her hands on the back of her head. The ceremony began as they all do: a long, boring chant and an excess of concentration. Though it was only a memory, Ethan could feel the intensity of the link created between the two women.

Annette's breathing became ragged and her eyelids fluttered, baring glimpses of her white eyes beneath. Adrianna rose with a stuttered moan. Annette's hands drifted to her shoulders as she did.

Adrianna's mouth hung open, breathing deeply and smiling at the power being drawn into her mind and body. "Oh, Annette, it's so beautiful."

Annette continued to chant, neither hearing nor seeing anything. The room filled with a shimmering light that made Adrianna smile and cry joyfully. "I can feel everything. The joy, the love, the hopes..."

Levi shook his head and tried to move off the rock, but he could not move. "No."

"...and the pain, the sorrow, the loneliness." Adrianna frowned. "It's so much." Tears sprung from her eyes. "How can it be so beautiful and so ugly?"

Annette started to withdraw her hands, but Adrianna grabbed them, pulling them back to her. "No, I can take it. I'm not afraid. I can't have one without the other." Annette pulled away again, but Adrianna started chanting, drawing the energy into her deeper and stronger than Annette could resist against.

Annette screamed, and the connection broke for all of them.

51

E THAN AND LEVI STARED blankly at Adrianna as she withdrew her hands from them. Ethan could feel the wetness of tears on his cheeks, but whatever emotion had compelled them was fading too fast to hold onto.

"You did this to yourself?" Levi asked her.

Adrianna held up her hands, balancing the scales.

"Yeah, I get it. You can't have one without the other, but you grabbed the wrong power. Earth power is neutral. You drew that power from souls. Positive and negative alike."

Adrianna shook her head and showed the scales again, wobbling more dramatically up and down. She beat her chest and pointed at the altar. She drew her hand downward, clasping onto an imaginary object. She smacked her chest again and showed the scales balancing.

"Annette stopped the ceremony too soon," Ethan suggested, hoping he was getting the signs right. Adrianna nodded fervently. "You..." He glanced at Levi, unsure if he should be helping translate since what he was about to say was likely going to set him off. "You want to go through the ceremony again and absorb the neutral earth power to balance you out?"

Adrianna pressed her nose and smiled at Levi. He just shook his head. "And Annette won't do it." She nodded somberly. "Because it's crazy!" Levi scooted off the rock and turned a brandished finger to Adrianna. "You know, Addy, you are frustrating as hell, but I was willing to put up with your jumpy, paranoid personality, and even the major creep vibe I get when we touch, because I thought deep down you were a good heart trapped in a crazy mind, but now... You are just a power-hungry witch, and I want no part in this."

Adrianna reached for him, but he pulled away and stalked off. Though she couldn't call after him, she still followed him and pestered him with hand gestures. He wasn't sure if Adrianna deserved the animosity that Levi was throwing at her, but he was right that finishing the ceremony was insane. If the first attempt did this to her, what would another do?

Ethan slipped off the rock and headed somberly to the exit. He wasn't sure what time it was, but he was tired.

Wait, a voice said in his mind.

"Damn it," he mumbled before turning back to the dragon that was re-entering the room from her adjoining cave.

52

"DON'T DRAGONS HAVE ANY concept of timing?"

The serpentine movements of the dragon were more obvious as she approached, but once she sat back on her haunches to strike up a dialogue, her features seemed more mammalian—like a cat, but with a bigger ego.

You should speak to me with your mind. You'll sound like a schizophrenic speaking without a partner.

"My brain doesn't work that way. I'm a little under-practiced. Maybe you could develop some vocal cords."

I have vocal cords, but this is far more efficient.

"Why didn't you start talking when Annette was here?"

Because Annette is not who we need to speak with. Annette is an excellent occultist and her devotion to my kind is admirable, but in the end, she is a glorified drug dealer.

Ethan snorted, but stifled his laughter. "That really isn't fair. She does good things with the help of your blood."

Forgive me, I didn't mean to belittle her character, just her income. At any rate, the purpose of your summoning has nothing to do with her.

"What do you mean? She was the one who invited me here."

She invited you because you were worthy enough to hear the mind of a dragon. That was our doing.

"The blood..."

...has nothing to do with it. The dragon you have named Penelope chose you to help us. Annette has a great deal of respect for you, as do many people that you interact with.

Ethan shifted, feeling a little uncomfortable. He would not deny the compliments, but he wondered what it meant to receive such accolades from a creature so... so...

Old?

"Hey, stay out of my brain. I mean, put in, don't take out. I'll say what I want you to hear."

We mean you no harm, Ethan. Despite your distrust of this experience, we are the ones seeking your help. If any debts will be incurred, it will be for you, not against you.

"Help with what?"

Adrianna.

"How's that?"

She is dying. She senses it, but she doesn't know for sure. She is doing her best to balance the spectrum of human emotions coursing through her as raw magical energy, but without the neutral earth power to balance it, she will be torn apart by it.

Ethan shook his head. "You need me to convince Annette to complete the ritual?"

Yes.

"Then just tell her yourself."

No. She must not know we have spoken to you. She must remain under the suspicion that you hallucinated the conversation with Penelope.

Ethan sighed. "Of course she must. Because communing between dragons and humans is what... forbidden? Taboo?"

No, it's damned annoying.

"Is that a personal dig, or do dragons have a sense of humor?"

Penelope said that Annette respects you. She said that you would be able to convince her to do this. Was she wrong?

Ethan looked over the magnanimous creature. He wasn't sure there was etiquette for turning down a dragon. Given the creatures' efforts to stay obscure, he couldn't reject the honor of their revelation by saying no to them. "Of course I'll do it, but since I have your attention, I was hoping to glean some knowledge from you."

And what purpose would that knowledge serve? To enlighten you, to benefit you, or just to amuse you?

"Depends on what knowledge you offer, but I imagine my first priority would be to understand you."

Perhaps one day we can begin a conversation for that purpose, but for now, save the girl.

"You're not even going to tell me why?"

Annette was right about her. She is special. She may be important to our kind in the future. She may even be important to you if the future continues to unfold as we predict, but she must find a more stable neutral power or she will die. Only Annette can provide her with the earth power she needs.

Ethan was used to taking orders from a lot of people, but somehow the giant turquoise lizard before him didn't exude the authority for him as it did Annette. However, he didn't doubt the animal knew what she was talking about. And if Adrianna was dying, he couldn't stand by and watch it happen.

"How long do I have?"

The girl will deteriorate beyond reparation in one month's time. She can sense it coming, but her desperation will only make her seem more unstable to her friends. You must be the voice of reason.

"I think I can wear that hat."

53

E THAN MADE HIS WAY back to his quarters. He still had no idea what time it was, but judging by the dimming coal fires that were supposed to be lighting his way, it was after curfew. The days went too fast without the sun to mark the change.

As he drew open his curtain to enter his room, he noticed that Levi's light was still on. There was movement within, shadowed against the curtain by his lantern. At first, it was difficult to discern what was going on, but the rising crescendo of pleasurable moans made it very clear why Levi was still up.

Silence followed the culmination, minus heavy breathing and a few whispers.

Ethan smirked, offering his new friend kudos for not letting his strange lifestyle affect his love life. He slipped into his room and began to close the curtain, but a flurry of movement behind Levi's curtain kept his attention. The curtain parted and Adrianna stepped from the room, loosely clothed and back to her beautiful hydrated self.

She paused to catch her breath. She leaned on her knees, exhausted. She looked drained by her tryst, physically and mentally. When she was ready, she darted down the stairs.

Ethan drew his curtain and wondered why Levi hadn't mentioned his relationship with Adrianna. Clearly, he felt some affection for the girl, since he was concerned for her wellbeing, but nothing in his tone and manner had suggested that they were intimately involved.

Or perhaps Ethan had just witnessed their first encounter.

He didn't bother drawing conclusions on it until he spoke with Levi. He had more important things to do, like sleep.

"WHY ARE WE RUNNING?" Nevia argued with him from the entryway of the kitchen. Daniel expected she would contest his decision to take Gypsy's warning seriously and leave the city. Which was why he hadn't brought it up last night. It was hard enough to convince her to sleep in the bedroom with Cori, so he could be the first line of defense in case someone came through the door.

It didn't matter in the end, since she only spent half the night in there. She snuck out in the early morning to finish what they had started on the dance floor that night. With his ears and her nose on high alert, their excruciatingly quiet evening was an effort in control that he hadn't practiced in a while. The morning after, however, she was not without her volume.

Cori, no doubt woken by the argument, trotted through their colliding opinions in pursuit of the fridge. She yawned her good morning, seemingly unaffected by the yelling. She was either unimpressed or immune, since her stomach was empty. She started pulling out eggs and cheese, and a few breakfast items that passed her sniff test.

"I'm not running, Nevia," Daniel said as he poured himself another cup of coffee. "I am doing my job, which is to protect Cori. Although, judging by last night's debacle, she may not need it."

"Debacle?" Cori questioned, chewing on the first strip of cheese that would not make it into her omelet. "How far I've fallen from my awesomeness," she said with mock forlornness.

"You're still awesome. The debacle was my doing," he conceded before snagging a piece of cheese himself.

Cori offered him a sympathetic, possibly even an empathetic, smile. She looked like she had some words of wisdom to share, but she gave up the deliberation and went back to cooking.

"They were trying to kill us," Nevia objected. "You did what needed to be done."

"I'm not arguing that point. I'm arguing that if that is the type of situation we are to expect in the future, then I don't want to be a part of it. Do you understand that?"

"No." Nevia stepped up to him, cornering him between the sink and Cori. Cori glanced over at them, uncomfortable with being so close to the argument, but she wasn't retreating without food on her plate. "I don't understand that. I think you should make a stand against Frederique and her followers to level the playing field for Leona and Callin."

"Feck, woman, it is the same argument with you over and over again. I am not getting in the middle of this."

"Why not?" She raised her hands to stop his preparation to start the yelling again. "I know you don't care about all this political shit, but... what about for me?"

"What *about* for you?" He furrowed his brow and pushed his glasses up further on his nose.

"Why not do it for me?"

Daniel shook his head. They were right back where they'd started. "Because it's like bringing a gun to a knife fight, or in my case, a nuclear bomb."

"Some violence can stop death. A nuclear bomb stopped World War II."

"No, it didn't! Those bastards were fighting for weeks after that. The outlying forces fought for months and years after that. Don't feed me your Americanized abridged war history to defend what you want me to do. I know exactly what will happen if I get in the middle of this fight. Lots of death! I don't want that on my conscience!"

"I don't want that either, but after a display of your power, Frederique—"

"Frederique got a display of my power last night!" Daniel set down his coffee and grabbed her shoulders to shake her gently. It gave Cori pause, but Nevia knew it was out of frustration, not anger. "Do you know what her response will be? She's going to try to kill me. You know why? Because that's what werewolves do!" He shoved her back just enough to get past her to the freedom of open space.

"They are fecking dogs fighting over the last bone, and they don't recognize anything as *too big to fight*. Believe what you want about her, but I know the truth. Next time, she will bring fifty werewolves and count on it. They'll be armed. I can't stop all the bullets, and as awesome as Cori's Magneto impersonation is, she can't, either. Last time I checked, we were all still susceptible to bullets."

Nevia approached him to object to some part of his statement or add another argument, but he didn't give her the chance.

"I guarantee Frederique is done making me offers. She will come after me purely to kill me, and then she'll kill the both of you for breathing the air next to me. She is an exceptional bitch and I will not put my friend's wife in danger just because you want to use me as a weapon! And no amount of your pussy is going to change that!"

Nevia's slap was more painful than he'd expected. He had expected it, and deserved it, but he hadn't anticipated how much it would wound his heart to see her face frowning up at him, layered with disappointment. She held her face high, proving at least to herself that she didn't regret hitting him. He could see her shaking, desperately fighting off the tears that were too stubborn to fall from her eyes. She walked away slowly to the bedroom. He knew she didn't want to make it seem like she was stomping off, even though she was.

Cori shoved aside her skillet and shut off her burner. She wiped her hands off on a towel before slapping it on the counter. Whether she was really angry at him was irrelevant; her second X chromosome mandated that she support her fellow female. She moved to leave the kitchen, but he grabbed her by the arm. "Don't," he said.

"She needs to talk," Cori said, glancing down at his hand on her.

"No." Daniel was fairly certain Nevia would prefer to be alone for a while, but that wasn't why he stopped Cori. "She needs to hate me right now."

"Why?" she asked, flabbergasted.

"She needs to make a decision once and for all. I'm sorry to sound like the asshole in this, Cori, but it's either me or that ludicrous war. No matter what I say, she's always going to hope that I'll be able to stand up and make it all better with a big boom." Cori glanced at the exit, but she didn't fight him. He released her arm, and she went back to her breakfast.

He returned to the counter for his long since abandoned coffee. Cori didn't bother searching for a plate. She took a bite of her omelet straight out of the pan. When she caught him staring at her, she frowned. "Did you want some?" she said over a full mouth.

He chuckled and shook his head. "No, mama, you enjoy."

She stuffed in a few more bites before she returned her attention to him. "I know what you mean about not wanting to kill anyone else. I've killed. I suppose it's not comparable, but I didn't like the way it made me feel. I guess *inhuman* is a good word for it."

Daniel nodded introspectively. Inhuman *was* a good word for it. He turned to face her, abandoning his coffee again. He probably didn't owe her further explanation about his relationship issues with Nevia, but he wanted to defend his character. "Nevia sees me as powerful and she wants to utilize that power to reach a goal. Her purpose is noble and I do respect it. I respect *her* more than any woman I've ever met. But... Cori, you saw what I did last night to Frederique. That wasn't power, that was evil, and there's no sugarcoating it. I enjoyed watching her writhe. I wanted to hurt her for causing you and Nevia pain. That's not what the good guy does."

Cori sighed and shook her head. "Oh Daniel, good and evil are such definitive descriptions. I hold the memories of a woman who was willing to kill her boyfriend *because* she loved him. I just recently had my life saved by a man who, on multiple occasions, has tried to hurt and/or maim me. That woman from last night who was supposedly trying to save us was only six months ago trying to kill me in an alternate reality."

Daniel's brow furrowed.

"The wish thing, long story. Anyway, my point is, I think you should stop trying to be the hero or the villain and just be a man. You have a wonderful and awful power, and I know you have a sordid history with it." She looked sheepish, like she wasn't sure that information should have trickled down to her. "But you are a good man, Daniel. I know me stabbing Gypsy in an alternate reality doesn't quite compare to what you did to Frederique, but I don't regret doing it one bit, and if I had been given the option of hurting her more, I'm sure I would have taken it." She shrugged. "I'm pretty sure that takes me out of the running for the hero hall of fame, but I haven't really lost any sleep over it."

Daniel smiled and kissed her forehead. She was right that it didn't compare, but she was right about everything else, too. "You should finish your breakfast. We're leaving as soon as possible." He rubbed her arm, extending a little non-verbal gratitude for the talk. She nodded and dove back in for round two of her breakfast.

55

DANIEL STEPPED INTO THE living room and found his cell phone in his coat pocket. He glanced at his bedroom door, but he had no intention of going after Nevia. Heaton's voicemail picked up and beeped for him to leave a message.

"Hey, man, it's Daniel. Shit just hit the fan with the Queen Bitch. We're all okay, but I'm taking Cori to the farm to hide out. I know you're on vacation, but give me a ring and let me know you're okay." Daniel hung up the phone and marched straight to his room.

He shoved open the door and walked in without knocking. Nevia was sitting on the edge of the bed, her eyes red from tears that had already come and gone. She looked up at him, stiff-necked and too proud not to look away. Her nerve even in the face of this was commendable.

He shut the door and took a few steps toward her. He wasn't brave, but he could fake it. "What's your decision?" Her brow was already dipped in anger, but it slipped in response to his question. "Nevia, I need to know. We've been dancing around this for six fecking months, and I know it's not fair to just throw my cards down in the middle of the game, but I'm done playing. You have to know, deep down inside, you have to know. Is it me, or is it your cause?"

She didn't answer. He kneeled down in front of her. He raked his hand through his hair. "Please, Nevia, just say it. Rip the bandage off once and for all, so we can both move on. You know damn well I'm not the guy you want to introduce to your parents and walk down the aisle with and have kids with. I don't want to make you miserable." He touched her hand and his words caught for a moment. "It's okay, baby, just say it. I know you want to."

After a short pause, she whispered. "I choose you."

"What?" His jaw went slack.

"I don't want to leave you, Daniel. I want to be with you."

Daniel shook his head. "I'm never going to be that guy for you. I'm always going to be selfish, inconsiderate, and slightly inappropriate."

"I know. I'm always going to be aggressive, stubborn, and assertive."

"So, we're perfect for each other?"

"I don't know about that, but who else will have us?" She smirked.

Daniel tucked his hands under her legs and drew her forward a bit. He moved between her knees and hugged her. Her body draped over him and once again he found the intimacy of the nonsexual act satisfying. "Well, then, now that we have that settled, it's time to go meet my mother."

56

C ORI TROMPED UP TO the small cottage that was surrounded by barns and farm equipment. The occasional crow of a rooster penetrated the landscape, but otherwise it was only the wind. Nevia had hung back to pay the cab driver. Daniel was slightly ahead of her, carrying his bag as well as hers. She wasn't sure he would have taken it if she weren't pregnant, but she appreciated the gesture, since she already had plenty to carry.

Daniel reached the door, but before he could knock or check the knob, it opened with a creak. A woman in her seventies with a graying mop of short hair peeked out. "What the blazes? Daniel! Oh, my boy!" Mrs. McGrath—Cori assumed—grabbed Daniel's face and squeezed his mouth. She gave him a lip kiss that he objected vociferously to, but didn't pull away from.

"Ma! Stop!" He gripped her arms and she turned in Cori's direction. Cori smiled cordially at the woman. "Ma, this is—"

"Oh, my goodness!" Mrs. McGrath looked down at Cori's swollen belly. "Oh, my boy, why didn't you tell me you'd gotten your girl pregnant?" She squealed and pulled

Cori into a muscular hug that was not to be denied. She looked helplessly over the woman's shoulder at Daniel.

He rolled his eyes and shook his head. "Ma! Ma! This is Cori!"

"Cori?" Mrs. McGrath pulled back and looked her over. "Oh, I thought it was Nancy or Navy—oh, never mind that. Come inside, girl, and put your feet up."

"Ma'am, I'm—" Cori tried to interject as the woman pressed her forward.

"Oh, none of that ma'am shite. You can call me Ma, or if that's too soon for you, you can call me Maggie. Who's this?" Mrs. McGrath finally noticed Nevia coming up the path.

"Ma, if you'd shut your gob and quit being a header, I'd a' told ya."

"Watch it, lad, you're not too old for my hand!"

"Got plenty of that already today," Daniel grumbled. "Ma, *this* is Nevia, my... girlfriend." Daniel glanced back at Nevia as if he needed permission to use this term.

"It's a pleasure to meet you, Mrs. McGrath." Nevia reached out her hand for a handshake. But the stout woman just looked at it like it was a foreign custom.

"Oh, that's gas." Her eyes looked Nevia up and down. "Are you trying to kill your dear mother, Daniel?"

"No, Ma, she's my—"

"I heard ya! Did you pick the smallest American girl you could find just to see if you could break her?"

"What?" Daniel's face pinched with honest befuddlement. "What's that mean?"

Nevia let her hand drop.

"How's she gonna give me a grandson on those stick legs? She's liable to fall over at three months. I'm surprised you even fit in 'er."

"MA! Jaysus—"

Mrs. McGrath threatened to smack him and he bunched up his face, preparing for the impact. "Curse the Lord's name again and see what it will get you. Now, who are you?" She looked back at Cori.

"I'm... he... we..." Cori stammered, unprepared for the interrogation.

"That's Ethan Pierce's wife, Ma—my old partner. I told you about him."

"Oh." Her mouth rounded perfectly, and her eyes softened and she smiled. Cori smiled back, but she felt more like she was just mimicking for the sake of surviving the introduction. "Looks like *Ethan* knows what it takes to make a baby." Mrs. McGrath tugged Cori along into the house. She glanced back at Daniel, fearful of what might lie within. Nevia walked past him, following Cori; he mouthed an apology to her, but she didn't offer any response.

57

"Y OU CAN SLEEP IN here, love." Daniel's mother showed Cori into the spare bedroom, and he followed her in with her bag. "And you can take Daniel's old room." Maggie continued down the hall. Nevia followed her to the next room, but not before giving him a look that would have seemed brave to any that didn't know her subtle facial expressions.

"Your mom's scary," Cori whispered to Daniel before he could leave.

He grinned. "Aye, she is."

"Seriously, I was ready to promise her visiting rights to my baby to make her happy."

"Oh, don't do that," he mock threatened. "She'll never give it back." He gave her shoulder a touch that he intended to be a reassuring pat, but his urgency to rescue Nevia before his mother starting measuring her hips turned it into more of a chummy slug.

Inside of his old room, Nevia was sitting on his bed. A decade of fantasies came true in one moment. "You'll be sleeping in the barn." His mother popped out from the closet, ruining his already plotted and soundtracked day dream. He was about to object, but his mother raised her brow. "I don't see a ring on her finger or a baby in her belly, so in the barn you will stay."

"I'll sleep on the couch. I won't leave either of them alone in this house. We have some pretty mean beasties after us, and I won't assume that they won't follow us here."

"The only beastie is in your pants, and I won't have you defiling an unmarried woman in my home."

Daniel's mouth tipped a little as he thought about his first defilement of Nevia. Despite their unwed relationship, he found great pride in knowing that he was her one and only. Even more so than that, he was going to get to keep it that way.

"Barn it is," Maggie announced.

"No, Mother. Couch," he said with his most assertive and calm adult voice. "It's not negotiable."

"Oh, really!" She perched her fists on her hips and he smiled at her. His mother was a hardass, but he loved her for it. "Don't think you be sweet-talking me, Daniel."

He ignored her attitude and gave her a long-overdue hug. "Howya, Ma?"

"I've been like a blue-arsed fly trying to keep up with this farm."

He pulled back from her. "Why don't you hire someone? I sent you enough money."

She scoffed. "I did, but I still spend as much time directing him as I do doing it myself." Daniel shook his head. She would argue this until her dying day. "Have you a mouth on you? I could start supper."

"Please." He nodded and offered her leave.

"You're not one of those vegetarians, are you?" His mother looked over Nevia carefully.

"No, ma'am, I'm not picky."

"Good." She paused at the door and eyed Daniel. "Couch then."

"Yes, ma'am." He smirked at her, but she was too stubborn to smile back.

He looked over Nevia, but before he could even contemplate the things he wanted to do to her, his mother called for his assistance in the kitchen. He rolled his eyes and shrugged apologetically. She looked just as disappointed, but she put on a braver face than Cori had. "I better go, or she'll bring up the barn again." He paused in the doorjamb and knocked on the wood before turning back. "I really enjoyed calling you my girlfriend."

She offered him a shy smile. "I really enjoyed hearing it."

He grinned even as his mother yelled again. "I have to... thank you for not shooting her."

Nevia laughed and gave him a full-on smile—a rare treat, and it was hard to walk away from, but his mother was too persistent to ignore.

58

AFTER SUPPER, EVERYONE HEADED into the family room to watch television on a flat screen that was as big as the wall it hung on. Mrs. McGrath seemed embarrassed by the awe that Cori gave the television, mistaking her technology deficit attraction as judgment of her opulence.

"I told Daniel I didn't need such a large television." Mrs. McGrath sat down in her small easy chair and picked up her remote to switch on the monstrosity.

"And I told you; I can afford it." Daniel sat down on the stiff floral print Victorian sofa that was designed to keep your guests from getting too comfortable. Daniel's ever slouching seated posture made the couch seem loungeworthy.

Nevia sat down beside him and he lifted his arm tentatively, inviting her into the crook of his arm. She paused only a moment before she shifted into position to rest her head on his chest. Something had changed in their relationship. Given this morning's incident, Cori would have thought that they would be in opposite corners ready to fight at the hint of a bell, but they were cozier than she had ever seen them.

Cori sat down on the chair on the opposite side of the sofa. It was the ugliest shade of brownish yellow she had ever seen, but it was very comfortable. There was room for a lot of philosophical discussion in that contrast, but she just chalked it up to: look with your eyes, decide with your butt.

"Affordable or not, you shouldn't waste your money on me."

"And who would I spoil if not you?" Daniel objected.

"You could spoil a wife and children if you'd bother getting them."

"Yes, Ma." Daniel rolled his eyes. Cori smiled at the interaction.

"If you could only meet a nice, sturdy girl like Cori." Cori frowned. She had not thought of herself as sturdy. Granted, she was not the slight woman that Nevia was, but she hardly compared her figure to a table. Daniel shook his head at her, reading her disappointment.

"I have met someone, Ma. She's sitting right here, listening to your passive-aggressive insults." Daniel kissed Nevia's forehead, but Cori couldn't see if she was hurt by Maggie's comments.

"How far along are you, dear?" Mrs. McGrath asked her, ignoring Daniel's comment entirely.

"Um... ah, about eight months."

"Where is your husband?"

"He's in China." Cori glanced at Daniel like he could somehow draw the attention back to himself, but he was already engrossed in the television.

"Will he be back in time for the birth?"

Cori smiled, but it was only to pretend that she was brave. "I hope so."

Daniel finally glanced over. He looked her in the eye for a long moment, but the appropriate words must not have come to mind. He turned to his mother instead. "Ma, what are you stitching now?" Daniel pointed down at his mother's needlepoint, and she was more than happy to pull out her partial project and flaunt her talent.

After an hour or so of television, Cori took a bathroom break and got hung up in the den. The wood interior and leather furniture were classic and manly, but the computer that sat on the desk was bright white with a glowing blue trimmed monitor.

Cori sat down at the computer and quickly found the internet icon. In the search engine, she placed her full maiden name. She wasn't sure why she was doing it, or what she thought she would find, but Gypsy's comment about being on a milk carton made her wonder if more people had noticed her disappearance from the real world than she'd thought.

When she first left the prison, Vince's precautions had kept her cloistered. Since most of her recent friends were in London, she wasn't likely to run into anyone in

Paris. Without technology, she had no idea if anyone had mourned her disappearance.

The numerous results that came up made her think that there was another Corinthia Ellen Reiger running around. The name David Reiger, however, stopped her in her tracks. She clicked on one of the sites and found a small article that claimed to be posted in the New York Times.

Cori read the article that explained that David Reiger was trying to raise money to find his daughter Corinthia, who had disappeared in transit to his ex-sister-in-law's funeral. The topic of female slave trade was brought up: prostitution, drugs, and underground organizations. It was the usual soap box speech against a business that is created and propagated because of the super-rich.

Cori switched to another article that started out with the same rendition of headline kidnapping, but then veered off into left field regarding the politics of combatting slavery of women, long after the slavery of men has ended. The article even went so far as to bring up women's liberation—as if fighting for fair wage was the same as fighting off drug-mule rapists.

The next article discussed David's long search coming to an end. Cori read on and found the article to be somewhat critical of him. It explained how after a long two-and-a-half-year search for his daughter, David Reiger abruptly announced that he would lay his baby to rest in mind, if not in body. The article continued to accuse him of raising money for his own purposes and not with any intention of finding his daughter.

Cori did a quick calculation and found that her father's unexpected exhaustion of her search landed just after her wedding. His announcement would have coincided with Danato's courtesy vacation that allowed her and Ethan a honeymoon—such as it was.

Despite the gesture, Cori had found it strange that Danato was willing to leave the prison for such a long time. He had never shared anything about his time away, and considering it was his first real vacation in many years, she had expected photos or stories.

Cori sighed and shut down the window. She didn't want to think about Danato having yet another secret. What Danato did or didn't do wasn't what was really bothering her. It was the fact that her father—who hadn't written or called her more than three times after she'd moved to England—made a national story out of her disappearance. Bitterness and raging teenage aggression aside, Cori couldn't help but think it was too little, too late.

Cori may have missed out on a father during her formative years, but now she had three very good men to care for her and protect her, each in his own way. Even if the blood she shared with David Reiger was thicker than water, there wasn't enough of it to compete with the bonds she had now.

59

ETHAN SMIRKED AT LEVI as he shoveled down his breakfast. "Hungry?"

"Hmm?" Levi mumbled between bites. "Mmm."

Ethan chuckled at him. "What?"

"How long have you two been involved?" Ethan lowered his voice, even though Adrianna hadn't joined them yet.

"What's that?" Levi said, going for another bite.

"Don't tell me last night was your first time with her? I guess I can't judge. Cori and I tend to be drawn to each other through conflict."

Levi's brow furrowed. "What the hell are you talking about?"

"You and Adrianna." Ethan grinned. He was surprised that Levi was going to be that secretive about it. So far, he had been an open book.

"Who?"

Ethan lost his jovial view on the topic and leaned back to look him over. He recalled the other times he had mentioned Adrianna to him. He seemed dumbfounded that her name should come up in conversation. "Adrianna... Addy."

Levi's eyes glinted with understanding, but he was quick to return to his breakfast. "What about her?"

"How long have you been sleeping with her?"

Ethan heard a gasp behind him and he knew before he looked, it was Adrianna. It was not a shock to see her eyes wide with panic. It was a little more surprising to see Annette behind her, with her lips pursed in disappointment.

Ethan cleared his throat. "Um, good morning ladies, we were just..." Ethan turned back to Levi for some help, but his open-mouthed gape made it clear he wasn't available for comment.

"We know exactly what you were doing," Annette scolded. "Really, Levi, isn't it enough that you treat her like a dimwitted child, but do you really have to converse about your sex life as if it were a sport?"

"What?" Levi squeaked, but that was all he got out before returning to his aghast expression.

Adrianna looked mortified and Ethan couldn't help but take the blame for the incident. "It wasn't him." Ethan stood to confront Annette. She was still glaring reproachfully at Levi, but he managed to get her to glance at him as he spoke, which seemed to ease her anger. "I brought it up. I was just being nosy." Ethan looked at Adrianna. "He didn't divulge anything. I just happened to catch you... leaving his room last night."

"*What?*" Levi yelped and stood up. The bench behind him flopped over with a thump and everyone stared at him. His reaction seemed wrong, even for someone in such an embarrassing situation. He pushed his fingers into his hair, ripping at it. All of a sudden, he slammed his hand into his wooden bowl, sending it and its contents to the other end of the table. "We had sex?"

Ethan looked at Adrianna, seeing a new interpretation of her shock at the situation. He looked at Annette, who was also finding Levi's confusion disconcerting.

"You... we..." Levi's confusion faded as a thought—or perhaps several thoughts—dawned his understanding of the situation. He frowned at Adrianna. He looked more than hurt. He looked defeated. "You bitch," he said quietly, almost to himself.

Adrianna shook her head, but without a verbal defense, she had even less of a chance of convincing him not to be mad at her. Ethan stepped back, allowing him to storm out. Annette's displeasure for him had transformed into concern, but she didn't try to stop him from leaving. Adrianna tried to follow after him, but Annette extended her hand in front of the girl. "We need to talk."

60

ETHAN WASN'T SURE IF he should follow Annette and Adrianna into the altar room, or try to find Levi to get his interpretation of what had just happened. When it became clear that the conversation between the ladies was going to take place behind a veil of magic, Ethan decided to go where vocal cords were still required.

Ethan gave Levi's curtain a gentle waggle that alerted him with the rustle of the grommets.

"Go away!" Levi snapped from within.

"Okay," Ethan mumbled, surrendering without an argument.

"Wait. Ethan? Come in."

Ethan pushed back the curtain and found Levi sitting on the edge of his bed, staring at the floor. He glanced up at him and they exchanged a look of mutual embarrassment.

"Look, I'm not sure I quite understand what just happened, but I'm sorry. I didn't mean to—"

"What did you see last night? Did you just see her leave?"

"No, Levi, I heard the both of you. It was unmistakably a mutually pleasurable evening." Ethan sat down on the bed while Levi mulled that over. "Do you seriously not remember any of that?"

"No," Levi said disgustedly. "To my knowledge, I've never touched her, except hands and lips, and never to anything but my hands and eyelids."

"What does that mean, exactly? I mean, I assume she was making you forget, but why?"

"I don't know!" Levi grimaced and shrugged apologetically for his tone. "I guess I don't even care why. I mean, what excuse could she have for...?" He looked at Ethan with wide eyes. "This is like rape or something, isn't it?"

"No," Ethan said quickly. "Rape is brutal, ugly, and without any love. What happened here last night may have been influenced and erased, but you were not being brutalized in any way that you weren't enjoying."

"Still, she can't just do with me as she pleases and then erase me."

"No, but she must have had a reason. She cares too much for you to hurt you intentionally."

Levi scoffed. "Yeah, right."

"You don't see it, do you?" Ethan smiled, but Levi didn't join him. He stood up and leaned against the wall across from him. "How many people around here does she touch? I mean, without necessity of spellwork."

"None."

"She touched your hand to get into the pool."

"That's different. The floor was wet. She's a klutz."

"She stays pretty close to you when you're together." Ethan could see Levi thinking hard about that, but he didn't say anything. "You're pretty hard on her most of the time. Do you think anyone would just put up with that if they didn't care about you?"

"Fine, whatever, it still doesn't give her permission to do that."

"No, it doesn't," Annette said as she pulled back the curtain, surprising both of them. She glanced at Ethan before sitting down beside Levi. She tucked her hand under the crook of his elbow and forcefully held his hand. He drew away slightly, surprised by the intimacy. "I owe you an apology. Multiple, in fact, but hopefully you can accept a blanket one."

"What do you mean? For what?" Levi asked almost suspiciously.

"I'm sorry that I didn't see what she was doing to you. I knew that you two were having sex. I assumed consensually. However, instead of suspecting any wrongdoing on her part, I interpreted your dismissive behavior to her as insensitive and semi-abusive."

"I wouldn't... she's just so... I'm not trying to be a dick, but..."

"I know, Levi." Annette caressed his cheek. "You are frustrated with her, and given the influx of magic she has been directing at you over the last few months, I can't imagine—"

"Months?" Levi looked to Ethan as if he might be able to define the word as something other than a really long time. "She's been doing this for months?"

"I'm afraid so."

"Why?"

"To balance her powers." Annette released his hand and leaned onto her knees so she could speak to both of them equally. "As you know, Adrianna is very powerful, but her powers are ever changing within her. That is why she always appears so weary and frail. It isn't her true form, but it is how we view her, because it is what our minds see when we look at her. Much like my youth, but mine is entirely intentional. When you came to us, Levi, I saw a way to help balance her power. That is why we use you in so many of our rituals. You are a microcosm of stability."

"I am?"

"Yes." Annette smiled warmly at him. "You may not feel it within yourself, but you demand it in others around you without even knowing it. We could stop wars simply by placing you in the right room at the right time."

"Really?" Levi said again.

"Yes, Levi. Unfortunately, Adrianna has been taking advantage of your gift through a sexual ritual. Even if you were a willing participant, I wouldn't condone it. Magic of this nature is short-lived and addictive—for obvious reasons. She was desperate to get control of her energies, and she used you. I'm so sorry that I didn't see this sooner, but of course, she is very powerful."

Levi paused, taking in her words before looking up at her. "I thought you hated me."

"Oh, Levi." Annette nearly broke into tears at hearing that. "My beautiful boy, please forgive me."

When Annette didn't move to embrace him, Levi pushed himself into her arms for a hug. "Of course I forgive you. You saved my life. There is nothing you could do that can erase that in my eyes."

61

ETHAN STEPPED OUT OF the room to offer Annette and Levi privacy while they discussed Adrianna's indiscretion in a little more detail. After a few minutes, Annette came down the stairs, dragging her hand along the wall for support. Ethan offered his hand for the last few steps.

"Ethan." Annette sighed. "How uncomfortable for you. I'm sorry."

"Don't worry about it. I'm used to drama. I'm just glad for once not to be involved in it."

Annette grabbed a lantern and headed back down the tunnel toward the main entrance. Ethan followed a few steps behind. "Annette, if Adrianna is imbalanced, why haven't you tried to balance her?"

"It's too dangerous."

"More dangerous than a woman with an overdose of unstable magic?" Annette paused in the main entrance—aka the garage—and looked back at him. She seemed annoyed that he was questioning her. "I'm just trying to understand," he said softly. "Adrianna doesn't exactly look... healthy."

Annette looked down ruefully before continuing into another passageway that Ethan had not been through—one of the many exit options from the garage.

"She isn't well, but there is nothing I can do about it. I can't reverse what has happened to her."

"If you don't mind my asking, what exactly did happen to her?" Ethan asked as he clumsily climbed a set of stone stairs dimly lit by the residual light from her lantern.

"She was supposed to absorb earthen magic, but she... reached too deep, as it were. She took in mortal magic," Annette stated it as if the mention of it should make Ethan mourn for her.

"What is mortal magic?"

"Mortal magic is the magic of man." Annette paused in her ascent and he heard more than saw her unlatch a door. "Some would call it black magic."

Light flooded the stairwell, and Ethan followed Annette into the room beyond the door. Within the room were the same moisture-steeped stone walls that offered claustrophobic ambience. A massive hearth on the back wall afforded the room warmth and soft light. Wooden shelves lined another wall, housing what Ethan could only assume were ingredients for medicinal tonics and other such *potions*.

There was a table and chairs in the center of the room near but not too near the fire. Tucked in a corner away from everything was a small bed. Ethan assumed this was Annette's version of living simple, but something about the tiny mattress made him wonder if Annette had ever loved a man.

"Many," Annette answered his thought, and he snapped to face her.

"How did you know I was...?" He gaped, hoping she wasn't secretly psychic.

"Because you're young, and still wildly in love."

He took a breath in relief and smiled. "And you? Were you wildly in love with any of the many, as you put it?"

"Oh, yes, all of them, I imagine. I've lived a long time, Ethan. Don't confuse being alone for being lonely. Not everyone is cut out for pairing." She sat down at her table and lit a candle.

He joined her at the table, and glanced at the label on the scented candle she had lit. He expected something floral or woodsy, but it was Tahitian Breeze. "You were saying about black magic."

"Ethan, I know you see Adrianna and you want to fix her, but you need to trust that I know what is best for her."

"And you need to trust that I don't speak out of turn unless I have something to say." Ethan could see Annette debating on how to handle this unexpected show of authority. "I know you don't know me well, but when I ask you questions, it is not to usurp your authority or disrespect you. It is to exchange knowledge. You, *as you put it*, have lived a long time. I would not patronize your wisdom; however, youth isn't without its fresh perspective."

Annette stared across the table for a moment before a smile spread on her face. "He chose well, didn't he?"

"Yes, he did. Now, if you would be gracious enough to bestow your knowledge..."

"If I were only a jubilee younger, boy, I might add you to my many."

"I... ah..." Ethan flushed, unsure of how to respond to that.

Annette cackled raucously at his reaction. He was pleased to have humor back in the situation, but he couldn't help but wonder if that was her way of regaining control of the situation. She was definitely a sweet and wondrous woman, but she hadn't become a powerful earthen witch by letting people step all over her.

62

"BLACK MAGIC IS DRAWN from the energies of humans," Annette continued to explain.

"But black magic is evil, right?" Ethan asked, cracking open a peanut from the dish Annette had offered him when she was through teasing him—returning his image of her back to the grandmotherly woman who desires nothing more than to fatten him up and pinch his cheeks.

"Not necessarily. There is dark magic that is drawn from negative emotions, which by rights is very powerful on its own, but the truth is, good or bad, still depends on how you use it. Dark magic can be used to kill, but depending on who you are killing..." Annette weighed her hands. "Murder or justice."

"What about positive emotions?"

"White magic can be just as dangerous, but it is harder to come by. The only time you can get a draw of positive emotions is when a large group of people feel happy simultaneously together, like a holiday. Negative emotions tend to cluster more often than the positive, which is why any magic drawn from humans is generally considered dark magic."

"Adrianna draws from dark magic. That's why she is unstable?"

"Yes, but she isn't drawing on it as she needs it, as a true witch does. She..." Annette repositioned to raise her hands for emphasis. "I reach out to the heavens to wield the power of the earth like a tool. My goal with Adrianna was to open her up so she could take in the power."

"She houses the power."

"Yes—well, no, she funnels the power. She is constantly connected to it, but it flows through her. If she tried to hold onto it, it would kill her."

"She isn't exactly bubbling with life now."

"She is a reflection of the love, hate, and indifference in the human race."

Ethan nodded. "The world weeps, and she feels it."

"Oh, yes, that's why you can't touch her. That much pain can't be contained without great concentration. She can draw on the positive energy when she needs to, but it is hard for her to maintain."

"You said she was using Levi to balance herself. How...?" Ethan wasn't sure he should be getting into Levi and Adrianna's personal life, but since it was just as misunderstood by Levi, he thought it should be okay.

"Adrianna drew on her power to appear to him in a healthy form. She claims that she didn't use any exterior magic to seduce him. I believe her. I don't doubt that Levi is offended that she made him forget the encounters, but

Adrianna is a beautiful woman. I can't imagine he would say no to her in her true form."

"Why sex? I mean, couldn't she just draw from him in a ritual?"

"A ritual of that caliber would drain Levi. Sexual magic creates and exchanges power. The effects can last days or weeks."

"How often was she doing it?"

Annette looked into the fire. "Levi's been with us for almost a year now. She started six months ago, increasing in frequency to weekly." Annette frowned. "How do I begin to reprimand her for this? It's laughable to assume I have control over her. As much as her behavior displeases me, I know that she is in this situation because of me."

"There is only one thing that you can do. Finish the ceremony."

63

ANNETTE STARED AT HIM with the same displeasure that she had at the beginning of the conversation. Ethan couldn't help but buckle under her gaze. He wasn't afraid of Annette, although perhaps he should have been, but he didn't want to disappoint her.

"Annette, if Addy is willing to go to this much trouble to balance her power, something must be wrong."

"Adrianna has been like this almost two years. Nothing has changed."

"How would you know?" Ethan asked without thinking.

"I would know." Annette's voice dripped with disdain.

Ethan frowned and cleared his throat. This approach would not work. "I am clearly insulting you, but I don't understand any of this enough to willfully do so. Please, Annette, just tell me why you are so opposed to finishing the ceremony. You intended to finish it before. Why did you stop? Why did you never continue?"

Annette sighed and tapped her fist on the table. "I never meant to put mortal power in Adrianna. I never meant to put the earth power in her either. I only meant to connect her to a portion of it. Mortal power, albeit useful, is still an emotional power. It should never be housed inside of a witch."

"But it is. The only way to balance it—"

"Adding earth power does not guarantee that she will be balanced. She might simply go insane, like your wizards."

"I kind of get the feeling that was a risk the first time around."

"Yes, it was a risk the first time. However, insanity is not the worst prospect. If she were to absorb too much earth power..." Annette looked into the fire. Ethan wanted to press, but he knew now wasn't the time. Whatever she was thinking about was making the fire dim unnaturally. "Adrianna isn't the first I've tried to do this to," she continued, taking her attention from the fire. As she did, the blaze returned to normal.

"In my youth, I attempted to do it to myself, which was a laughable attempt. Trying to exert and harness that much power is like trying to light a fire during a hurricane. In truth, and I only say this because I consider it fact, I'm the only witch strong enough to singularly imbue another with earth power."

"Who else did you try it on?" Ethan asked, trying to refocus her.

Annette's eyes faltered shamefully before she answered. "There was a young boy, not much older than

Levi. I thought he would be strong enough, but his mind severed under the weight of the world, quite literally. He developed multiple personalities that he called North, South, East, and West. He referenced his emotional states like seasons: winter, summer."

"Was he powerful?"

"Very. He created the passageways that we walk through. He did it in less than a day." Annette looked back at the fire.

"And? I know this story doesn't have a happy ending."

"He was going insane. He started out loopy and careened into wonky. When he started cutting off his fingers, I decided that there was no hope for him. I tried to remove the power, but he was too strong."

"You had to kill him."

She looked back at him sternly. "Yes, I had to. He was dangerous."

"Why did you even attempt it again?"

"Adrianna was special. So much stronger. I was stronger. It was arrogant to assume that it would turn out better, but... I've never been one to play it safe."

"You're afraid if you finish the ceremony that she'll go insane like your other attempt."

Annette chuckled. "No, sweetheart, I'm afraid that if I finish the ceremony that I will have created the most powerful sorceress in the history of the world. Pure earthen power directed by mortal magic—there's no going back from that."

64

"Hey," Ethan offered the only commiseration he could think of when he found Levi sulking in the altar room. His arms were wrapped around his knees like a child huddling scared in the darkness. "Do you want to be alone?"

Levi looked over at him and shook his head. The movement stopped as quickly as it started, and he glared behind Ethan. Ethan turned and saw Adrianna in the doorway. She glanced between them and crept in slowly, as if she was now at risk of scaring away the wild animal before her.

"What do you want?" Levi mumbled.

"I should go," Ethan suggested.

"No," Levi said quickly. "You're welcome, she's not." He motioned for him to come over. Ethan slipped onto a lower part of the rock outcrop and glanced between Adrianna and Levi.

All three dragons lumbered into the cavern from their passageways. No one seemed to mind the intrusion, but Ethan got the feeling the dragons had an agenda other than food. They paused around the altar and watched them. Apparently, they were just as eager to see how this conversation went.

Adrianna licked her lips and opened her mouth to speak, but nothing came out. She stepped forward, and Levi fixed a finger on her. "Stay away."

She looked torn between obeying him and demanding that she be heard. She caught Ethan's eyes, and she seemed to have an idea. Judging by the way she tip-toed toward him, he knew he wouldn't like it.

He leaned back suspiciously and grimaced when she motioned to her neck. "I know you can't speak, Adrianna. I can do my best to translate, but—"

She tapped her head and then her throat again. After she motioned a flow from her mouth. She pointed to her brain again and repeated the throat and mouth sequence on him.

He sighed and tipped his head. "Is this going to hurt me?"

She shook her head vigorously.

"Am I going to be... conscious?"

She nodded.

He glanced at Levi, who was taking an interest in the exchange. "Are you ready to talk to her? Cause I'm not going to do this if you're just going to walk out."

Levi examined Adrianna's torn face. She placed her hands in prayer and pleaded her case through a crumpled brow. "Yeah," he said finally, "I have some questions, anyway. Do you mind? I don't want her in my head right now."

"No problem. Okay, shy girl, you're up. Just don't make me sound too girly."

She offered him a small smile to humor him. He expected she might touch his throat or link hands with him, but instead her eyes glazed and she focused on his eyes. He felt a cool pressure settle in his throat. He swallowed to alleviate it, but it didn't help.

When she looked away from him to Levi, he started to ask her what he needed to do, but his voice was gone. Frozen, stolen, or just incapacitated, he wasn't sure. He gripped his throat, but there were no holes to speak of, no damage.

"Levi," he heard his voice crack from Adrianna's mouth. It was his voice, perhaps him with a cold, but he knew his own voice. "Please let me explain."

"Annette explained," Levi interrupted, glancing at Ethan. He was probably a little thrown by his voice coming from her, too. "I don't want to hear the reason you did it. I get that. I don't want to hear why you chose me. I get that too. I just want to know why you made me forget it."

Despite the newly acquired vocal cords, Adrianna was silent.

"Tell me the truth, Addy. Did you think I would reject you? Did you just not want to be with me? Is that why you didn't want me to remember being with you?"

"I..." The voice trailed off as she brimmed with tears. She turned away a moment, but quickly returned to face him. "I needed the balance."

"I know why you—"

"I needed *you*!" she yelled. The voice was already hoarse and barely recognizable as anyone's. "I wanted the magic at first. It was conniving, but you didn't turn me down. I made you forget so you wouldn't tell Annette. She would not have approved. I returned to you each time with the same new experience for you, but each time you were more... loving with me. You held me so close and so tightly. I couldn't help falling in love with you."

Levi blanched at the statement, but didn't move to her. "Why wouldn't you tell the one you love that you are sleeping with them? Why wouldn't you let me remember those nights that were so precious to you?"

Adrianna glanced at Ethan. He wasn't sure what show of support she expected from a now mute man, but one glance at the dragons reminded him of what it was she was about to tell Levi. He nodded for her to go on, and she looked back at Levi.

"Because I'm dying, Levi."

Levi unclamped his legs and anger lit his face—a shield against the truth, and a weak one at that.

"I didn't want you to fall in love with me, too. I didn't want you to mourn the loss of me, as I will mourn you when I go."

Levi shook his head and puckered his lips in bitter defiance. "No, you can't die. You're too strong. I've seen what you can do." He slipped to the edge of the rock and jumped down to face her. "You are too magnificent! You aren't dying!"

"I am, and even if you choose to ignore it like Annette, it is coming. I can feel it. I've tried to spare you, because I love you."

"Spare me? Spare... you didn't spare me anything." Levi frowned, looking over Adrianna's face. "I love you too, you stupid twit." He walked away, but turned back to face her. "I don't need those precious memories to be in love with you. They were only ever precious because I was already in love with you."

He continued to storm off, and Adrianna followed. Ethan offered a few frantic hand gestures to remind her that she was still playing Ursula to his Ariel, but she was too distracted. He wasn't sure if there was anything normal about this particular relationship, but he was almost certain that the yelling would stop soon enough—assuming Adrianna could hold back her mortal magic long enough to give him a proper memorable first kiss.

65

*W*ELL, NOW YOU'LL HAVE *to speak to us through your mind*, the dragon on the far left said inside his mind.

Ha. Ha. Very funny. Ethan concentrated on thinking the words. *Any thoughts on this evening's performance?*

Have you made any progress with Annette?

No. Ethan frowned and jumped off the rock to face the dragon that was thinking to him. *She is convinced that the ceremony will make Adrianna too powerful.*

Powerful, yes. Too powerful... that is dependent only on the sturdiness of her virtues.

You think that Adrianna won't take advantage of the power?

Her heart is pure, three voices chorused in his mind.

Hey, easy on the simulcasting. Ethan was glad the dragons were in support of Adrianna, but only because he really wanted to save her. The truth was, though, he didn't trust them, not like he trusted Annette.

You would trust her over us, the dragon interrupted his involuntary thoughts.

He crossed his arms and glared at her before shrugging. *I get that you are hundreds, thousands, forever old, but there are rules against creating sorcerers.*

These rules do not apply to us, the dragon stated simply.

They do apply to me. I am supposed to be protecting the world from supernatural influence, not supporting it.

There was a long pause. *Your loyalty to your duty will not be contradicted by your actions here.*

Ethan shook his head. *That's exactly what I am doing. How can you ask me to convince Annette to do something that I know Danato would disapprove of?*

Danato's opinion of these events is not relevant to us at this time.

Ethan threw up his hands. The dragons either had no concern for anything but their own agenda, or they were just avoiding revealing too much information. Either way, it was making trusting them difficult.

Trust is earned through reciprocity, the dragon continued responding to his unintentional broadcast. *We put a great deal of trust in you, Ethan Xavier Pierce. Our secret has not been exposed to humans for thousands of years. Our request has been laid at your feet above all others. Our faith in you places greater weight on your shoulders than simply the life of a girl.*

Ethan sighed. *I don't mean to offend. It is a great honor, but I would feel more comfortable with the burden of it if I understood your purpose.*

Purpose?

How do I know that this isn't just a plot to create a sorceress?

It is guidance, but not a plot. We are only interested in preserving the girl; the outcome of her powers is negligible to us. Whether she is titled a witch or a sorceress is no matter to us, but sorceress, I imagine, would be significantly more beneficial to you.

Ethan furrowed his brow. *I'm not even going to ask what that means since you won't tell me, anyway. I don't suppose you have any tips on how to convince Annette to do the ceremony.*

She is a stubborn woman. Vain and selfish.

Ouch. So, do you like anything about her?

Those are observations, not opinions. Her nature is benevolent, just introverted in purpose. My advice is to ask her to do the ceremony.

Ask? Ethan looked at the other dragons in case they might have a second and third option.

Many of life's most difficult problems have simple solutions.

You want me just to ask her to go against her beliefs.

Not you. The dragons turned together and wobbled back to their exits.

Once again, Ethan was floored by his anticlimactic conversation with them. If Annette knew he had spoken to them, she would be dancing with joy, hoping that he held the key to the universe. All he knew for sure was dragons were reticent, a little judgmental, and smelled like cattle.

66

"**L**ook, man, I know you're probably ass deep in..." Daniel cringed at his own metaphor, and redirected his message to Heaton. "This is like the fifth message I've left you in two days, and that doesn't even count the calls I didn't leave messages for. Once again, *we* are okay, but since I haven't heard from you, I'm starting to worry. Actually, worry started when you didn't call me back after the first message. Seriously, call me back, text me, write me a goddamn letter. Just let me know you're okay."

Daniel ended the call, leaned against the barn, and sputtered his exhale through his lips. Nevia came out of a nearby shed with a pitchfork in hand. "No message yet?"

"Not a one."

She grimaced and rested her fork on the ground as she looked him over. "You want to go find him, don't you?"

"You know I do," Daniel said a little acerbically. He knew she knew what he was feeling even before he could verbalize it. "I can't leave Cori."

"I think I can protect her for a couple of days, Daniel."

"It's not that. It's the pregnancy."

"What about it?"

"Belus insisted that Cori be protected by me. If he was insistent enough to convince Danato that I was the man for the job, then he must have been worried about her. She's been under a lot of stress lately. It leaves room for concern."

"Do you know anything about delivering babies?"

"I've been present for dozens of births. It's a good luck thing. I've witnessed more than my share of difficult labors. I know enough to get the baby out without killing either one of them."

"Okay, then you stay and I'll go look for him."

"How would that ease my worry?" he asked, wide-eyed.

She smiled shyly. He'd thought she would have more trouble accepting their newly defined relationship, but it actually had relaxed her. The last six months had been frustrating, to say the least, but now that there was a label on them, it seemed far less complicated.

"Just a thought." She shrugged.

"I appreciate it, but I'm not risking either of you. Heaton's a big boy; if he's in trouble, he'll figure a way out of it." Daniel wasn't sure why he was putting up a fake bravado, since she could smell right through it. "Besides that, you aren't leaving me alone with my mother."

Nevia scoffed. "Please, the sun rises and sets on you. Cori might as well be the moon. I'm just a stray meteorite that's she's hoping will burn up before I can reach you."

"I like the metaphor, but technically my mother is the sun, so therefore the rising and setting on me, is just her being overbearing."

"Yeah, well, maybe you and Cori can take an orbit around her together and make her happy." Nevia yanked her pitchfork up and headed into the barn.

Daniel followed her in and stepped up directly behind her, only touching her incidentally. "Nevia, my mother has been the most important person in my life for a long time. The only reason she's not making this easy on you is because you are the first woman I have ever introduced to her as my girlfriend. She's testing you. You have to sense that."

"I sense territorial love. Beyond that, it's all very mixed."

"Mixed emotions would be Ma's specialty. Just ignore her. Trust me, she isn't the type of woman you can win a fight with. I gave up trying a long time ago."

"I'm not good at knuckling under, Daniel," she said firmly.

"I know." He smiled and kissed her neck. "I know you're struggling with this, and I would never ask you to be someone you're not."

"But it's your mother and you want her approval."

"Aye, as stubborn and infuriating as she is, I love her." She turned around and looked him over. Whatever she saw there didn't bring a smile to her face, but she was content with it. "What are you doing with that pitchfork?"

"Your mother *requested* I change out the hay in the horse stalls."

Daniel narrowed his eyes. "She hasn't kept horses for years. Too much work just to get saddle sores."

"*That's* why she was so smug about it. Damn it. I'll figure her out yet." Nevia dug the pitchfork into a bale of hay near the entrance to the stall and broke it up.

"What... you're not seriously going to do it, are you?"

"You want me to play nice? This is me playing nice."

"But..." Nevia scowled at him and he shut his mouth. He didn't quite understand her motive for continuing the useless task, but he figured it was a good way for her to take out her aggressions.

67

C ORI SET THE TABLE for dinner while Daniel stared aimlessly out the kitchen window. Mrs. McGrath shuffled about getting the finishing touches on her surprise meal. Nevia came in through the mudroom looking like she had taken a dirt bath.

Cori grinned at her. "What on Earth have you been up to?"

"Your stalls are ready for horses, Mrs. McGrath," Nevia said curtly on her way through the kitchen to the bathroom. "Should you choose to get any," she added before she was out of earshot.

Maggie looked after her. "Be sure to scrub hard, dear. Ireland doesn't wash off as easily as American soil," she called after her, though there was no guarantee she heard her.

Cori chose to ignore the dig at her heritage, but only because she wasn't entirely sure what the insult meant. Daniel checked his phone and shoved it back into his pocket. It was only the third time she had seen him do it in five minutes.

She stepped up to the window and looked out with him. "You seem agitated," she whispered.

"I'm fine." He forced a smile for her. "Just hungry," he added, louder for his mother's benefit.

"Mind your manners, boy," Maggie grumbled back, but her lips turned up as she continued to doctor her meal.

"You don't have to do that, you know."

"Do what?"

"Pretend. Despite appearances... and past evidence, I'm actually not that fragile."

"Fragile?" Daniel thought about that. "When I first met you, I had three different images of you in my head: the one Ethan put there, based on his rants; the one I put there, based on my view of women as a whole; and the one you gave me."

"Which one was more accurate?"

"All of them and none of them. I think you were honestly unprepared for the world that was thrown at you. Surviving your... past..." It was Daniel's turn to be concerned about his trickle-down knowledge, but she didn't flinch. "...acclimating to your present, and trying to plan your future, all while falling in love with Ethan. It must have been very hard. I think you bravely bite off more than you can handle, and then you foolishly forget that you can ask for help, but... no, I don't think you're fragile."

Cori tipped her brow at the evaluation of her character, but he wasn't necessarily wrong.

"Then tell me what's wrong," she said softly.

"I think Heaton's in trouble, but I can't do anything about it because of the situation we're in."

"Oh, Daniel, I'm sorry. This is all my fault. If I weren't here—"

"Then it would be some other danger, some other time," he said curtly, cutting her off. His intent was to take the blame from her, but his tone only made her feel worse.

"You could leave me with your mother and go check on him."

He looked her over like he was considering it, but shook his head. "I can't."

"Dinner's ready!" Maggie announced for the entire house to hear, though four of those ears were only a few feet away from her.

68

D ANIEL HAD NO INTENTION of leaving Cori, but since his reasons for not wanting to leave were only conjecture, he didn't want to worry her. He was more than willing to change the subject to supper. He sat opposite his mother at the table, and Cori sat opposite Nevia, who had arrived late from her shower.

He gave her a quick once-over, admiring the fresh, clean skin she had exposed. She was already in her frumpy pajamas with no intention of getting dirty again. He was always amused that she had so many extremes of clothing. She loved her designer casual wear, but on the job she looked the part of the ex-FBI agent. At night she had no qualms about wearing old t-shirts and sweats. He wondered if she would find it amusing that he found her most attractive in her timeworn loungewear, or perhaps she already knew that.

"What are we eating, Ma?" Daniel asked, dragging his eyes off Nevia.

"Boiled pig's feet," Maggie said with pride and lifted the lid of the pot before her.

Daniel groaned. Cori visibly convulsed upon seeing the delicacy. Nevia, to her credit, handed her plate to his mother so she could load her plate with several feet.

"Ma..." Daniel tiptoed around the topic. "Is that all you made? No tatties? Soda bread?"

"I wasn't aware I was running a restaurant," she said with feigned annoyance. She wasn't hiding her amusement well.

Cori looked at him fearfully. She was starting to turn green. He raised his hand ever so slightly off the table to tell her to wait. He passed his plate to his mother, and she loaded him up with more feet than he would ever consider eating.

"Cori, sweetheart?" Maggie asked cheerfully.

"I got it, Ma." Daniel used his knife to skin one of his feet and pick off the meat for Cori. She appeared more than relieved, but he was sure that she wouldn't make it past the first foot without leaving the table.

Nevia, however, was digging into her pig's feet like it was fried chicken. Judging by the vacant stare she held at the wall behind Cori, he thought she might excuse herself soon, too.

"Well, at least she has an appetite. God knows where she'll put it." Maggie pulled out a pig's foot for herself. "Probably go puke it up later," she mumbled.

Daniel glared across the table at his mother. "Mother!"

"Well, that's what the American women do," she defended coarsely. "The shallow ones, anyway."

Daniel slammed his fist on the table, making everyone but his mother jump. She had never been afraid of him. Not even after he killed his father. "That's enough!"

"Oh, is it? I wasn't aware that we were sharing a meal over *your* table."

"It's not my table, but it is *my* girlfriend you're trashing."

"Girlfriend." Maggie scoffed. "I know your lifestyle, Daniel. Forgive me if I'm being unkind, but at least I'm honest about the future she has with you." She turned to Nevia. "Don't let him fool you. Despite my greatest efforts, my son has turned out just like his father."

"I am nothing like my father!" Daniel jumped to his feet and Nevia was right behind him. He wasn't sure he needed to be restrained, but he knew if Heaton were here, he would be placing a calm hand on his shoulder. Her standing impassively next to him was enough to remind him he was too dangerous not to keep his temper in check.

Even with the events unfolding as they were, Maggie was still seated, unimpressed by his dramatic movement. "He was a philanderer, and so are you! I'm not going to watch you entice this girl with the pretense of a relationship that isn't going to happen."

"It *is* happening! We are together!" Daniel glanced at Nevia for confirmation of this, and she offered him a reassuring nod. She was stock still, but he knew she was biting back every comment, repartee, and defense that came to her mind.

"For how long? Don't do this, Daniel. Don't waste her time. Let her go while she can still find someone to give her what she wants."

Daniel shook his head. This was the argument all along. He was too old, too troubled, and too undeserving to have her. Yet, she was here. She pushed him to be more. She stayed with him even when he pushed her away. She was biting her cheek just to keep from disrespecting his mother, as he had asked. She was eating pig's feet, for feck's sake!

"No!" he answered. "I won't let her go."

"Oh, Daniel, why—?"

"Because I love her!" Daniel yelled at his mother. He said it with authority and not the childish tone he usually ended up using on her.

When she blinked at him, dumbfounded, he knew he had won this battle. When he looked at Nevia, she was staring down at her pig's feet. It was the first time he had ever said that out loud. It might have been too soon. He might have just scared her away.

He didn't bother sticking around for the uncomfortably awkward silence that was about to take over. He stormed out through the mudroom to find a haystack to sulk on.

69

"H ey." Nevia walked around the bound haystacks that created a wind shelter for his mother's land.

"Hey," he said back. He didn't know what to say beyond that, and she seemed to be struggling with words as well.

"I... um... you..." She attempted to crawl up the tall, rounded haystack, but like most beginners, she didn't understand the approach she needed to take. "Does this thing come with a ladder?"

"If you've come to let me down easy, I'd rather you stay down there."

"What?" She looked hurt. "I wanted to thank you for defending me, for defending us." She touched his leg, squeezing his shin.

He smiled at her, though it was mostly forced. He had too many emotions running through him to focus on any one. He imagined that was messing with her radar on him. She looked nervous and desperate to get close to him.

All the better to smell him.

"Daniel, please, either help me up or talk to me."

"Talk about what?"

"About what you just said in there. Did you mean it? You were angry; the vibe didn't really match the words, you know?" She tapped her nose.

"Why do you ask?"

"Daniel." She looked out at the field he was staring at. "It's kind of an important set of words. At least to me it is." She looked down at her feet before turning back to face him. When he didn't answer her question, she took in a steadying breath and cleared her throat. "The thing is... I love you. I guess I was too chicken to say it first, but if you really feel that way too... then I can tell you, right?"

Daniel didn't react to the statement so much as relax. He did love her, more than he'd realized until he heard himself say it. "I don't want to be your boyfriend, Nevia." He cruelly let the sentence hang between them, and she froze, wide-eyed. This might have been another rare time when she would cry, but he didn't want that. "I want to be your husband." He said it quietly, as if it might be more appealing as a plea than a question.

She gulped and returned to the haystack, searching for a way up again. She was letting her silence lie heavily between them on purpose. "Let me up," she finally demanded in frustration.

"Say the right word and I will." He was trying to be funny, but his heart was balancing on her answer, so he couldn't fake the levity.

"Let me up first." She snared him with her gaze and didn't look away.

He reached down and helped her climb onto the hay. Instead of taking the spot beside him, she straddled him and pushed him *flat* on his back. She yanked his hair hard, making him yelp as she pulled him into a hard kiss.

When she withdrew, releasing his lips and hair, she added a punch to his shoulder. "Ouch. Why the abuse?"

"You know why!"

"Are you going to answer me or just keep beating me?" he asked sourly.

"Ask me properly and I'll give you an answer," she said, giving away nothing.

Daniel sat up as she shifted back on his lap. He cupped her rear so she didn't fall back. He licked his suddenly dry lips and cleared his throat, so the words wouldn't catch. "Nevia..." He felt sick, but he knew she wouldn't offer him any leeway on this. "Will you marry me?" He could only manage a whisper, but she smiled, hearing the words just fine.

She leaned her head back, exposing her neck as she chuckled. He winced at the strange reaction, but let her have her moment. When she came back to him, she leaned in for a kiss. He pulled back slightly. "Say it."

"Yes."

"Are you sure?"

"Yes." She smirked, gently removing his glasses. "You have beautiful eyes, Daniel."

He shied away from her gaze. "You're the only one who would ever say that in the light of day."

"You are a magnificent creature, Daniel McGrath, and I want to claim you as my own. Are *you* sure about that?"

"You're not going to pee on my leg, are you?" He squirmed beneath her.

"No, but I will cripple any woman that touches you." He smiled at her joke, but he realized she wasn't joking. "You have to be sure, Daniel. If you choose me, it must be me alone. I try not to let my werewolf heritage control my life, but there are aspects beyond my control, and that is one of them."

Daniel nodded and tipped her chin up so he could kiss that sweet neck. "Will you keep yourself only for me?" he asked between kisses.

She shifted on his lap, pressing herself into him. "I will be yours alone."

Daniel had never thought of monogamy as a path for him, but knowing that he was the only man to facilitate her orgasms made him want to reserve all his sexual energies for her. It didn't seem like a commitment so much as an honor.

Daniel pushed forward on the haystack, sliding himself off and her with him. Nevia landed on her feet despite the lack of warning. He grabbed her too forcefully and shoved her against the warm hay. "Sorry," he said breathlessly.

"It's okay, I kind of like it." She reached for his pants, but he pulled her hands away.

"You first. It's the least I can do since I don't have a ring for you."

"I don't need a ring," she murmured as he slipped her pajama bottoms down.

"Will you wear one?" he asked curiously as he kneeled down and invaded her privacy in the best way possible. She gasped, trying to find a grip against the haystack.

"I'll wear whatever you want, just don't stop."

He chuckled and delved deeper into his decadent celebratory dessert.

70

AFTER HIS ATONEMENT FOR a ringless proposal, Daniel and Nevia snuck into the barn for a literal roll in the hay. When he had finally sated her romance-overloaded appetite, he was spent physically and mentally.

He sucked in air, trying to get his heart rate down. Nevia continued to kiss his chest and neck. "Say it again," she whispered and rested her head on his chest.

"I love you." She smiled up at him, half dazed. "I don't get that smile very often. I must have fucked the cynical out of you that time."

"I'm not cynical, just... wary, and serious."

He grabbed her and flipped her onto her back, resting his leg over her thighs so she couldn't move. "You're guarded." He pinched her nipple, making her wince a little. "Sorry," he apologized, before kissing the delicate flesh. "Why do you love me?"

"What do you mean?"

"I mean... I'm an arse."

"You aren't an arse... anymore."

"Okay, but initially, something in your brain said, 'Hey, I'd like to get me some of that.' What would ever possess you to choose me, one-night stand or otherwise?"

"I don't think you'll like the answer. It's another of my werewolf heritage things."

"Oh, yeah? How's that?"

"Power, strength; it's kind of a turn-on."

"No shit, you and every other woman seeking alpha males."

"No, you don't understand, the reason I was a virgin when I met you was because I've never found human men attractive."

"What?" He chuckled.

"I avoided male werewolves because I didn't see a future with them. It wasn't until I started researching that I found out the reason there was no future was because the Council of the Moon had been preventing normal family units for over a century. When I got the job offer to become a hunter, I saw it as an opportunity to make a difference. And I did."

"That you did." He smiled, though he couldn't hide his disappointment that she was in danger because of that opportunity. "So, humans—normal humans—don't do it for you?"

"No."

"But you didn't know that I was not normal when we first met." She shook her head, not hiding the guilty look on her face. "You didn't know until... oh." Daniel took a deep breath.

"Told you you wouldn't like it."

"You were turned on by me killing?" he asked, disgusted.

"I was turned on by a man with such a great power that he *could* kill, if necessary," she scolded him. "I'm not a sexual deviant, Daniel, but you must always take my werewolf heritage into consideration. There are certain aspects of my life I keep secret purely out of habit, but if you are going to be my husband you should know them, so you can accommodate as needed."

He flushed. "Like what?"

"I have many tradeoffs. You know I can smell emotions on a psychic level, and you also know I can't see worth a shit in the dark." Daniel snorted, but stifled his laughter when she glared at him.

"I find that particular trait romantically fortuitous, since I can see very well in the dark." He winked at her and her glare softened into a pout.

"Also, I don't turn into a werewolf on the full moon, but... I do have some pretty vicious mood swings on the night of one. PMS times fifty. You'll need to either avoid me, or... be extremely dominant."

"Dominant?" He struggled not to laugh again. "Are we talking about bedroom bondage?"

"Not necessarily, more like emotionally thick-skinned and quick on your feet. I've lost a few friends because of inconveniently timed visits." He smiled broadly. "It's not funny, Daniel."

"I'm sorry, that is definitely something we will have to work through, thank you for telling me," he said soothingly as he leaned in to kiss her breasts, which had been left terribly bereft of his attentions for almost a full two minutes. "Keep talking, baby. I'm listening." He sucked her nipple hard, making it pucker back up to full form before tracing his tongue around it.

"That is so distracting, Daniel."

"Not as distracting as I'm about to be. Keep talking. I love listening to you when you're in teacher mode."

"Really?" she asked as he shifted onto her, parting her legs.

"Aye, didn't you know I find brains hot?"

"Shut up, you do not!" She laughed.

"Hell yes, I do. Haven't you ever heard the expression 'fuck your brains out?' That's why I love blowjobs so much."

"You're so vulgar."

"I'm just getting started," he said, shifting to start round two.

"Wait!" Nevia's hand pressed hard against his chest and her head tipped up, offering her nose a better angle to the air.

"What's wrong?"

"We need to get dressed right now." He didn't know what she had smelled, and he didn't bother asking. The seriousness in her tone was undeniable. He was off her and almost dressed when the gunshots started.

71

CORI HEARD THE GUNSHOTS from the bathroom, where she was brushing the taste of pig's feet out of her mouth. She dropped her toothbrush and ran out of the bathroom. She could hear glass breaking, plaster chipping, and Mrs. McGrath screaming.

"Get down, Maggie!" Cori braced herself low in the hallway, avoiding the bulk of the mayhem in the kitchen and formal living room, though she did get dusted by the plaster falling from the walls.

When the bullets stopped, Cori crawled to the kitchen to check on Mrs. McGrath. She was huddled in a ball by the sink. Water was spraying out from the pipes and the window over the sink was shattered, but she wasn't hit. "Mrs. McGrath, move behind the fridge away from the outside wall." Cori wasn't sure where she was getting her cool, calm, and collected voice from, since she was having a heart attack herself, but she could only assume that it was stemming from her overdose of motherly hormones.

"Who is shooting at my home?" Mrs. McGrath was angry, but she was more than happy to do as she was told.

"I'm about to find out. Stay down." Cori created a veil of magnetic energy with her borrowed power that bounced from the stove to the fridge. She stood to peek out the window and found just what she'd expected to find. "Frederique."

She cursed as she watched a team of a dozen men and women walking up the drive to toward the house. Each one held a gun in hand. It was an unusual use of weaponry for a werewolf, but one that Daniel had predicted in response to their colossal failure the other night.

As they approached, they branched off, hiding behind the various outbuildings on the property. Frederique was left with two women behind her. Amongst the triad stumbled a man, barely keeping himself upright. Frederique stopped at the far end of the drive and said something over her shoulder.

The man stumbled around her, revealing his identity and his injuries. "Heaton!" Cori gasped at the swollen bruises on Heaton's face. He had taken a good number of hits. By the looks of his shirtless torso, he had received puncture wounds and burns as well. She cringed as he walked slowly toward the house.

She ran to the front door off the formal living room and waited for him to arrive so she could usher him inside. Halfway to the door, Frederique gave the nod and her female counterpoints shot him twice.

"No!" Cori screamed as Heaton went down to his knees. His teeth were clenched under the pain of the double calf injuries, but he didn't scream.

"You bitch!" Cori opened the door and threw fireballs one after another at the three women. Frederique escaped the firestorm by hiding behind her already burned team members. Cori attempted to go after Heaton, but the gunfire started again and she was forced back inside to duck for cover.

"Ma!" Daniel's voice echoed down the corridor from the kitchen.

"Cori!" Nevia's footsteps ran toward her.

"Here!" Cori peeked up from behind an overturned coffee table.

Nevia looked relieved to see her. "It's Frederique! I can smell that bitch a mile away."

"I know, and she has Heaton," Cori said as Nevia helped her up.

Nevia's eyes went wide. "Heaton? Shit."

"What about Heaton?" Daniel marched in from the hallway.

"He's outside." Cori glanced at Nevia, hoping to get some idea of how to gauge Daniel's familial level of devotion to his friend. Judging by the concern etched on her face, Cori knew she should tiptoe. "He's wounded. They are using him as bait to draw us out."

Daniel dipped his brow in confusion and marched to the window to see for himself. The image of Heaton, face down and bleeding on the McGrath lawn, crumpled Daniel's face into horrified pain. Tears sprang to his eyes, but they quickly melted off as his expression turned cold and deadly.

He moved to the door, but Cori and Nevia jumped in his way. "Daniel, no! It's what they want!" Nevia yelled at him.

Daniel picked her up easily and set her aside. "I'll kill them all," he said matter-of-factly.

"No, Daniel, they're hiding," Cori insisted, backing away as he moved forward.

"I'll destroy everything then."

"That's too much, Daniel!" Nevia dragged down his arm. "I know you don't want to kill unless you have to."

"I have to!" Daniel screamed, pinching his eyes shut.

"There are too many guns! You can't stop all the bullets!" Nevia brought his own argument back to face him.

"I don't care!" Daniel pushed her off brusquely, leaving Cori as the only thing between him and the door. "Move, Cori." His eyes leveled on hers, and she felt the same uncomfortable feeling she usually felt when they were eye to eye. She didn't understand how Nevia could stand his scrutiny. This time, however, she forced herself to look into the abyss. "Move, Cori. I don't want to hurt you."

"Daniel," she said soothingly, and took his hands in hers. "I don't want to hurt you either." She released a crackling shock that crawled up his arms and snapped in his face.

He narrowed his eyes at her, trying to discern whether she was bluffing or not. "Cori, I could knock you on your ass just as easily as you can me."

"Daniel!" Nevia hissed behind him.

"Both of you need to let me help my friend." Daniel reached for the doorknob but found his hands covered in a layer of thick ice that had essentially shackled his wrists together. He looked back up at her, impressed but angry.

"Daniel, I could put you to sleep right now, but I need you awake. Let's try this the hero-way first, and if that doesn't work, then I'll help you turn this place to ash." Daniel nodded and his face lit up with the thought of their mutual vengeance. "Now let's—"

Cori's vision blurred suddenly and, for a moment, everything was out of focus. Everything except the tattooed genie, who was suddenly in front of her. Before she could speak, the genie held up one finger in her face. The vision ended as fast as it started, and the genie was gone.

"Oh, shit." Cori looked around for the impending problem. "Minor inconvenience number one."

"What?" Both Nevia and Daniel asked, exchanging glances.

Cori felt her pants moisten, and water dripped from her pant leg. She looked down, as did Daniel and Nevia.

They each added their own particular colorful statement
to mark the moment.

72

"M a!" Daniel bellowed from the living room as he ushered Cori into the spare bedroom. "We need clean towels!"

"No, I can still help," Cori objected. "The contractions haven't even—ahhhh!"

"Started?" Daniel couldn't help but mock her. "Melt this shit off me now." Daniel extended his hands out to Cori and with great concentration she separated the ice holding his hands together. He didn't bother asking her to melt the rings around his wrists; he just smacked his cuffs on the doorjamb, shattering the ice.

"What's happening?" Maggie shoved into the room around Nevia. "Oh, dear, the baby. It can't come now!"

"Minor inconvenience, my ass!" Cori grunted as she leaned against the back wall, holding her stomach.

"I need to get Heaton. Ma, can you watch her?"

"You can't go out there!" Nevia yelled.

"You need to help her!" Maggie objected.

"Ma, you've given birth, I haven't."

"It's a hell of a lot different from this end, son!" Maggie scolded.

"The baby can wait. We can get Heaton together!" Cori groaned. "I just need to create a magnetic field so you can grab him."

"Cori, you're too distracted," Daniel snapped. "You barely got the ice melted."

"Daniel, you stay with Cori," Nevia ordered. "Your mother and I will go get Heaton." Nevia grabbed Mrs. McGrath by the arm and pulled her to the door.

"Yeah, okay... wait, *what*?" Daniel grabbed her arm and yanked her back. "You aren't going out there!"

"Yes, I am! And your mother is coming with me to carry Heaton."

"I am?" Maggie looked between them.

"Yes, Heaton is a tall, strapping man; it's going to take some of your hard-earned farm muscle to drag him inside."

"You... my mother... feck no!" Daniel stammered.

"Move the furniture to block any stray bullets in the front room. Then give Cori a damn rifle and prop her up. I'll go out the side door and lasso Heaton with that extension cord from the mudroom, so your mother can help me drag him back to the house. She won't even have to step outside. You clear out any unnecessary riffraff that happens to pop its head out while I'm roping up Heaton. Somewhere between all that, catch the baby and get her healed back up so we can put up a full fight."

"What about the bullets?" Daniel yelled, exasperated. "They will shoot at you!"

"Yes, they will, but they won't get me." Nevia slapped her forearm. "Natural Kevlar. Another tradeoff. I don't have a lot of strength, but what muscle I do have is bound tighter than a spidersilk quilt."

"Bulletproof?" he clarified, and she nodded. "Why the feck didn't you ever mention that before?"

"It's not something I readily share. Besides, I still prefer to be on the distributing end of the bullets." Nevia moved away, but he grabbed her and kissed her. He sensed his mother's disapproving eyes on him, but he didn't care. "I'll be okay, Daniel, I promise," she said when he released her.

"You better be, or I'll rip a hole in the fecking Earth to swallow all of them up."

"I know." She nodded, unfazed by his fury. "Come on, Mrs. McGrath."

"You're a werewolf?" Maggie stammered, looking over Nevia.

"One quarter werewolf, but don't worry, I don't turn."

Maggie nodded and followed her obediently. His mother may not have liked his choice of woman, but after tonight, she wouldn't be so heavy-handed with the insults.

73

CORI HELD THE RIFLE on the windowsill. The chair she was sitting in was sturdy enough to hold her, but the only thing protecting her from bullets was plaster and wood. The pain resonating on and off in her abdomen was no doubt normal, but far more painful than she wanted to admit.

After the last one passed, she couldn't keep from crying. She wanted to help save Heaton, but now she was a useless liability. She sniffled uncontrollably and Daniel looked over from his station beside her. He wasn't armed, but he didn't need to be. All he needed was to see his target.

"Hey." He touched her leg. "I'm sorry I was so harsh. I get... intense sometimes."

"I get that," she whispered, keeping her aim focused. "If that was Ethan lying out there, I wouldn't be any calmer."

"How's your pain?"

"It's okay," she lied, but her face scrunched up in a flood of more tears. "Daniel, I'm scared."

Daniel moved his hand to her belly. "Just hang on a little bit longer, and I'm going to help you through all that, okay? Can you help me save Heaton first?"

"I'll do my best." Daniel touched her belly gingerly, and she pressed her hand against his. "I know Belus trusted you with this, and I trust Belus."

"So do I." It was a lot of responsibility to put on his shoulders, but she knew he wouldn't buckle under the pressure.

Just as Nevia explained, she ran out to Heaton with her gun holstered and an orange extension cord in hand. The gunfire started immediately, but there was no one visible to return fire on.

Tiny unseen forces wracked and volleyed Nevia's small body. She had described herself as bulletproof, but that didn't account for the damage to her skin. Cori could see the puckering red welts from the bullet impacts and bleeding gashes all over her exposed skin.

Daniel ignited his power into the space between Nevia and the werewolves. The bullets ceased to disrupt her, and she was able to get Heaton lassoed under the armpits. She signaled for Mrs. McGrath to pull, and the rope tugged Heaton toward the house. If Mrs. McGrath struggled at all with his weight, it didn't show.

Three of Frederique's men attempted to follow Nevia inside, but crossing Daniel's line of sight proved deadly. Cori fired a few shots, but her aim was too poor to do more than threaten a bruise.

"Daniel!" Mrs. McGrath dragged Heaton in under his arms and laid him out in the back of the room, away from the windows.

Daniel jumped to his side and started healing his more desperate wounds, starting with the holes in his calves.

Nevia stepped over the healing in progress and took the rifle from Cori. "Mrs. McGrath, get Cori prepared for birthing, and then take over the rifle."

Cori was glad that Nevia was barking orders, but Mrs. McGrath's bitter beer face hinted that she disagreed. She did, however, collect Cori and take her back to the bedroom to disrobe. She handed her an oversized nightgown that appeared to come with the room. "Put this on, dear. You won't want anything too confining."

Cori put on the gown and groaned as another contraction pushed her to one knee. "Daniel?" She puffed and crawled toward Daniel just outside the door.

"I'll be right with you, mama girl," Daniel said, not looking up from his work on Heaton's torso.

"Mrs. McGrath!" Nevia barked from the front windows. "We got creepers!"

"Coming!" she hollered and jumped over Cori to take up her rifle position. After a few cracks of the rifle, Nevia gave her congratulations on a good shot. "It's not my first tango with werewolves, dear."

"I'd love to hear that story," Nevia said before she cracked a few shots with her pistol. Mrs. McGrath joined in firing the rifle.

Cori sidled up beside Heaton's bruised and broken body. "Heaton, are you awake? Daniel's working on you, so don't mmmmmove!" She leaned her head on his upturned shoulder to bury the pain.

His hand reached up and caressed her face. "Heaton, thank God!"

"I'm sorry." His voice choked, and blood dripped from his mouth to the floor. Cori glanced at Daniel and he noted the disappointing revelation of the internal damage, which he wouldn't readily be able to access. He repositioned to gain access to the other leg.

"I tried not to tell her," Heaton croaked. "She just wouldn't let up."

Daniel's jaw clenched, but he focused his attention on the damage he could see.

"Shh, it's okay, Heaton," Cori assured him. "We don't blame you. We blame that sadistic bitch," she said coldly, and for the first time since she was lying under Gypsy Grace, she wanted to kill someone. Cori winced and panted through another contraction.

"Baby?" Heaton looked her over.

"Yeah, I thought I'd complicate the situation a little more."

"Daniel!" Nevia barked from the windows again. "Hurry this along; they're trying to double back. Either get Heaton fixed, or get Cori back in commission."

Daniel looked over Heaton. Aside from his bruises, the only thing left to fix was internal, and he couldn't fix that right now. Heaton was too exhausted to expect him to be useful. "Okay, baby mama, your turn."

Cori frowned as he picked her up. She wasn't quite as ready for her turn as she'd thought she would be. He carried her into the spare bedroom and set her on the edge of the bed. She groaned through another contraction and spurted a cry that she couldn't contain.

"Okay, Cori, your job is really simple. Just wait until it feels right, and then push as hard as you can."

Cori shook her head, but she wasn't sure why. She knew there wasn't any way around this.

"Yes, you can," he answered her unspoken objection. "I know this isn't the way you want to do this, but I need that not-fragile girl right now." Cori nodded feebly and leaned back on the bed in preparation for her brave performance.

She closed her eyes, too mortified to watch as he lifted her gown to proceed. She felt a stinging sensation, and she was vaguely aware of the blood dripping down her legs.

"Are you ready to start pushing?" Daniel asked soothingly. She had never thought of Daniel as sincere, competent, or gentle, but at that moment she would have told him she was ready to paint a gorilla with superglue as long as he asked nicely.

74

"STOP! STOP PUSHING, MAMA!" Daniel popped up from between her legs and grabbed her shoulders. "Cori, I need you to stop."

"I can do it!" she said, determined to finish what she had started.

"Yes, you can, but there's a problem." He saw her eyes widen with panic. "No, no, nothing I can't fix. I just need to back the baby up a little. He's crushing the cord. I need to apply some pressure and reposition the cord. It's going to hurt like hell."

"It already hurts!" she cried.

"I know, but just for a bit, okay?"

"Daniel!" She sputtered his name, but all at once her face cleared and she nodded. "Okay."

"Good girl." He ducked back down to offer the manipulation that he needed to un-pinch the baby's oxygen flow.

75

SOMEWHERE BETWEEN FREEING OUT the baby and pulling out the afterbirth, Cori passed out. Daniel decided to speed up her healing process so she could help defend the farm when she woke up.

The baby squealed beside him, but he couldn't worry about that yet. Heaton crawled in as he was fixing up Cori and scooped the baby into his arms. He looked to be in as much pain as his bruises claimed, but he smiled and cooed at the baby to get it to quiet down.

"Daniel! I'm out of bullets!" Nevia yelled.

Daniel broke away from Cori. He was already past the marathon run stage and bordering on heat stroke. He would have to finish healing her up later. Heaton gave him a thumbs-up on the way out, letting him know the baby would be fine with him.

Daniel ran out to the front room and swung open the door. He was overheated and ready for a cooldown. The immediate outbuildings were easy sacrifices to his anger. The swirling mix of wood particles and paint chips dissipated, revealing six werewolves. He slowed his destruction to a precision that cooled his body back to a normal level. The resulting effect removed several layers of skin from his targets and virtually crumbled their weapons.

"Frederique!" Daniel screamed at the top of his lungs as bullets attempted to hit him from behind the barn. He wouldn't destroy the barn—too expensive to rebuild—but he did disintegrate the gun and hand that snuck around the corner. "I will kill you for this!"

Daniel heard glass breaking from inside and his mother screamed. He ran back into the house and found Frederique inside the living room with two of her goons holding his mother and Nevia. He noticed that the door to the spare bedroom was shut. Heaton, he thought.

"Don't even think about using your power, Daniel, or they'll snap their necks." Daniel didn't even bother trying to think of a rebuttal. He had no clever plans. Even if Nevia could get free, his mother wasn't quite that nimble. He needed a clear shot, or he had no shot. Frederique was starting to figure him out. His power was hot and heavy and all-encompassing, or distinct and measured. He couldn't kill her without setting off the others. He couldn't kill them all without killing his mother and fiancée with them.

"What do you want now?" Daniel asked.

"Nothing. I'll settle for your death, and hers." Frederique nodded to Nevia. "If I get that, then no one else has to die. I'll leave your mother and your friends alone."

Daniel stared down at the floor, wondering how big of a hole it would take to swallow both of them up. If he was going to die, he might as well take her with him.

"And I thought your sister was a bitch," Cori said, startling everyone.

Daniel jumped forward to get to Cori, but Frederique was between them. She put up her hand, effectively stopping his approach. She stared quizzically at Cori. She looked exhausted and positively crazed. The yellow nightgown was splattered with blood, and her hair was disheveled. She might as well have just stepped out of the nuthouse.

"Did you just give birth?" Frederique frowned.

Cori grimaced and tears pricked her eyes. "Yes, I guess you can add another to your list of casualties." Maggie gasped from her position in her captor's arms. Daniel was almost positive that Cori was faking to protect the child, but the part of him that was unsure thought immediately of Ethan.

"You might as well snap my neck too, because as long as I walk the Earth, I will never stop hunting you."

"Oh, girl, you are so trying. All of you. Such a cavalier attitude when you are so far out of your league. Don't they teach you anything at that prison, Cori?" Frederique stepped toward Cori and grabbed her neck. "Fem-wolves are not to be messed with." Daniel tensed, prepared to knock everyone into the back wall together and see who stands back up. It was only the small smirk on Cori's face that stopped him.

Frederique's grip lifted her off the ground. Cori grappled at her throat, but couldn't offer more than a massage for the fem-wolf's thick, muscular neck. Even the futility of her fight didn't keep Cori's smile from growing. "What are you smiling about, you...?" Frederique coughed. "What...?" She coughed again, spurting a spray of water as she did.

Daniel took his opportunity and threw Nevia and her captor into the back wall. His mother's captor was ready to rip her head off, but a precision attack peeled his face, sending him stumbling back, screaming.

Frederique's intermittent expulsion of water forced her to drop her prey. Cori kept her hands in contact with her neck, while she watched her writhe in pain from the endless ocean in her lungs. He didn't know how it was possible, but he sensed Cori was experienced in this particular torture.

Nevia stabbed her captor in the eye with a shard of glass and shoved him back again when he tried to lunge at her. Nevia watched the scene of Frederique drowning with the same concern etched on her face that she had the other night after watching him almost rip her apart.

Daniel felt the same way from this perspective, and yet what could they do? She would never stop hunting them. However, seeing the eye patch Gypsy had forced on her, he decided she could be an example—an example that might once and for all end this battle with the Council of the Moon.

The question was: which was more humane?

"Cori." Daniel stepped over to her and held his hand over hers, not touching, but forcing her to break concentration. "Let me take care of this. This is our mess." Daniel glanced at Nevia. "Let us clean it up."

"But she'll never stop," Cori objected.

"There is one thing that will stop her."

76

C ORI WAS IMPRESSED THAT one phone call to the number on Daniel's black card could cause the uproar that was transpiring at the farm. Within twenty minutes, a helicopter arrived with sharpshooters to discourage the errant werewolves from leaving the scene of their crime. Within an hour, two more helicopters arrived with enough weapons and soldiers to collect the remaining werewolves and deliver them back to where they belong.

By the time the militant fashionista Gypsy Grace arrived, most of the questions had been asked and answered. An assessor had even been through the house to determine the damages that Mrs. McGrath would be suing the Council of the Moon for. Cori wasn't sure anyone had been thinking about restitution, since the gunshots were so distracting, but the litigation seemed to be a high priority, even more important than prosecuting the criminals.

Gypsy stepped through the open front door, crunching the glass beneath her boots. She looked over the scene, settling on each of the exhausted faces she had been *introduced* to the other night. A man handed her a clipboard, and she glanced over the scribbles that filled her in on the details of the event without actually speaking to anyone. "What's this?" she asked, folding the paper over the metal clamp. The second page seemed to disappoint her just as much as the first. "You still didn't kill her?" Gypsy turned her question to Daniel. He was comfortably lounging in an armchair he had flipped back over.

"No," Daniel responded despondently, peering at Gypsy through hooded eyes. Cori was exhausted—with good reason—but the worry of the last few days had definitely caught up with Daniel. "We didn't want the Council trying to avenge her death."

"We also didn't want to martyr her," Nevia said from behind Gypsy at one of the broken-out windows. Her skin was spotted with puce bruises, and she was shaking, but she was still clutching her gun—perpetually on guard, despite the presence of thirty or forty well-armed soldiers meandering through the property.

Gypsy looked back at her. Cori expected her to return with a smug, condescending smirk directed at Nevia's behavior, but she was inexpressive. "I see you finished what I started, though." She scanned the document. "You blinded her and two of her henchmen. Six of them are going to the burn unit for skin grafting. Not to mention a few shattered knee caps."

"That was her." Daniel pointed accusingly to Nevia, but she didn't seem to mind the attention for her good aim.

"A couple of those were from Mrs. McGrath." Nevia passed on the blame and glory to Mrs. McGrath, who stammered behind Daniel for a moment before surrendering a shrug.

Gypsy smiled at the elderly woman before resting her eyes on Cori and her fresh bundle of joy. She reflexively pulled the child a little tighter to her. "My men are checking out Heaton as we speak. If he needs surgery, we will airlift him to Dublin immediately." Gypsy paused, eyeing her cautiously, but with a hint of the ever-present amusement that Cori would forever associate with her psychopathic nature. "Would you like them to check you or the baby?"

Cori narrowed her eyes, but stopped when she realized it was a perfectly reasonable request. Her nightgown was covered in blood and all manner of unpleasantness. Her clammy-skinned baby was obviously fresh into the world. She glanced at Daniel, unsure of what to say. He seemed to understand her reluctance, but only gave a noncommittal shrug. "Thank you. I think we're good."

"Let me know if you change your mind. We'll be here for a while." Gypsy glanced over the report once more. She pulled an envelope from beneath the layers of paperwork and handed it to Maggie. "Mrs. McGrath, this should tide you over until the Council can provide restitution."

Mrs. McGrath snatched the envelope. Her staunch scowl disappeared as she peeked inside the envelope. "Oh, sweet Jesus." She signed the cross before promptly stuffing the envelope into her blouse.

"As for the rest of you..." Gypsy tucked the clipboard under her arm and pulled a canvas pack from her side cargo pant pocket. She pulled out a pinch full of hundred-dollar bills and handed it to Daniel. "You can distribute that as needed—hotel, flight, whatever. Needless to say, that also goes as hush money." She winked at Daniel as he took the wad of cash. He eyed it coolly before turning his lazy gaze to her.

"Seriously, who the feck are you?" he asked unceremoniously.

Gypsy smiled. "We are new and not yet affiliated with your group."

"Yet?" Cori asked.

"We hope to be." Gypsy bowed her head slightly. "There is a lot of paperwork and red tape left to go, but one day we might have a mutual goal."

"Which is?" Daniel asked.

"If you are the hunters, we would be the enforcers for the remaining supernatural beings living amongst the human population. The police, if you will."

"Why are you getting involved in a werewolf war?" Nevia asked suspiciously. "Werewolves aren't under anyone's jurisdiction, but their own."

Glass crunched under Gypsy's feet as she turned to face Nevia. "You may have incited Leona to start this war, but it's going to take a lot more than grandstanding to win it."

Nevia shifted slightly, dipping her head imperceptibly toward her. Gypsy stepped closer, tossing her clipboard on a tipped settee. Daniel gripped the arms of his chair, prepared to leap between the two women if necessary. Gypsy unbuckled her equipment vest and pulled it open, exposing her black undershirt.

Nevia's eyes narrowed, affronted by the woman's candor. She took the offering and inhaled the woman's scent. Her lips parted after, like a cat, letting the bouquet linger on the back of her tongue. When Nevia finished, she didn't look happy, but she backed away.

"My employer is particularly interested in being on good terms with the werewolf population. As the strongest mortal race on Earth, they will make excellent recruits in our future endeavors. He has chosen to align with Leona during this upheaval, and it is my job to make sure that he has not backed the wrong horse."

"Why are you being so forthcoming today?" Nevia asked. "You seemed reluctant to reveal anything before."

"What can I say? I love telling secrets."

"How about telling us who your employer is?" Cori asked.

Gypsy turned her attention to her, stepping back to the center of the room. Her perpetual amusement was, for once, disrupted. "I don't know."

"What do you mean, you don't know?" Cori persisted.

"He's a little flamboyant at times, but he's not stupid. Until our alliances are secure and our usefulness indispensable, he will remain an unseen financier."

"How fecking nuts does someone have to be to get involved in a werewolf war?" Daniel griped. "No offense, love," he added when he noticed Nevia's scowl.

Gypsy smiled and braced herself on the armchair as she leaned in over Daniel. "Pretty fucking nuts," she whispered before moving away to retrieve her clipboard. "At any rate," she said as she pulled a lighter from her pocket, "I may be seeing you all again in the future, so you should save your tear-jerking farewells." She pulled her remaining paperwork from the clipboard and set it on fire as she walked out. Once thoroughly alight, she let the pages drop on the lawn and rejoined her team.

"What did you smell?" Cori asked, when she was well out of earshot.

Nevia holstered her gun gruffly, her composure momentarily lost in irritation. "Nothing."

77

ETHAN WOKE THE NEXT morning—probably morning—and headed for the kitchen. He hadn't expected to see Levi and Adrianna there since they had spent the night together. There was nothing to be said for any extracurricular activities, but he had heard them talking, or at least heard himself talking.

After a quick voice check, he found his vocals to be back in working order, albeit a little scratchy.

When he entered the kitchen and saw Adrianna and Levi sitting together, he almost walked back out again. "It's okay," Levi assured him.

"I take it from the frog in my throat you guys had a lot to talk about."

Adrianna blew him a fervent kiss, and he smiled at the emphasis she managed to place on such a singular gesture.

"You're welcome. Glad I could help you clear the air." Ethan sat down at the table. An overly muscular kitchen worker slapped a bowl of food in front of him. At first, he thought the man might have been a mythical creature, but upon closer inspection, he determined he was just ugly. "I don't mean to ruin the moment, but there is something we need to discuss."

"Oh, you probably want to get out of here. We keep distracting you." Levi grimaced.

"No, I mean yes, but not until Adrianna is safe."

"Safe?"

"Not until Annette gives her the remaining earth power she needs to balance her mortal magic," Ethan said bluntly. He didn't want to dance around it any longer. Adrianna looked at Levi, just as he looked at her.

"Would that really work?"

Adrianna shrugged.

"It's a risk, but as I understand it, the mortal power can't be removed. The only option is to add more power," Ethan explained. "Unfortunately, Annette is convinced the transformation will corrupt her and make her too powerful. She won't do it."

"She could at least try. If it will save her." Levi's eyes flickered between Ethan's before lifting behind him. "You have to try, Annette," he pleaded.

"What have you told him, Ethan?" Annette scolded behind him, but he didn't turn to look at her.

"She is dying," Levi explained.

"She isn't dying," Annette snapped.

"Yes, she is!" Levi snapped right back. "She's been dying since you did this to her. This is all your fault and you won't fix it because you are jealous!"

"What?" Annette moved to the table looking down at Levi, but he wasn't having any of it. He stood up to face her.

"The only reason you wanted to offer her raw earth power to begin with was so you could access it through her. She was to be your basin of power, but now, with mortal magic, she won't just provide it; she'll command it as well."

"That is exactly why I won't complete the ceremony." Annette raised her chin, trying at least physically to dominate the conversation.

"You won't complete the ceremony because she'll be stronger than you." Levi took a step closer to her. His height would never offer the intimidation that he probably wanted it to, but Levi knew he was right.

Annette was only momentarily flummoxed by his accusation. "She will transcend beyond any living being ever in existence! She'll be stronger than any sentient being! No one should wield that kind of power."

"You do it every damn day," Levi snapped. "You do it for profit." He shoved his hand into his pants pocket and pulled out the bare lint-filled innards. "I don't have anything to offer you. I'm flat broke. The only thing I have in this life is you and her." Levi glanced back at Adrianna. "Please don't tell me you'll let her die, or I'll lose both of you."

"Levi..." Annette's brow crumpled with hurt.

"Please, save her life. Fix her... for me."

"Don't you think I've thought about this?" Annette glanced at Ethan, including him in the statement. "I want to fix this, but it's too dangerous. I can't take the mortal magic from her without killing her. Her *od* is too tightly wound to it. Adding more magic seems logical, I know, but it is precarious."

Annette turned to Adrianna to plead for her understanding. "Adrianna, you are the only one that can understand what they are asking me to do. To funnel that much power into you... even if you were healthy, it would take a miracle for you to come through it unscathed. What if you die?"

"She's already dying," Ethan said quietly. Annette gave him a glare that was usually reserved for Levi, but he didn't react to it defensively or otherwise. She had lost this argument the minute Ethan had given Levi hope of a normal—mostly normal—life with the woman he loved.

"What if you don't die? What if the power corrupts you? Destroys your moral compass? I can't be responsible for creating a sorceress that will harm people."

Adrianna shook her head and closed her eyes. Her body and face changed into the youthful, rosy-skinned woman she should have been. When she opened her eyes and scanned each of them, Levi took in a deep breath, as if it was a relief to him to see her natural self.

"I know you are scared, Annette." Adrianna spoke with a tiny feminine voice that belied the authority she was capable of exerting. "I am frightened too, but what you don't understand, what you cannot fathom, is that I am already being pushed and pulled by the good and evil within this mortal magic. Controlling my mind takes every measure of my strength. I am far more dangerous to the world now than I would be if I had control of my mind. The only time I feel remotely in control of myself is when I am with Levi."

Levi stepped closer to her, and she slipped her hand into his. He glanced down, concerned, but when he realized she wouldn't radiate negative emotions, he relaxed and let his eyes flicker over her face. A moment of nonverbal communication was exchanged, and they looked back at Annette as a couple, as one.

"The mortal magic is irreversible. Only the earth magic can stabilize and heal me. I know this is against the rules, but I promise you, my heart is pure."

Annette pinched her lips. "Pure or not... I'll lose you either way," she whispered. "You know that."

Adrianna nodded. "Death is always in the future. At least let me choose how close."

78

ETHAN SAT QUIETLY ON the rock while Annette explained the procedure once more to Adrianna. The young woman politely shook her head each time Annette asked her to reconsider. Levi approached Ethan and pressed his hand to his overhanging calf. Ethan looked down at his pained expression.

"Thank you. I am indebted to you."

Ethan shook his head slightly. "You're welcome, but you don't owe me anything. I have a good number of people in my life I am lucky enough to call friends. They've taught me that loyalty is free. If you don't mind being added to that list, you can write off your debt."

Levi smiled and gave Ethan's leg a pat before resting on the rock with him.

The dragons lumbered in, as if the dinner bell had been rung.

"Why do they do that?" Ethan asked Levi, since they would be unlikely to respond telepathically to the query in the presence of others—despite it being the number one benefit of telepathy.

"They like the magic." Levi shrugged, suggesting that was the best answer he had for it.

"They aren't as... fun as I thought they'd be," Ethan said quietly. One of the dragons looked over at him, but he pretended not to notice.

"Tell me about it. I thought I'd at least get to ride one, but apparently that is insulting and disrespectful." Levi rolled his eyes.

"Yeah, all I got was a few scars and wheat grass shakes."

"Wheat grass?" Levi scrunched up his nose.

"The protein shakes." Ethan raised his brow.

"Oh, yeah, Annette has me drink those once in a while. She uses peanut butter, though. What does that have to do with the dragons?"

Ethan crooked his smile and shook his head. "Never mind." There might have been some amusement in revealing the truth to Levi, but he couldn't bring himself to ruin a man's enjoyment of peanut butter forever after.

"Ethan!" Annette snapped. He looked over and saw her by the door. "I need help collecting my supplies."

Ethan exchanged a look of dread with Levi before following Annette to her room to gather her magical incendiary ingredients.

As he followed her around the room, holding out a crate for her to load with small jars and sticks that might have been wands, he couldn't help but smile at her attitude. She was a magnanimous woman with power that demanded respect, but she was still giving him a silent treatment tantrum, just like any other woman might.

"Something amusing to you?" Annette pinned him with hooded eyes.

"You," he said simply. "You're mad at me, aren't you?"

"Of course I'm mad at you, and if you had any idea what I'm about to do, you would be mad at you, too. You started this. I thought I was abundantly clear that this was inadvisable."

"Yes, you were," he conceded somewhat sheepishly.

"And yet you insisted on encouraging it. I am so disappointed in you, Ethan, and so will Danato."

Ethan tossed the crate of goodies onto the table and crossed his arms over his chest. "You do not speak for Danato."

"I have known Danato for years. He—"

"You haven't known *me* for years." Ethan shook his head. "I know I went against you and I'll accept your anger, but *disappointment?* I don't think so, Annette. Whom do you think Danato hired to run his prison? I might be disciplined and dedicated, but I'm not an automaton.

"What you have failed to observe in my character, outside of Danato's praise, is my fortitude and objectivity. If you are disappointed in my actions, it's not because I failed to meet your expectations, it's because they failed to meet me. I am not going to stand by and watch someone die when there is something I can do to help."

"But—"

"I have listened to your concerns, but yours is not the only view to consider. Ultimately, this is Adrianna's decision, no matter who weighs in." Annette pulled a long knife off the shelf, and Ethan eyed her carefully. When she did nothing with the knife, he perked an eyebrow. "If you are trying to intimidate me..." Ethan narrowed his eyes, hoping that Annette was above physical retaliation.

"I'm waiting for you to retrieve the crate. I need this knife for the ritual. I can't very well stab her without it."

79

ETHAN PROBABLY LOOKED GREEN when he came back. He felt green. Levi looked up from his almost touching encounter with Adrianna. He was concerned for his depressed expression, but he smirked and looked back at his girl. He no doubt blamed his change in mood on Annette's bitter reprisal.

Ethan set his crate on the altar and abruptly headed over to one of the dragons for an impromptu neck scratch. He hid behind the big beast, scratching her until a vibrating purr that could easily be confused for a growl resonated from her throat.

"She has to stab her?" Ethan hissed in as hushed a tone as he could manage, as well as thought it at her.

The dragon said and thought nothing.

"Answer me!" He growled low. *I have no reason to trust you. Annette's devotion to your kind does not extend to me! Give me one reason I should trust that this will help Adrianna. Now!*

The dragon didn't answer, but the low rumble in her throat stopped and she shifted her position to her haunches. The other dragons did the same, before offering a shrill howl that sounded nothing like a dragon, a cat, or any animal Ethan could think of.

"Oh, my stars!" Annette clasped her hands and bowed down to the creatures. "They are singing! They are offering their blessing for the ritual! Thank you! Thank you!" Ethan looked to Levi and Adrianna and they were smiling widely.

It wasn't the reason Ethan was looking for, but he imagined if the beasts were willing to offer such a display to comfort the others, he certainly couldn't be the one to start second-guessing the plan.

80

ETHAN KNEELED DOWN ON one side of Adrianna, while Levi kneeled on the other. He was pleased that he did not have to be naked for this ritual. Adrianna and Annette remained cloaked as well.

The dragons had finally settled, but were watching the ceremony intently. After lighting several bunches of sage leaves and incense, Annette pulled a small knife from her line of necessities laid out before her.

She reached out her hand, demanding Ethan's. He raised each hand, palm up, as he was instructed in the pre-ritual rehearsal. With little warning, she cut each palm, making them bleed rather profusely.

"Take her by the arm," Annette instructed, and he grabbed Adrianna's tiny limb. He felt a wave of misery, but it subsided as she concentrated.

Annette made the same cuts on Levi's hands, and he gripped her other arm.

"Is this really necessary?" Ethan whispered across to him.

Levi nodded. "Don't worry, it heals fast."

"No, I mean holding her."

Levi nodded again. "She's about to catch the whole world inside of her. We'll be lucky if we are strong enough to keep hold of her, even with the blood bond."

"If you don't keep hold of her..." Annette interjected, "she'll be ripped apart by it. This is far more power than I ever intended to give her. This is far more than..." Annette cringed at her train of thought before finding her track again. "You are her anchors to this realm. Release her and her mind will be lost to another plane and her body will die."

Ethan frowned. He didn't even want to know about other dimensions. He had once upon a time lived in a world where magic was make-believe. It was hard enough getting the rhythm of a world with goblins and glow-y rings. There was no room for schisms in time and space.

"We are all part of this now," Annette said, losing the ire in her voice for somberness. "I will do my best. I only ask that you each do yours."

Ethan nodded. Levi leaned into Adrianna and kissed her gently. When he pulled back, he looked terrified. "I love you," he whispered, barely audible. She smiled and nodded, mouthing the words back. His fear seemed to subside slightly, hinting that the near-death experience coming at them wasn't the scariest thing he would do today.

Annette started chanting, and Ethan glanced at the dragons.

Be strong. The thought came across clearly from one dragon.

Have faith, another thought.

Don't let go. The last thought was more a command than encouragement, but he nodded imperceptibly at them.

Ethan lost track of time as Annette's words put him in a trance. He could see everything that was happening, but it was disinteresting to his addled brain. He imagined this was what it felt like to be a sacrificial helper like Levi.

The thunder was the only thing that really woke him up. Cold wet rain pelted his face before immediately drying on the hot stone altar. Sand cyclones threaded with lightning were dancing around the room. The shaking that he thought was his own trembling dropped several stalactites from the ceiling of the cave.

The wind had only begun, but he was already feeling Adrianna's body pulling. His hands were still firmly locked on the super glue that was his blood bond, but there was an underlying current that was threatening to separate him from her. He glanced at Levi, but he seemed to still be in his hypnotic trance.

Annette yelled over the wind, demanding the Earth's offer to this vessel. She was holding the large knife that might eventually kill or save Adrianna, but she was not ready to use it. The Earth still had to test her worthiness for the gift.

The lightning danced around the altar between them until they reached Adrianna. Her body was wracked with the electricity, but Ethan didn't feel it. All he felt was the link that was trying to rip her away from them. He realized that although it might take his physical strength to hold her; it was not her body that was pulling away. It was her essence, her spirit, her soul.

Ethan felt the water that came next, but it was not wet so much as a cold weight pressing against them. The wind whipped them, stinging their skin raw, but he held on, and so did Levi.

When everything died away, Ethan took in a relieved breath, happy to be alleviated from the pain of pelting rain and sand. Unfortunately, that was when Annette stabbed Adrianna in the chest.

Adrianna screamed horrifically, tipping backward. The recoil of her body was nothing compared to the whiplash of her life-force. Levi gasped as he was thrown off of the altar completely. His body rolled and lay still against the sandy floor.

Ethan felt the wind rise around them again. The gift was about to arrive.

He shifted behind Adrianna, moving his second hand to her other arm. The blood bond didn't fight his change, and he was able to clasp just as tightly onto her other arm.

The walls around them shed rocks, and creaked as if the Earth were going to open up and swallow them. Adrianna's chest arched upward as an unseen force ripped the knife from her chest. The blood from her wound mixed with the tornadic winds all around them. Ethan ducked behind Adrianna, pressing his head against her to further prop her up as the winds started to not just blow against them, but suck into her.

Ethan could feel the rebuff of Adrianna's body. Her soul wasn't prepared for this kind of power; no one's was. Despite the struggle, the offer had been made and accepted, and saying no was not an option. He didn't really understand anything about creating a sorceress, nor did he comprehend the power of the earth, but he was pretty sure he was about to be educated on both topics.

The ground vibrated, and Ethan had to grip tighter to keep hold of Adrianna as her body vibrated with it. The temperature of the room increased and decreased in second intervals. He didn't know if he was being frostbitten or burned.

The creaking sound continued to get louder, and Ethan felt the cave shift. He wasn't sure whether his eyes were lying, or whether the room had actually tipped upside down. Up and down were no longer a matter of fact, but conjecture and conceptualization.

What was certain was gravity.

The pressure against Ethan was tormenting. Nothing was touching him, and yet the weight of the world was pressing him down, back, and away from Adrianna. He felt his hands slip, so he gritted his teeth and clamped on tighter, disregarding the bruises he might give her. He fought through the pain of his overexertion, roaring in tune with the cacophony of creaking rocks. He had come this far; he wasn't letting go.

Adrianna was a beautiful, happy woman despite the savage magic that coursed through her every day. He knew she was worthy of the gift being offered, and he was going to make damn sure that the earth didn't rip her essence from her body to give it to her.

He felt something pop in his muscles, and he feared his arms might rip off, but he didn't let go. The weight abruptly released, and the weather and temperature fluctuations in the room stopped. He fell forward onto Adrianna's stooped over body, once again understanding the concept of down, and knowing that it was his only option for directions at the moment.

Even when Annette screamed at him to let her go, Ethan kept one hand on her arm while they examined her. He vaguely understood the panic in Annette's eyes as she looked her over. He forced himself to sit up and look at her.

He expected to see the beautiful, vibrant girl, newly balanced by her earthen gift, but she wasn't beautiful or vibrant. As much damage as he could feel in his sore muscles and battered, sand-blown skin, she was so much worse.

The pale skin she usually bore now looked gray. Her eyes were sunken and haloed by dark skin and the cheekbones that he had once thought made her look malnourished jutted out sickeningly above hollowed cheeks. He imagined under her robe would be a body that even an anorexic would shy away from.

If Ethan hadn't seen her chest rising with breath, he would have assumed she was dead. He got up and moved to help Annette carry her, but his efforts were met with a slap across the face. The slap startled him, justified though it was. He dropped back down and watched Levi pick up his love. He glanced at Ethan with a sorrowful sympathy that he didn't have time to give him in words.

Ethan couldn't remember when the last time he cried was, but he was sure he was due for a little now. He lay back on the platform, holding his arm over his eyes, and sniffled a few times before speaking to the surrounding dragons.

"Tell me she's going to be okay," he demanded. "Tell me that it was still the right choice."

No one answered.

81

DANATO WATCHED EFRAT AND Belus argue about the feasibility of aim when dealing with electrical energy. He didn't imagine that he would ever be lonely enough to subject himself to that. He would rather answer Cori's endless questions about his wife than listen to Efrat whine about his power, like it was a cancer that needed to be treated instead of conditioned.

"For the last time, you can't steer lightning!" Efrat's voice echoed through the gym.

Belus took in a deep, sobering breath before aiming the elemental weapon at Efrat. The electrical surge danced to Efrat, and he retaliated by throwing out a stray bolt and diving for cover. The energy joined and bounced around into oblivion.

"I don't want you to steer it. I want you to aim it, like I aim this weapon. I can't guarantee that it will hit the target as you have demonstrated, but I can certainly point it at the fucking target. Now get up!"

Danato shielded his smirk with a well-timed nose scratch. He was usually good at backing up Belus's bad cop act, but since Belus was well past the point of *acting* pissed off, it was becoming farcical. Efrat was turning out to be more than Belus had anticipated. He wondered if Efrat's military experience was working against the process.

Unlike Daniel McGrath, Efrat didn't hold nearly as much guilt for his actions over his incarceration as Danato would have preferred. In Efrat's opinion, he was a prisoner of war. Anything he did while under lock and key was simply civil disobedience or survival instinct.

"Now shoot the target!" Belus pointed at the metal shield on the far wall.

Efrat glared at him, grinding his teeth. Belus looked like he was going to explode. Danato shifted on the small set of bleachers just in case he needed to pry Belus off Efrat. The air crackled and a burst of electricity shot out from behind him, hitting the shield.

Everyone looked at the door, where Cori's arm was still outstretched. "Cori," Danato said happily, but then he noticed the lack of a bulge under her shirt. The cold expression on her face seized his heart.

Ignoring everyone but Efrat, she moved over to him. "Let it pool in your hand and release it like you're blowing a really messed up kiss at someone."

Efrat shot his hand out, and the energy splayed, dancing all around the shield. Cori looked at the shield and then wrinkled her nose at Efrat. "Premature electrification. Shit, Efrat, you've had this power for years and I can still run it better than you."

He narrowed his eyes. "You don't have the full strength," he seethed, his teeth baring like a wild dog.

"Pool it in your hand..." Cori raised her hand, showing the blue trickle that she was immune to. "...and release it." Her hand spread like she was throwing the electricity. Though it was fast, Danato noticed that the surge was more like a tiny ball of energy rather than the erratic tentacle attacks Efrat usually offered. "Now you."

Reluctantly, Efrat tried it her way, and he hit the shield dead center. Despite it being an accomplishment, Efrat seemed almost disappointed to have achieved it.

"Again," Cori said softly.

Efrat did it again, with the same happy result, but the same not-so-happy expression.

"Again," she commanded.

Efrat repeated the process several more times. His anger faded, replaced by disinterest and possibly even despair. Danato was sure there was more to know about Efrat's displeasure with this accomplishment, but he wasn't interested in pursuing the topic at that moment.

"Cori!" Danato climbed off the bleachers and crushed her in a hug. A little too late, he thought about how sore she might be and released her. "What happened?" He moved his hands to her hips, hoping that perhaps he was just confused, and blind, and very stupid. "Did you... oh, Cori... is the baby...?" He waited for the answer, but her proud smile gave it away. She nodded behind him, and he turned.

Daniel had entered the gym holding a baby—Cori's baby. "Danato," Cori whispered behind him. "I'd like to introduce you to your grandson."

Danato gasped at the word. He'd never felt right calling Cori his daughter, though emotionally it was true enough, but this child born and raised within the walls of this prison would know no other man as his grandfather.

Tears sprang to his eyes as Daniel brought the baby to him. The blue blanket should have been a dead giveaway, but he hadn't even noticed it until he was carefully transferring the baby to his arms. "Have you named him?"

"I can't. Not until Ethan gets back."

"Oh, Ethan's going to be so proud. So proud." Danato's leg shimmered with pain, and he faltered. "Daniel, take him, please." Daniel rushed back to rescue the baby, just as Danato collapsed, panting, sweating, and crying for a new reason.

82

DANIEL STARED IN AWE at the mountain of a man crumbling before him. Danato had been reduced to a shaking mass by an unseen force. Cori was instantly by his side, begging for answers, but Danato was barely containing the agonized scream written on his face. Even Efrat seemed to be concerned.

"What's wrong with him?" Efrat asked Belus, who was oddly calm.

"I need to get Danato to the infirmary," he answered.

"Clearly," Efrat said with irritated sarcasm, "but what is afflicting him?"

Cori's head whipped around, wanting the same answer from him. Belus pinched his lips shut as if he were refusing to tell, but after a moment's pause, the truth fell from his lips, just as every other truth had only days ago. "It's sorrow demons, Cori."

Cori looked at Danato, horrified. "Your leg?" she whispered, and he nodded. "Danato... all these years?" Danato wailed and grabbed his leg, fruitlessly trying to stop the pain. "Oh, Danato!" Cori leaned her forehead against his.

"What is a sorrow demon?" Efrat asked, almost crossing his arms—forgetting he couldn't. The annoyance in his tone was directed more at himself.

"It's a demon that feeds off of grief," Belus said, approaching Danato. "The long-term effect is very taxing on the body and the mind. Danato has been fighting his demons for many years, but he can no longer stand the pain."

"We have to help him!" Cori wailed to Belus.

"There is only one thing left to do, but I won't do it unless he gives me permission."

"What?" Cori asked, volleying her frustration between the two men.

"We have to amputate his leg," Belus said somberly.

Cori froze, absorbing the information slowly. When the reality dawned, her face mutated into a grief Daniel had never seen before. "No, no, no..." She gripped at Danato's shirt, pulling at him, though it was only she that moved from her angry tugging. "You stupid, stupid man—both of you!" she sniffled and glared at Belus. "How could you keep this from me? How could you endure this alone, Danato?"

"You can't just cripple the man," Efrat murmured behind Cori. "There has to be another way."

Belus shook his head. "There isn't."

"Yes, there is," Daniel spoke up, finally getting his bearings in the conversation.

"Daniel, yes!" Cori brightened, but Belus was already shaking his head.

"They aren't exactly easy to see."

"I only need a glimpse of the bastards."

"Can you do it without taking off his leg in the process?"

"Even if I can't, that was already the risk." Belus glowered at Daniel. "My skills have improved significantly over the last year," Daniel said to appease him. It was true, though. Even if Daniel had known about the big man's affliction years ago, he may not have been any more useful than a surgeon's scalpel. "Here, someone take the baby." Daniel leaned over to pass Belus the baby, but he waved him off instantly. Cori noticed the slight and took the child from his arms almost defensively. "Okay, Danato, hang in there. Let's just take a peek."

Daniel rubbed his hands together and kneeled beside Danato. He pushed him up to a kneeling position, which made his breathing labored, but he held himself still. "Okay, Danato, just think about that beautiful baby boy."

Danato winced, and Daniel leaped to look over his shoulder. He gasped and flung himself back from the onslaught of seven or eight fat and happy demon critters writhing near Danato's leg. Their slashing claws just missed his face. "Jaysus!" Daniel shook his head at Belus and he surprisingly wilted under the unspoken accusation. "She's right, you know! You are both stupid, stupid men."

"Can you help him or not?" Cori asked.

"Yeah, I can help him, but it might take a while. Those little buggers are quick to hide." Daniel looked to Danato, who seemed surprised by this answer. "You know they grab on tighter when threatened?"

Danato flushed, but he nodded. He glanced at Cori. Without words, Belus caught his meaning. "Cori, you should go," Belus said gently, coming to her side.

"What? I am not leaving him to go through this alone."

"Cori—" Belus started to plead his *suggestion* again.

"No! Forget it! I'm not leaving!" Cori crushed the baby to her bosom, protecting his precious ears against her volume.

Daniel expected Belus to yell back at her, but instead, he extended his hand to her. "Let me take you home. You don't want to watch him go through this pain, and he certainly doesn't want an audience for it."

Cori wiped away an eye full of tears and looked to Danato for permission, one way or another. He nodded at her and she wiped her hand on her pants before taking Belus's hand. He drew her out of the gym, only stopping to give Daniel a look that told him he was placing Danato's life in his hands. There was a good amount of irony in that action.

"I'll help?" Efrat said, maneuvering around Danato.

"How?"

"Nerve interference," he said simply. Danato seemed just as confused, but was beyond verbal communication.

"Pain is just an electrical impulse, sent from nerve fibers to the brain. If you overload them, the message gets lost in the shuffle. I can't say it won't hurt, but it might make the pain more tolerable."

"Well, aren't you just useful?" Daniel mumbled. "You good with that, Danato?"

Danato gave a weak nod, and Daniel kneeled down in front of him. Efrat kneeled off to his side, clutching his leg around the thigh as far as his fingers would reach. "You know not to get in my way, right?"

Efrat gave a vague nod.

"No, seriously, I'm going to be using a pretty intense power, so don't be an eejit."

"Hands and fingers inside until the ride comes to a full and complete stop. Got it."

Daniel smirked at him. "Aye." There was also a good deal of irony in this moment as well. The man Danato had not so long ago asked him to execute was now assisting him to save Danato's leg. Life was strange; stranger still inside the walls of this prison. "Okay, Danato, think happy thoughts."

83

CORI HALF EXPECTED THE house to not let her in, but the fire lit with the warm embrace of an old friend. It had only been a week, but the incident was long forgotten. Cori was glad her residence wouldn't kill her, but there was also something insulting about being forgotten so quickly. She really was nothing more than an insect to this entity. Their quarrel was at best a bee sting to her—painful at the time, but forgotten as it healed.

Belus cleared his throat at the door. She didn't remember letting go of his hand. She was surprised he had offered it, but more surprised that he let her keep it for the walk back. "Why doesn't she let you in?" She ignored his hint.

"You know why," he answered simply.

"She imprinted on you too?"

He shrugged. "Something like that. I doubt she remembers why she does it, but... as you know, you can't argue with her."

"Come in." She waved him in. He stepped inside, shutting the door and hanging his coat. Without any further invitation, he moved to the liquor cabinet and poured two short glasses of brandy. "Belus, alcohol and nursing don't mix," she said, sitting on the couch.

"It will be out of your system in two hours." He held the drink out to her. She questioned his knowledge of breastfeeding, but he knew alcohol well enough. "It's been a long six months drinking alone," he added, almost pleading for her to join him.

She took the glass of brandy from him and clinked it to his before he moved to settle into Danato's chair.

"What are we drinking to?" he asked before sipping the liquor.

"The house not killing me on entry?" She shrugged and took a sip. It was the usual pungent taste that made her wonder why Belus insisted on keeping her as a drinking partner. She knew nothing about alcohol, and even after tasting every liquor in Danato's cabinet, she still knew nothing about alcohol. "I suppose you must have done most of your drinking with Danato at one time," she said, swirling the liquid in her glass, because that was the only thing she knew about brandy.

"I used to do a lot of things with Danato, *at one time*... but the drinking I usually did with Olivia." Belus held her gaze a moment and she froze under his scrutiny. She could only imagine what it might mean to Belus to replace his drinking partner, or the honor she should take from it. As his gaze returned to his glass, she pushed away the unnecessary sentiments that were threatening to overwhelm her.

After a moment of silence that demanded conversation, Cori found a new emotion to concentrate on. "I should be yelling and screaming at you," she said as she readjusted the baby so her arm didn't go numb.

"Daniel was the best choice to—"

"No, Daniel was... wonderful. I mean about Danato's leg."

He nodded introspectively. "Why aren't you?"

"Because I know you were only respecting his wishes."

"If it makes you feel any better, I think that's the last of the secrets."

Cori stared blankly at Belus while he lost himself in the scent and taste of another sip. "Are you sure about that?" she asked, knowing full well that it wasn't the last secret.

"What do you mean?" he asked, honestly confused.

"Belus, I know about my father."

Belus's brow deepened further. "Your father?"

"I know that he was looking for me after I went missing—"

"Looking for you? Your father is alive?" Belus gaped at her, wide-eyed and open-mouthed.

"Yes, I thought..."

Belus slumped back in the chair, pondering a number of things that were putting more and more ire on his face. "Son of a bitch." He pounded the chair with his free hand.

"You really didn't know about this?"

"Please tell me you didn't try to contact him."

"No, of course not, but..." Cori suddenly felt guilty. "I read that he was looking for me, but he suddenly called off the search around the time that I got married. I wondered if Danato's vacation had anything to do with that."

Belus rubbed his face. "I can almost guarantee it. I knew he was being very generous with trusting Ethan so early on, but I assumed he was just testing him." Belus frowned, suddenly looking guilty himself.

"What is it?" she asked.

"Since we've dragged out the last of the skeletons, you should know that I never sent for him."

"What do you mean?"

"The trouble with you and the transmorphs. I told Ethan that I called Danato and he refused to come back, but I never called him."

"Wow." Cori's heart fell and she bit back tears. "I guess we weren't exactly close then."

"No, Cori, it wasn't like that. Danato couldn't have helped you. In hindsight, I think his presence would have kept Ethan from figuring out how to find you. I sent for the man that I thought *could* help you. Daniel was ultimately your savior, not Danato."

"I bet Danato was angry about that."

"Yes, but given his deceit, it's no wonder he didn't make a bigger deal about it."

"Do you think Danato... threatened my father?"

"No, but he probably blew a good deal of bribe money on him, though."

"I guess it shouldn't surprise me that it worked. My father was done with me long before he signed the last child support check."

"Cori, I don't mean to add to the burdens that come with our particular employment practices, but you need to understand, Danato listed your immediate family as deceased. He must have bribed your father to cover his tracks with the board. If you contacted him in any way..."

"I didn't, Belus, and I won't. I swear. I would never do anything to jeopardize my life here. This is home. This is where my family is."

Belus stared at her a long moment. "I'm glad you're back, both of you." He winked and looked down at the baby in her arms.

"Do you want to hold him?" she asked.

"No." He shook his head. She thought back to his reaction in the gym and she couldn't help but feel rejected on her child's behalf. "If you pout any harder, your lips are going to fall into your lap." She rolled her eyes and downed her drink. "Look at me, please," he said in that magical way that disguised his gravelly voice as soothing. She looked at his smirking face. He was delighted at her acrimony. "I'm not going to hold that baby before his father. Ethan's already got two men ahead of him, and I know him well enough to know that will irritate the shit out of him. So, I will wait patiently for him to return and then you may pass the baby to me as much and as often as you like."

Cori suddenly burst into tears. She knew it was mostly her residual hormones, but Belus, thinking of Ethan's territorialism over himself, was just the breaking point for the last week. He poured himself another drink, politely ignoring her breakdown while she collected herself.

"I'm sorry. I just can't believe I never considered what Ethan would think about everyone meeting his son before him."

"He'll be bitter for a little while, but you'll remind him that he is and always will be that baby's one and only father. Truth be told, the only reason I'm offering that little concession is because Ethan and I have never really met eye to eye on a lot of things. I think one less pebble under the skin is best for all of us."

Cori released a yawn she didn't know she had been holding back.

"Tired?" Belus asked.

"Yeah, but I don't want to sleep in this house alone yet. How long do you think it will take for Daniel to remove those demons?"

Belus frowned. "I don't think you should hold your breath. I'll stay if you want to take a nap."

"You don't have to babysit me. I know you'd rather go check on Danato."

He drew in a long breath. "I thought we'd decided that you shouldn't speak for me. You're really bad at it."

"Sorry," Cori mumbled and yawned again.

Belus set down his glass on the coffee table and adjusted a pillow on the couch for her. "The truth is, I don't want to watch him go through that. Not when I'm the one who caused it."

Cori grabbed his hand. "You are not to blame for his sorrow."

"You know I am."

Cori shook her head. "She gave you no choice."

"Right or wrong, I still pulled the trigger."

"Belus—"

"Enough." He pulled his hand away. "I didn't bring it up to get your sympathy. Lie down. Get some rest."

"You are so frustrating." Cori shifted back onto the pillow he laid out for her, shifting the baby onto her chest.

"Back at ya, kid." He pinched the tip of her nose and then gently caressed the baby's head. "Sleep." He picked up a newspaper off the end table and sat down in Danato's chair to read.

Cori closed her eyes, and she felt the stress in her muscles and mind ease, and the exhaustion take hold. "Belus," she whispered when the room was almost gone. She heard his paper crinkle. "I love you."

For a long moment, he said nothing. She kicked herself for saying it, knowing full well that her neediness only repelled him. "I love you too, Cori," he finally answered, and she was almost positive it wasn't just a waking dream.

84

CORI COULD HEAR DANIEL and Belus, but she couldn't recognize the other lowered voice coming from her kitchen. She started to shift to sit up. When she realized the weight against her was gone, she flung herself upright in search of her baby. "The baby!" she gasped, looking around the couch, suddenly fearful that he might have slipped between the cushions.

Visions of her suffocated son stopped dead when she saw Daniel near the sink, holding him in one hand and a fresh beer in the other. "I got him, mama," he said reassuringly, and the tension released from her muscles. She blinked away the overeager stray tears in her eyes.

Belus glanced back at her from his position, leaning on the island with mild amusement on his face. She must have looked comical, pitching up from behind the couch in such a panic.

The third voice she had heard was Efrat. He was leaning against the fridge, sipping on a beer. She caught his eye, but he looked away. She wasn't sure why he was there, or why Belus or Daniel had taken it upon themselves to invite him into her home, but that was not the topic of conversation that was burning to be discussed.

"How is Danato?" Cori moved into the kitchen to join the conversation, taking up residence as close to her baby as possible without actually pulling him away from Daniel. Once again, she and Daniel were faced with a new level to their friendship. Her life was indebted to him, more than once, and now she had her child's life to add to that.

"He's good," Daniel answered. "Better than me, I think. He'll keep his leg, at least." Cori could see the darkness under his eyes. His wide inhuman pupils had shrunk just enough to give her a rare view of his golden-brown irises. Whatever he had done to save Danato's leg took both spectrums of his powers. "You want him back?" He leaned forward, offering the baby.

"No, he's sleeping so nicely," she conceded.

"Aye, but you're salivating." He winked and laid the baby in her arms.

She wasn't sure if it was normal, but Cori felt like her left arm had just been returned to her. "Why is he here?" Cori murmured to Daniel, though Efrat would easily hear her.

Daniel glanced at Belus. "I was just explaining to Belus that I owed Efrat a beer for helping me. He took away a lot of Danato's pain."

"Pain?" Cori looked at Efrat and he waggled his fingers. "You electrocuted him?"

"Shhh." Daniel wrapped his arm around her shoulder and pulled her against him. "Don't wake the baby." He kissed her forehead and turned slightly to whisper into her ear. "Do you have complete control over those rings?"

Cori looked up at him wide-eyed. She had more control than she used to, but Efrat incited a lot of emotions in her. She could never be certain of anything around him. "You were saying," she said calmly, and Daniel squeezed her arm before letting his hand drop.

"A small charge of electricity can overstimulate and blind the nerve receptors," Efrat answered. "It's something Dr. Frank, and I had played around with while I was still developing my powers. I didn't char him to death, so I guess it worked." He smirked slightly and Cori clenched her teeth, willing herself not to yell.

"That's very amusing, Efrat," she said sourly. "You know how much the thought of my dead friends just tickles me into uncontrollable giggles."

Efrat scoffed and shook his head. Daniel downed his beer and pulled the baby from her arms smoothly. She didn't resist since she knew containing her volume didn't count as containing her anger.

"I didn't mean to be gruesome," Efrat grumbled, taking a swig of his beer. "I was trying to lighten the mood."

"Successfully. You've relieved me of several moods; care to guess which ones?"

Daniel moved into the living room, rubbing the baby's back to keep him asleep.

"When are you going to get over this vendetta? Because I thought saving your ass in the elevator would win me some brownie points."

"Brownie points?" Cori chuckled and moved toward him with a brandished finger. She paused her ensuing argument to look at Belus. She was expecting him to intervene, but he was only observing the situation.

"You might as well get it out of your system," he conceded, looking at Efrat with the same capitulation. "Neither of you are going anywhere."

Cori returned to her previous attack, minus the finger pointing, since her digits were just as lethal as Efrat's. She propped her hands on her hips and made an effort to be reasonable in her ass-ripping. "Yes, you saved my life, and I am grateful, but if you want points for saving my life, then we have to subtract for the number of times you tried to kill me."

"This again?"

"Again?" Cori strained to keep her voice low. "No, not again, *still!* I have saved your life on more than one occasion too, Efrat. I risked my position in this prison to help you and your friends because I believed that you were righteous and misunderstood. And what did I get in return? You tried to cut my hands off!"

"I know the backstory, Cori! I was desperate and depressed! It was the wrong way out! I understand why you are mad! I just don't understand what you want me to do about it!" He shrugged and bowed his head to look her in the eye. "The only place I could think to start was to apologize, but you wanted none of that."

"Because I don't believe you!" she shrieked. "You don't give a damn about anyone but yourself. I know you, Efrat, better than you think." She tapped her brain, where vague memories of a long since dead woman still rattled around on occasion. "You were a career-driven egomaniac a decade ago, and even though your career has been shattered to hell, you still think you should get the respect of your rank. You hate taking orders when there's no one for you to give them to. Well, I got news for you! You are at the bottom of the freaking barrel and if you want someone to look down on, you better get a dog."

"I thought I already had someone to look down on." Efrat thrust his chin behind her to Belus. It was another joke, probably intended to *lighten the mood* since she was spitting her rage in his face, but the insult to her mentor was too much.

She slapped his face hard, and he groaned and withdrew to the floor. His face bled from the razor thin water spray she unwittingly wielded against him. Unsatisfied that her retaliation hadn't left him howling in pain, she charged to slap him again. Belus intercepted her and grabbed her arm. He twisted it behind her back with the strength he usually hid and knocked her knees out from under her. She landed abjectly in front of Efrat.

"Okay, that didn't go quite how I wanted it to," Belus said. "Efrat, perhaps we should call this a night."

"Yeah." He nodded, touching his bleeding cheek. He looked Cori over and regained his feet, towering over her. Cori panted and gritted her teeth, double-dog daring him to make another joke, but he didn't. "Thanks for the beer, man." He nodded curtly to where Daniel was rocking her baby.

"You want me to fix that?" Daniel asked.

"Nah, she wanted me to have it," he said, glancing back at her. She felt a twinge of guilt at his sullen face, but she reminded herself that it was just his crestfallen ego, not actual distress.

85

"Why am I the one getting yelled at?" Cori shrieked as she shuffled the skillet on the stove. She had only been gone a week, but Danato had eaten every reasonable thing in the house. She was being forced to get creative. Since Belus and Daniel were both hungry, she decided to make them her guinea pigs.

"*I* am not yelling," Belus clarified from the stool at the end of the island. Daniel was next to him, sans baby. Since the house seemed to be doing okay with her presence, she'd slipped the baby into Danato's room for a proper nap after his feeding. "*I* am having a frank discussion with my protégé. You, however, are getting upset."

"Have a heart, Belus; she's still teeming with hormones." Daniel slapped Belus on the back and ignored the glare he got for it. He was on his fourth beer, so his defense of her was going to boil down to comic relief. She wasn't sure if he would have contributed anything different sober, since Belus was his mentor as well.

"Pregnancy or not, it is those base emotions that make her overreact."

"Over...react? I was defending you."

"From... what?" He mocked her tone.

"He insulted you!" she hissed, cracking an egg into her... concoction.

"Oh!" Belus put his hand over his mouth and gave Daniel a horrified expression. Daniel snorted, making no attempt to hide his amusement. "My God, I've never had anyone insult me before. Certainly no one in this room has ever insulted me."

"I have always respected you, Belus! I just get frustrated with you." She eased back her tone.

"It was a joke. A rather funny one at that, but you used it as an excuse to let your claws come out. Christ, it's like day fucking one with you, all over again."

Cori looked at Daniel for help. "Don't look at me." He shrugged. "I've been through anger management with him. Believe me, you and Efrat haven't said anything to him that he hasn't heard from me. Trust me." Daniel grimaced for effect.

"What do you want me to do, Belus? Forgive him? I don't think I can."

"Cori, every headstrong, idiotic, fortuitous mistake you have ever made has been made because you care too much—"

"So you want me to stop caring?"

Belus slammed his hand on the counter. "Stop speaking for me! I was going to say I want you to *start* caring again."

"What?" Cori pulled her skillet off the burner and started loading the plates with food.

Belus glanced at Daniel. "Listen, kid, I know Efrat's betrayal and that incident with Gypsy has jaded you."

"Gypsy?" Daniel chimed in, but Cori shook her head at him. She didn't want to get into all that yet.

"I need your help," Belus asked humbly, but she could tell he hated having to. "Everything you said about Efrat's personality is right. He doesn't listen to me. He fights me every step of the way, and I can't figure out why. In case you haven't noticed, he listens to you."

"That's ridiculous." Cori shoved a plate in front of each of them.

"Maybe, but it's true." Belus frowned at his meal, but picked up a fork to taste it. "I need you to put your anger aside and go back to sympathizing with his situation."

"I only sympathized with his situation because I was..." Cori shook her head vigorously. "She—Dr. Frank was in love with his best friend. Without those memories... he's just some asshole who tried to kill me."

"I don't believe that for a second. You put my life in his hands long before any memories of Dr. Frank came along. You brought out his gooey inside just like you do for every man you meet."

"Gooey? Don't you mean hard?" Daniel smirked at her, but she was too distracted by the *gooey* comment to react.

"I need you to draw him out again, so we can make some progress," Belus continued, ignoring Daniel as well. "And I need you to do it before the auditors come."

"Auditors?" Cori still wasn't finished compiling the demands he was making on her goodness, but she needed to keep up or lose her place in the conversation altogether.

"I know Danato would have danced around this for another few months, but I don't see the point. We will be audited at the end of the year. Our loss of income with the military has hit us hard, and they are going to start weeding out unnecessary expenses."

"What are they going to do, take away my cookie allowance? It's not like I'm getting paid."

"Living expenses, medical expenses, liabilities incurred. Everyone will be under investigation, from the breakfast cereal they eat to the amount of toilet paper they wipe their ass with. However, given that your heroic act of benevolence has caused us to go deep into the red, you will be under particular scrutiny."

"Shit," Cori whispered.

"I..." Belus cleared his throat. "I appreciate your loyalty, Cori. I really do, but I need you to grow a very thick skin and prepare yourself for a lot of very hard fights coming up. Danato and I are both in agreement that you are not going anywhere."

"Why? Where would they send me?"

"There are a few small operations in the Americas that deal with minor vampiric attacks."

"Hunters?" Cori scrunched her nose. She couldn't imagine herself being any good at that.

"They're more like dog catchers." Daniel shook his head. "They're amateurs and hicks. She's not going there." Daniel gave Belus a stern look, causing him to narrow his eyes in annoyance.

"As I was saying, we will fight to keep you here, but you have to make it hard for them to dismiss your actions as self-serving. And honestly, the only way you can do that is by making Efrat the most important asset we have in this prison."

"And how do I do that?" Cori shrugged, no longer fighting her duties.

"You need to get his powers under control so we can recruit him as a guard."

Cori's eyes widened, but she restrained the cuss words she wanted to offer her mentor. She glanced at Daniel, who was cringing in preparation for her reaction. She glanced down at her plateful of food that she had already lost her appetite for. When she looked back at Belus, he too was waiting for her sarcastic, impetuous response. "When do I start?" she said, resigning herself to her duties.

86

ETHAN HAD ATTEMPTED TO calculate how many hours it took to get back home and what day that put him on, but somewhere in the intense mental challenge, he concluded that it was... night. It could have been an hour after dinner, or an hour until breakfast. It didn't matter. He was home.

He stepped off the dock, vaguely wondering how many more steps he could take before he was officially sleepwalking. He wanted to go straight home and crawl into bed with his wife, but he decided to take a detour while the prison was still mostly empty.

He pulled the lever to the hangar door containing Penelope, their resident dragon. The metal squawked and groaned as it rose. He expected to see the scaly beast sleeping, but she was sitting on her haunches staring at him, as if she was waiting for him to arrive.

He didn't bother asking the obvious questions. He checked outside the door for observers and approached her. "How is she?"

Adrianna will survive. We owe you a great debt, as does she. It will not be forgotten.

"I don't care about debts. I just want to know that what we did was the right thing."

It was. When there is an imbalance in nature, it must be corrected.

"We nearly killed her."

Nearly is not dead. Her capacity to heal is intact. She will awaken when the powers within her are balanced.

"How long will that be?"

As long as is required.

"That's a nice evasive answer. I take it you're only psychic when you want to be." Ethan gripped his hair, trying not to be mad at the dragon for something he knowingly agreed to do. "Annette will never forgive me. You should have let me explain your part in this."

Annette does not seek knowledge unless it pleases or benefits her. Her forgiveness and approval is unnecessary for our purposes.

"Are you going to tell me what your purpose is?"

We have been guardians of the Earth long before man walked in stride and we have been the guardians long after. When a time arises that we are required to protect it, we will do so by the means of enlightened forethought.

"What the hell does that mean?"

It means that we can see further ahead than you, and one day you will be grateful for the preparations we have made.

"Fine. Good enough. I trust that I shouldn't mention to anyone that I can talk to you guys."

Your silence is not required, but it is most assuredly preferred and appreciated.

"I can't blame you. Being around hundreds of years, I'm sure conversation lost its appeal decades ago." Ethan jogged back to the front of the gym.

Ethan.

"Yes, Penelope?" he said almost mockingly, but he smiled to let the dragon know he meant no offense.

I am obliged to prevent you from learning too much about the future. The future we predict. However, the offering of a name to my kind is something very special. It should be rewarded.

"Really?" Ethan crossed his arms and waited for the nugget of information about to be revealed.

I choose to tell you that your wife will betray you.

"Say again?" Ethan furrowed his brow and stepped forward.

However, you must trust her regardless of the duplicity. Sometimes the wrong answer is the right answer... when it is the only answer offered.

"What kind of betrayal?"

I cannot say more.

"Is she going to shoot one of us... again? Is she going to cheat on me? What?"

Enough talk, it's time to go meet your son.

"My son?" Ethan's mouth dropped open. "You mean she's already had the baby? I have a son!" He flounced back and forth trying to figure out what to do, but soon enough he dove on the hangar door lever and ran out of the gym toward his home, and his family—plus one.

74 1/2

CORI TOOK THE PINK champagne from a passing waiter and drank it down. Once again, she was surprised by the pungent taste that did nothing to quench her thirst. She looked down at the evening gown she was wearing. It was white and clingy—two things she would never choose for her body structure.

She caught sight of herself in a wall mirror and saw that she was still in a t-shirt and jeans in the reflection. She shook her head and tossed her champagne flute toward the nearest condescending trophy wife. She ignored the pretentious gasps that followed as she pushed on to find Cleos.

She wasn't sure which version she wanted to find, but she was relieved to see the friendly leer of his unconscious self leaning on the mantel of the fireplace. She wondered if that was where he always stood, or if it was just the image he wanted to portray. The suave, sexy, businessman. It was a cliché, of course, but so was Cleos, or at least that was what he wanted her to believe.

She knew Belus was right about him. He was just another tycoon that used his personality, money, and influence to get more money, influence, and *personalities*. The fact that he used psychic power didn't make him different, it just made him better at it.

"You look nice." Cleos's eyes traveled her body. "You must be getting more comfortable with the surroundings."

"Why am I here?" she asked.

"I presume you are unconscious."

"But I'm hundreds of miles away from you," she objected and plopped down on his tufted sofa. She expected the man already sitting on the sofa to leave, but he just ogled her tight dress and the cleavage it provided.

"If only that mattered." Cleos moved to the man near her and turned his chin to face him. "No." The man seemed confused, but left the couch, opening a place for Cleos to lounge next to her.

"So no matter where I am, or what I'm doing, if I'm not awake, you'll be there."

"Unconscious, yes. Asleep, no."

"Great, forever in the mind of a man who hates me," she grumbled.

Cleos moved closer, but didn't touch her. "There, there, Corinthia. Don't let his bluster hurt you. He's more afraid of you than you are of him."

"I doubt that," she mumbled. She noticed a young woman sitting across from them in a similar tufted leather armchair. She was staring intently at Cori. She shifted to keep the blonde out of her line of sight. "He's going to leave the prison, you know."

Cleos shrugged. "Yes, I suppose they'll let him go, now that they know his intentions were not malicious."

"You don't sound very pleased with that. Isn't that a good thing?"

"Cleos always gets what he wants in the end."

"And what does he want?" she asked, glancing across to the glassy brown eyes that were unsettling her like Daniel's usually did.

Cleos sighed and brushed the back of his hand along her cheek. "I think he has good intentions... for once."

"Who is that?" Cori whispered, and motioned with her eyes to the overly curious female sitting across from them.

Cleos looked over at her and smiled. "That, my dear, is your house entity."

"What?" Cori jumped up, prepared to fight to the death, but the woman only observed her movement. Cleos, however, grabbed her and tucked her arms to her side in a strong, sideways hug.

"Easy, girl."

"You took her in?" she fumed, staring at the woman with a newfound concern. The creep factor was blooming into full-blown fight or flight. She didn't want her unconscious anywhere near her.

"I told you I would."

"Cleos, she isn't a human! She's a freaking... She isn't human. You can't just take part of her as a trophy!"

"It's just a sliver. She's a great deal more than I anticipated, I admit, but she is contained."

"Cleos, she could take over your mind!"

"Hush now, you're insulting me," he scolded soothingly.

"This is insane." She turned and whispered as if the creature three feet away couldn't hear them.

He turned to look at her. His face was so close she could feel his breath on her face. "This is what I do, Cori. I explore the minds of others. Sample bits and pieces here and there."

"You can't take a bit or a piece. She isn't a fragmented human psyche! Her mind is all she is. You didn't take in part of her personality. You took in part of *her*."

"A benign part," he assured her.

"There *is* no benign part!" she hissed and glanced at the woman again. "Cleos, please, listen to me. You are putting yourself *and me* at risk. It is going to start pulling your strings like a marionette, and consequently, mine, too."

His eyes flickered over hers. "You underestimate me."

"You are underestimating her."

"I think I hear your exit coming," he said dryly, as if he were bored with her company.

"Damn it, Cleos." She grabbed his tuxedo jacket and forced him to face her. "I won't remember this, so you have to listen to me! You have to tell Cleos what I've told you. She isn't benign. She is a very powerful being from another dimension that will do anything to get a grip on a mind in this dimension. She will make you her possessed vessel. I know your mind is vast, but that just gives her a spacious interior for the ride. You have to tell Cleos to let her go! Promise me you will tell him!"

Cleos's eyes floated to the entity behind her. She yanked on his collar, but he didn't have a chance to make his promise before she woke again.

FELICIA JEDLICKA

MAGIC & MAYHEM

Book 9

THE WARDEN

Magic & Mayhem

Sneak Peek

GYPSY LEANED ON THE stucco pink wall, watching the cars pass with an attentive eye. She could smell the noxious Mexican food that permeated the street and ostensibly the whole fucking country. She had already smoked an entire pack of cigarettes, trying to alleviate her olfactory sense with a different abuse, but apparently, she hadn't burned enough of her nose hairs to diminish the experience.

She knew it was important for Callin to get the allegiance of Mexico's clans. Not just to help overthrow Frederique—which was now a definitive outcome of their efforts, give or take a few loose ends—but also to make Leona's rise to power uncontested. She also didn't trust anyone else to handle Callin's security, so she made the trip with him.

Still, she hated Mexico on principle.

Maybe it was the obnoxious bright colors that pretended to compensate for the rampant poverty. Or perhaps it was the cuisine that only redeemed itself after it escaped the borders. Better still, it was probably the endless potential threats lurking in the shadows. There were always a good number of bottom feeders poised to benefit from the hubbub of a parked limousine and private security.

Even now, she could sense movement in the alley across the way. So far, she couldn't get a bead on the voyeur. She couldn't tell if it was a man or woman, human or werewolf, but she wouldn't take any chances. She gestured that it was time to go through the large picture window beside her, which was barely a window since the entire menu was painted on it. Callin barely glanced away from his dinner party and nodded when she signaled that he should take the alley exit.

She repositioned and radioed for the driver to get closer to the alley and keep the engine running. He grunted a "yes, sir" and clicked off. She imagined that the men she led had originally intended to piss her off with the masculine designation, but frankly, as long as it started with yes, and ended with them doing what she said, they could call her Sugarlips for all she cared.

They were very much under the mistaken impression that she was sleeping with their boss in order to get the privilege of leading such an esoteric operation. Little did they know she hadn't even met the mysterious benefactor. She had hoped someday to meet him, but had resigned herself to the Charlie's Angels feel of her contracted employment. The money was good, and the work was helping to hone her skills, so she couldn't really complain.

After another half-hour, the heavy metal door leading from the restaurant kitchen into the alley opened and a small Mexican man stepped out to peek around the alley. He caught sight of her and his mouth dropped open slightly as he took in her hard-edged military style.

The only color on her was a silver crescent moon necklace—a *gift* from Frederique that she had graciously accepted after their first face-off. She had never gambled to wear the necklace in front of her, but now that the fem-wolf was blind, the risk was minimal.

The little Mexican man tucked back behind the door and said, "Si, si, una chica."

Gypsy gripped her gun and stepped to one side to see around the door. Callin tipped the man generously, and he thanked him before scurrying back to his kitchen duties. She narrowed her eyes on Callin and waited for an explanation.

He stepped into the alley, making sure the door was properly latched before he turned around. He was only wearing blue jeans and a white-collared shirt with a V-neck gray cardigan, but it could have easily been an Armani suit, since he was never without his suave demeanor. "Well..." He paused to place his money clip in his front pocket. "You can't be too careful."

She waggled her head. "I suppose, but it does present the appearance of mistrust."

"Not at all. I trust you implicitly," he said, bowing his head slightly.

"But not with your life?"

He shrugged apologetically. "I appreciate that you are here to keep a watchful eye where I can't, but..." He trailed off.

She crossed her arms. "Oh, please, go on. You won't hurt my feelings. What few I actually have aren't usually wasted on other people's opinions."

His lips turned up slightly, and he tipped his nose up almost imperceptibly to get a whiff of what she wasn't revealing in her expression. His faint smile disappeared entirely.

"Must be the Mexican food," she responded with a brow lift when his sense of smell didn't offer him the interpretation he was seeking.

His smile returned even broader, and he pursed his lips and nodded. "Alright, have it your way. Grace, was it?"

"Call me Gypsy," she said, offering the borrowed nickname from Cori—or herself, if she bought into the backstory.

"Gypsy." He rolled the name off his tongue as if he was tasting it; or at least making a point to memorize it this time. Since she had intrigued him, she must have risen above the status of *no name guard*. "I find it amusing that you are still purporting to be my bodyguard, when it is obvious that anyone who could be a threat to me is clearly going to be a bigger threat to you."

She frowned, looking him over. His face softened, and he raised his hands, surrendering his insult. He opened his mouth to no doubt offer an apology for his macho, albeit accurate, statement. Rather than let him waste her time groveling because of a misunderstanding, she interrupted. "So, you don't want me to take care of that red dot that's trying to lock aim on your throat?"

"What?"

Thank you so much for reading. I hope you enjoyed the ride and if you aren't getting off here, I encourage you to sign up for my newsletter so I can return your generosity with new release updates and special offers.

Sign-Up

You can also find me on Facebook or visit my website. Keep reading!

Website

Facebook

AUTHOR

As a Nebraska native, and a small-town girl at that, I have very little to occupy my time beyond imagining a world outside of my own reality. By the grace of God and the seat of my pants, I have kept my waning attention span on the task of becoming an author.

So here I am, an indie author, peddling my words in cyberspace and enduring my comeuppances with an unwavering determination. I may not be a professional, and I certainly am not perfect, but if you've made it this far, you have to admit, this smartass yokel does spin quite a yarn.

From the self-inflicted sweatshop conditions of my unairconditioned childhood home, to the arthritis reaping positions of a sedentary lifestyle, I bring to you: my sarcasm, my oddity, and my heart. Take it with a grain of salt or a teaspoon of sugar, but take it for what it is: a story born of the mind, translated to paper, and gifted to you.

I thank you for your readership and even more for your support. Please recommend this book to your friends and family via any social media that you use. Word of mouth is still the best advertising and is greatly appreciated.

Most importantly, keep reading. I'll keep writing.

9 781946 092557